Checkmate

A.M. Offenwanger

AMOVITAM PRESS

amovitam press

Note: This book uses Canadian spelling and punctuation.

Also by A.M. Offenwanger

Contents

CHAPTER 1

T HE GIRL WAS BACK. Catriona had seen her in the rear garden of the library at least three times over the last week. She usually sat under the old walnut tree against the tall stone garden wall, her back to the library window, hunched into herself with her knees drawn up to her chest and her head buried in her arms. But every time Cat had stepped out the back door to say hello, or to see if she could help, the girl had scampered—out the old plank garden gate which was rusted in place in its open position, and away around the corner before Cat could get more than a glimpse of her. Cat had even considered greasing the back door hinges, so the squeak wouldn't give her away—she figured that if she could only get close enough to the girl, maybe cut off her retreat out the gate, she would have a chance to speak to her. She was not very old, this visitor to the back garden of the town library of Ruph. From the few glimpses she had had of her, Cat guessed her age to be close to that of her own stepdaughter Bibby—no, Bina, as she insisted on being called now—so maybe around nine.

1

"Ma-ma!" a small voice called behind her, "Ma-ma-ma-ma!" Cat turned away from the window and smiled at the red-headed baby boy in the playpen that stood next to the big reading table in the middle of the library room.

"Hi Yaya!" She scooped the little boy up and gave him a kiss, then put him back in the playpen and handed him a couple of wooden toys. "Look, there's hippo and rhino to play with."

"Po-po," said the baby, banged the two animals together and took a bite at the round little stump which was meant to be the horn of the rhinoceros.

Cat rolled her shoulders and with a groan pushed her fists into the small of her back. She had been on her feet since six o'clock that morning; Yaya had woken and wanted to nurse, and by the time he was done, the other three boys were up and needed breakfast. It had been a long time since then. Five children under the age of ten, in addition to her work at the library, left her very little energy at the end of a day.

Yaya threw his wooden hippo out of the playpen. "Po!"

"Are you ready to go home?" Cat said to him, wiping the drool off his chin with a little cloth that hung over the playpen's railing. "I just need to finish going through these books, then I'm done sorting the carpentry instructions and they can go back on the shelf. I'm going to have to tell Uncle Sepp about this one." She waved a dark brown leatherbound volume at the baby. "I think he'll find it interesting. It's got some information about joinery from three hundred years ago; and they're even talking about how to use the wood of the spikeberry bush."

"Yepp," little Yaya agreed, "Yepp Yepp." He gnawed on the rhinoceros.

"Yes, Uncle Sepp. Maybe the spikeberry bush wood could be good for carving? It doesn't say here if it's any particular colour or texture, but you never know, do you?" She put the book aside.

Cat's attention wandered back to the window. She could still see the girl's white-blonde head under the walnut tree. Should she give it one more try to talk to her? But she would have to go out through the little back room attached to the library, which was Nikor Archivist's living space. She hadn't seen him in the last hour, which made her think that he might be taking a nap; she did not want to disturb him. He was getting old and needed his rest.

She stepped over to the small-paned window and looked out. The girl was still curled up into a ball and her shoulders were hunched in a pose of acute misery. This was not right; Cat had to do something! But suddenly the girl's head came up like a deer that had scented danger. With one lithe motion she sprang to her feet and darted out the gate, her pale blonde hair streaming out like a flag behind her.

Cat shook her head. She would ask Aunt who this girl was, she generally knew what went on in town. Cat couldn't remember having seen her before, she had to be from a new family. That long fall of white-blonde hair was unusual enough to be noticeable.

She turned back to the baby in the playpen. "Well, Yaya, I think it's time to go home." She gathered up her bag and cloak that were draped over the chair, and adjusted the baby sling over her shoulder.

"Ba-ba-ba," said Yaya.

"That's right, we're going to see Papa. I think he's at Uncle Sepp's house with the boys. Let's go find them."

—ele—

"Checkmate!" Randor moved his rook over one square, and grinned at his uncle across the table.

Guy groaned. "Not again! Nicky, this outlander game of yours is going to be the death of me!"

A petite woman with a head of blonde curls came through a side door, stepped over to the kitchen table, and looked over his shoulder. "He trounced you again, did he? Well, don't blame me; complain to your wife. It was her idea to teach everyone to play chess. Hi, Cat," she called through the door, "you're just in time! Randy came over to find someone to take him on at chess, and Guy has a problem with his cousin's eleven-year-old being better at the game than he is."

Cat followed Nicky into the room and deposited her cloak on the bench beside Guy. "He'll just have to prac-tise more," she said. She leaned over her husband with the baby who was strapped to her front with a long woven shawl. "Here, Yaya, give Papa a kiss," she said with a grin.

Guy recoiled. "Not before he's had his nose wiped, he won't!" he said, pulling a handkerchief out of his pocket. "I'll have a kiss from you, though; you don't drool."

"Where are the boys?" asked Cat, "out back? We should get home, it's getting on for suppertime."

"I suppose it is," said Guy. "The days are getting so much longer, it's hard to tell how late it is already. Yes, I think the kids are all outside; the little ones anyway. I'm not entirely sure about Cory and Tor; I haven't seen them in at least an hour."

Nicky laughed. "Ari wanted to play house, and Cory was supposed to be the papa," she told Cat. "For some reason he was not interested. I suppose at the ripe old age of almost seven it's against his dignity. She didn't even bother asking Tor; she knows better than to bug her brother about little-kid games like that. I think she got your other two boys into the game, though; Dyllie didn't want to be the baby, but he said he'd play if he could be the dog. They've got a nice little playhouse set up in the garden shed."

Randor snorted with all the superiority of a pre-adolescent. "Playing house is stupid," he said.

"Don't be so hoity-toity," Cat said, "you and Bibby—sorry, Bina—did it lots when you were little."

"We did not!" he responded, outrage at such a shameful accusation making the freckles across his nose stand out even more than usual.

"Oh yes, you did," said Nicky. "Where did you think that collection of old dishes out in my shed came from?"

"Speaking of Bina," said Cat, "where is she? Didn't she come into town with you, Guy?"

"Yes, she did," replied her husband, "she's somewhere about, with Andy. There was something terribly important she had to tell him that came up in the five minutes between his leaving the pottery to come here and us setting out for town ourselves, and it absolutely couldn't wait until tomorrow morning."

The outside door opened, and a young girl with a mane of copper hair and brilliantly turquoise eyes stepped into the room, closely followed by a boy whose brown hair and red cheeks made him look like a robin. The girl turned back to the boy.

"See, Cory? I told you, Mumma and the baby are here, and everybody is ready to go home."

The boy pouted.

"Me and Tor weren't done our fort!" he said. "We coulda waited until they called us. And anyway, how did you know they were here?"

Bina rolled her eyes. "I—just—know. Sheesh, I've told you a hundred million times!" she said.

"Well, you can tell me a hundred million bazillion gafillion times, but we still wasn't done our fort and it's not fair! It's not fair, Mumma!" he appealed to Cat.

"'Gafillion' isn't even a word," said Bina in a superior tone, "and besides..."

"That's enough," Cat interjected. "Bina, go get the boys, please, so we can get ready to go. Cory, I know you wanted to play longer, but it's almost suppertime, so you would have had to stop soon anyway. And on top of that, once you're done building the fort, you want lots of time to play in it, so you wouldn't have wanted to leave then either! What kind of fort is it going to be?"

"Oh, Mumma,"—Cory's chocolate-brown eyes lit up—"it'll be the bestest fort ever! It's in the corner by the chicken shed, and we got sticks, and a big piece of wood, and we made holes in the bottom with Uncle Sepp's drill and we're putting in real wattle walls and..."

"How did you talk Uncle Sepp into letting you use his drill?" asked Guy with a raise of his eyebrows.

"They sent Ari," said Bina over her shoulder on her way out the back door.

Cat laughed. "That'll do it," she said. "Little Miss Ari only has to blink her big blue eyes at Sepp, twirl a golden curl around her finger, and go 'Pweeeease, Daddy?' and he'll let her have anything she wants."

"It's a good thing you keep that girl of yours in line, Nicky," said Guy, "or she'd be spoiled rotten."

"It didn't harm *your* girl any," said Nicky.

"What didn't harm me?" asked Bina, shepherding a red-headed little boy into the kitchen and pulling an even smaller one by the hand, who was sobbing.

"Having an indulgent father, dear," said Cat. "What's wrong with Dyllie?"

"Hi Mumma!" said the bigger one of the two boys. "Dyllie was being the doggie, and I tooked away Wuffer's bone because Dyllie's not a real doggie an' I didn't think Wuffer'd like it if Dyllie lickeded his bone. So then Dyllie cried."

Guy got up from the bench and picked up the distraught toddler. "Thank you, Kell. I don't think Mumma would like it either if Dyllie licked the dog's bone. Come on, Dyllie,"—he wiped his little boy's nose—"when we get home we can see if we've got a biscuit bone for little boy-dogs in the cupboard."

CHAPTER 2

B INA SKIPPED ALONG THE cobbled lane, trying to jump on each patch of late morning sunlight that fell through the gaps between the houses. One, two, hop on both feet, three, four, jump across! One, two... She was getting really good at this; next time they played hopscotch she would win for sure. Mumma had taught her that game; she said she played it as a little girl in that other world she'd come from. And then she and Aunt Nicky had had a game together, and giggled like little girls the whole time, and Mumma won hands down. Aunt Nicky had come from Ah-Mare-Icka, too, like Mumma when Bina was just tiny. Bina couldn't remember much of anything about that; only that there had been a time when it was only her and Papa, and then all of a sudden there was the warm lovingness that was Mumma, and Papa wasn't sad any longer. And then Andy came, and he was in the workshop with Papa most of the time. And not long after that, there was Cory, and then Kell and Dyllie and Yaya.

Bina checked on them all as she skipped over the two white cobblestones in Six Fishes Lane, and hopped the next ten black stones on one foot. Mumma and Yaya were in the library; she could feel Mumma's quiet happiness at being with all those books. The baby felt sleepy and content; he'd probably just had some milk and was about to take his nap.

Bina turned her attention to her home in the forest. Papa and Andy were in the workshop; she could feel their satisfaction at pottery dishes that turned out right. The boys—oh, right, they weren't at home; they were at Aunt Nicky and Uncle Sepp's. Cory and Tor were probably working on their fort, because Cory felt really proud, and he had his whole mind on what he was doing. It felt very different from when he was having lessons with Master Nikor, when his attention was splintered, with sharp edges. Dyllie was angry—with who?

Bina let her attention wander past her immediate family. Ah yes, it was Ari that Dyllie was fighting with; probably over that doll of hers, the new one Uncle Sepp had made her with the black yarn hair—Ari was angry, too, and was afraid to lose the doll. Dyllie wanted one for himself; Bina felt his wishing underneath the anger. And now Aunt Nicky was interfering in their argument, Bina could tell she was a bit frustrated. Kell was—somewhere, Bina could not tell exactly where, but he liked it there. He was probably with Uncle Sepp and Ben in the carpentry workshop; he felt very comfortable there. Ah, yes, that's what it was; Uncle Sepp's attention wasn't completely on his work, there was a little corner of him keeping an eye on someone else to make sure they didn't get hurt.

Bina pursed her lips and tried to whistle. Andy knew how to whistle, and so did Papa and even Cory. Andy had tried to teach Bina, and she kept putting her lips into the 'oo' shape he'd said to make and put her tongue in the right place, but so far all that came out was a puff of air; she couldn't get it to make a sound. Oh well. She straddle-hopped onto the cobbles on either side of the big stone in the middle of the lane, then jumped with her feet together out of the end of Fishes' Lane onto the marketplace.

The library was right across from her. She'd go tell Mumma about Dyllie wishing for a doll; there was no reason he couldn't have one. Dyllie's dolly. Bina giggled. She headed for the side lane that led around to the back of the library. She could go in the front, too, but she didn't like the big front doors. They were really heavy to pull open, but what was more, they were made of thick oak carved with pictures, and right next to the handle on the right-hand wing of the door was this face—it stared directly at Bina, exactly on the level with her own face, when she put her hand on the door handle. Ever since Mumma had told them the story of *The Christmas Carol* one snowy night last winter, Bina couldn't look at that face without expecting it to turn into the face of Marley's ghost. It was too creepy.

So she always went around the back and got into the library through Master Nikor's little room; he usually didn't mind. Half the time he thought she was Yeryl, Papa's sister, although Papa said she didn't look that much like her except for the hair colour. Master Nikor got a little confused about real people outside of books because they kept growing and changing.

Bina had never met Aunt Yeryl herself. She lived with her family in Ilim, the big city to the south, and hadn't been in Ruph since before Bina was born. Grandmother lived there, too; she was helping Aunt Yeryl with the kids. Bina had never met her, either. She thought it might be nice to have a grandmother—but then, they did have Aunt. She was Randy and Immy's grandmother, but she might as well have been their own, too. And she bossed around Papa and Uncle Sepp like they were her own sons, not just nephews.

Aunt was a Wisewoman—she knew things, about plants and animals and people and what you needed to do to make them better if they were hurt. It wasn't just from the Knowing, like Bina and Mumma had too, where you felt things about people you cared about. Mumma and Aunt didn't have it as strongly as Bina did, but that was because they were only Unissimae, only daughters of only daughters, while Bina was an Unissima Maxima—her born mother who'd left when Bina was a small baby had been an Unissima too, so Bina's Knowing was extra-strong. Mumma said she couldn't tell herself what everyone was feeling all the time, only when there was something wrong. Bina always knew—she couldn't help it.

Sometimes that was hard. That time when Aunt Nicky had almost died, giving birth to the little baby girl who did die, that had been awful. Horribly, horribly awful. Bina wasn't very big then, no more than Kell now, and she had cried so hard she thought her heart would fly apart into little pieces. Papa had to hold her really tight in his arms, for a long, long time, and *his* heart was so terribly sad, too, it had felt like a dark hole; and Mumma and Aunt had been so worried and working so hard to keep Aunt Nicky alive, and then they were so awfully sad when the little baby girl didn't make it. And Uncle Sepp—Bina couldn't even bear to think about how Uncle Sepp had been feeling. It had all been AWFUL. But then, a year later, Ari was born, and that time Aunt Nicky wasn't sick at all, and when they were all done being worried about her and she got through the hurt of having the baby, everyone was double as happy about Ari as they usually were about a new baby. And Uncle Sepp, he was clean crazy about his baby girl. He loved Tor lots, too, of course, but Ari was special. Bina found her little cousin annoying sometimes, but she could forgive Ari her annoyingness because of how her being born had made those big black sad holes in Uncle Sepp's and Aunt Nicky's hearts heal over.

She reached the rear of the library building. A six-foot-high wall made of crumbling red stone closed in the little back garden. Bina walked around the corner, and turned in at the wooden gate with its rusted iron hinges that was set in the middle of the wall. As she did every time, she was about to set her hands against the gate to try to push it open a little further, just for fun—but she stopped in mid-motion.

There was someone in the garden!

CHAPTER 3

C AT PUT THE LAST volume of the red-bound
Chronicles of Ruph back on the shelf. Nikor had
finished entering last months' events, ending with the
marriage of Elymas Farmer and Kinris Bakersdaughter. It
hadn't been a great surprise, that marriage; in fact, it had
been about time—Kinris was definitely showing. Aunt
figured the baby should be due in October sometime. But
at least Elymas had taken care to have a proper home ready
for his wife and child before he gave her the wedding chain
and took her home; there was something to be said for
that.

Cat corked the ink bottle that Nikor had forgotten
about, and locked it into the little cupboard that stood
against the end cap of the bookshelf in the middle of the
room. She rubbed the back of her neck, trying to massage
the kinks out of it, and yawned. Her eye fell on the stack of
books on the shelf right next to the cupboard, which she
had put there because they needed mending; but that had
been at least a month ago. She just did not have the time
or energy to get to it.

She heard voices in the back room. Ah, Bina must have come in her usual way—Cat was well aware that there was something on the big carved entrance door the girl was afraid of. Cat didn't blame her; some of those designs on that door gave her the shivers, herself. And Nikor didn't mind Bina coming through his room and chatting with him a little bit. He'd probably forget again within minutes that something had interrupted his book.

"Mumma!" shouted Bina, "look, this is..."

"Shh!" said Cat automatically (the librarian's instinct to shush still had not worn off). Then she noticed that Bina was not alone—she was towing the white-blonde visitor from the back garden by the hand.

"Sorry," Bina said, only a smidgen more quietly, "but Mumma, look, this is Rhitha!"

"Oh!" said Cat. "Welcome to the library, Rhitha!" She held out her hand.

"See," said Bina to the girl, "she's nice!"

The girl had her head tipped downwards, the fall of pale hair hiding most of her face. Now she shyly looked up and took Cat's offered hand.

"Hello," she said in a near-whisper and quickly dropped her eyes again. Cat let go of her hand. In spite of the shyness, the girl's handshake had been firm enough—maybe she was just afraid of strangers?

"So this is my Mumma," Bina said, "she's the librarian here. Well, Master Nikor Archivist is really, but Mumma does most of the stuff. Master Nikor just reads lots of books. And oh, this is my baby brother. He's sleeping." She towed Rhitha over to the playpen by the big reading table, where Yaya was curled up under a multi-coloured crocheted blanket, his thumb in his mouth and his diapered bottom sticking up into the air. "He's my littlest brother," Bina continued. "I got three more. Do you have any brothers?"

Rhitha half-smiled and shook her head.

"Just my big sister," she said in a whisper, "the one..."

"Right, the one you told me about!" said Bina in a normal voice. "She sounds awful. Why are you whispering?"

"Because we're in the library," whispered Rhitha with a side glance at Cat. "You've got to be quiet in a library!"

Cat laughed. "A girl after my own heart!" she said. "I've been trying to teach Bina that from the time she was two! But we're not very strict about it here. For one, half the time nobody is here except us, and then, the library is used for a school room, too, to teach the younger kids in town to read. So I think the people here never got into the habit. You're new to Ruph, aren't you?"

"Yes, Mumma, she's just come back here!" Bina said. "But she was born here, and so was her sister! They've been away for eight years—right?" She looked at the other girl.

"Seven," said Rhitha, still in an almost-whisper. Cat smiled to herself—the habit of silence-in-the-library was a hard one to break. "We left in the Year of the Thunder."

"Then you were still here in the Year of the Mouse?" Cat said. "That's when I got here, seven-and-a-half years ago. I might know your family—what's their names?"

"My father was Esseld; my mother is Shamira," Rhitha said softly.

"Esseld... and Shamira? I know those names—wait! No way—is your sister Kashinka?" Cat couldn't suppress a wrinkle of her nose.

"What is it, Mumma?" asked Bina, "do you know Rhitha's sister? Why don't you like her?"

She'd picked up on Cat's feelings again; for the hundredth time Cat resolved to keep a better lid on her reactions when her daughter was around, for the girl's sake.

"Yes, I remember Kashinka," she said, ignoring Bina's other question. "And I remember you too! Not very well; but I remember a cute little blonde girl in that family—you must have been, what, four?"

"Yes," said Rhitha with a shy smile, "but I don't remember anything about this town. Or not much, anyway. But we still had family here, so we came back."

"Hold hard!" said Cat, looking from one girl to the other. "If you're Kashinka's sister—that means you two are cousins!"

"What?!" shrieked Bina, and was instantly shushed by both Cat and Rhitha, which made all three of them laugh.

"But no, Mumma," said Bina, bouncing up and down on the balls of her feet, "is Rhitha *really* our cousin?"

"Yours, dear," said Cat, "not of the rest of us, more's the pity." She smiled at Rhitha.

"I don't get it," said Bina, "why just me, and not... Oh, now I see! From my mother's side, right?"

"Exactly," said Cat.

Rhitha looked confused.

"You see," Bina explained, "Mumma isn't my real Mumma, except she's been around since I was really little, so

I keep forgetting. My real mother, the born one, was called—Ashya, I think?"

"Yes," Cat said. "And Ashya was Kashinka's cousin—your cousin, Rhitha, since you're Kashinka's sister. Or actually—wait a moment..." She stepped over to the shelf with the Chronicles of Ruph and let her fingers walk along the spines of a set of dark purple volumes. "Hmm, where is it? I'll have to ask Nikor."

"Where is what, what?" asked the little old librarian from right beside Cat, making her jump. He had shuffled up behind them without her noticing.

"The volume with the family trees," she said, "the fourteenth one, with the M's to R's from the last hundred years in it. It's not where it's supposed to be."

"Yes yes, quite quite," Nikor said. "Took it to look up Manuska's children's children, I did. Bring it back presently." He shuffled off in the direction of his back room.

"It should be all in there," Cat said to the girls, "the whole family tree. I think the ancestor of yours that that particular section of the family tree starts with is Rahikun. Bina..." She nodded her head in the direction in which Nikor had disappeared. Bina took the hint and went after him, returning with a purple-bound book a minute later.

"He *almost* brought it," she said, "but his open book caught him. He was stuck in his chair, reading, with this one pinched under his arm."

She gave the volume to Cat, who took it over to the table, let it fall open two-thirds of the way through, and turned the thick pages until she found what she was looking for.

"See, here," she said, "just as I thought. Here is Rahikun; that was your great-grandfather. He had two sons, and they had one daughter each: Ashya and Shamira. So your mothers were first cousins, which makes you second cousins. I noticed that when I saw it because Kashinka always said she was Ashya's cousin, but it's actually her—your—mother who was the direct cousin. Not that it matters; around here, everyone who's not a brother or sister is a cousin, even if they're around three corners and twice removed. But I just noticed it."

"And there is Grandmother!" said Rhitha, who was leaning over Cat's arm, studying the family tree. "See, Urnhild, married to Belock."

"Of course, Urnhild is your grandmother, isn't she!" said Cat. "She's a nice woman, I like her. You remember, Bina, Mistress Urnhild, she's quite small—not much taller than you are—and she makes those delicious quince sweets. Aunt took you there once or twice on a visit."

"Yes! And she had a little doll's cradle she let me play with when we were there; I put the kitten in it and it wouldn't stay. I remember, even though I was really little. But—Rhitha isn't even written on this page!"

"You're right," said Cat, "this must not have been updated in a long time."

"It doesn't say that grandfather died either," Rhitha said quietly. "Or father—but that was quite recent. Grandfather was a long time ago, before we left."

"I'm sorry to hear about your father," said Cat.

19

"It's why they came back here," explained Bina, "they came to live with their grandmother, Rhitha and her sister and her mother."

Cat gave Bina a look. She was surprised her daughter seemed so unaffected by hearing of the other girl's loss; normally her compassionate nature would be deeply moved by hearing of something like this. Did she know something Cat did not?

"Oh look!" Bina said. "Your mother was an only child too! Like my grandmother, see, and my mother—my born mother, I mean, on the page here. Mumma is an Unissima, too, but that's not why I'm an Unissima Maxima. It's because of my born mother, because I'm the only child of an Unissima. If you didn't have your sister, you'd be an Unissima too!"

Rhitha did not say anything. She turned her face aside and traced the edge of the book with her finger. Bina looked at her, and her turquoise eyes were taking on a thoughtful expression.

"So," Cat said, deliberately turning the subject, "do you like books, Rhitha?"

The girl's grey eyes lit up. "Oh yes!" she said loudly, then gasped a little and clapped her fingers to her mouth. "Sorry!" she whispered, "yes!"

Bina leaned over, put her mouth close to Rhitha's ear, and in a penetrating stage whisper hissed, "WE DON'T MIND IF YOU MAKE NOISE IN HERE!"

All three of them burst out laughing. The baby in the playpen woke up and started crying.

"Well, we don't mind on account of the books," Cat said with a smile, "but the baby might be a different matter." She picked him up out of the playpen. "Look, sweetie, this is Rhitha! She's come to live in Ruph. I think she'll come visit us lots in the library; won't that be nice?" He gave a little hiccup and regarded Rhitha solemnly from his big brown eyes.

"Hi, baby," the girl said shyly.

"His name's Yaya," said Bina, "well, Iawar. But nobody calls him that. He's too little for a big name yet. So, see," she continued, "we even have babies in the library here. Well, not most babies, but the ones from our family. So your sister was talking nonsense about children not being allowed in here. I bet she's never even been in the library herself!"

"Who, Kashinka?" said Cat. "True enough; at least not in the time that I knew her when she still lived here."

"Oh, Mumma!" Bina said, "could Rhitha come help with the books sometimes?"

"Would you like to?" Cat asked Rhitha. "I certainly could use some help!"

Rhitha nodded eagerly.

"That's great!" said Bina. "Then we can both help!"

"That would be a novelty," said Cat with a smile. "Bina's never been all that interested in sorting books for me."

"Yeah, but it's different when there's someone else to do it with!" said Bina. "It'll be lots of fun!"

The heavy front doors creaked open and a stocky man in an innkeeper's apron stepped through the doors.

"Ah, Catriona Bookwoman!" he said. "I was hoping to find you here."

"What can I do for you, Druce?" Cat asked. "Do you need another book on coopering for those oak barrels of yours?"

"No, I'm good with the one you found me last time, Mistress Cat. It's you I need—there's a message needs taking to your man. Tell him there's a couple of strangers at the inn, just come from Rhanathon, away at the coast, who want to see him. They want speech with Dyniselm Potter, the Septimissimus."

CHAPTER 4

B INA KICKED HER HEELS against the thick legs of the pottery work table she was perched on.

"So who were those people that wanted to talk to Papa the other day?" she asked Andy, who was at the other end of the table, wedging clay pieces in preparation for throwing on the wheel. "And how come you didn't go along this time, too?"

"They mostly wanted speech with the Master, it seemed to me," he said in his slow voice which had deepened to a mellow bass over the last few years. "And while you might think I'm the most important person in this pottery, Little Bee, not everyone is of that opinion." He gave her the little half-smile that was reserved especially for her.

She wrinkled her nose at him. "You do make at least half the dishes in this shop," she said, "and all of the fancy sculptures that people buy for special. But who were those folks?"

"It's a craftsmaster and his journeyman, from Rhanathon. They deal in clay work for sale overseas, they said."

"Hmm. Rhanathon is a long ways away, isn't it?"

"Yes, about five days' travel, I believe. We get some of the glaze minerals from there—the cobalt we use in the blue dishes, for one. And I think the fragrance wood Mistress Cat cooks with is brought in by ship through the harbour there, too."

Bina swung her legs. "Mumma calls it cinnamon; that's the word they use in her old world. Yum, it's my favourite. But if they have all those special things in that city, what do those people want here in Ruph? We don't have any of that stuff."

"By the sounds of it, they wanted to hear about our clay here. And about Master Guy's special work, the Septimus dishes he makes." Andy reached for the fifth lump of clay and began to knead it into the round snail shell he needed for shaping it on the pottery wheel.

"That won't do them much good; they can't make anything like those special cups and pots if they haven't got the powers Papa has. And he's only got them because he's the Septimissimus."

"Yes, they seemed to know that—or at least, the master did; the journeyman asked a lot of questions that made me wonder. Either he does not know much, or he is after something else that he was not letting on about."

"What are they like, those people? Do they look like us?"

"You mean, do they have two eyes and ears and hands and feet?" Andy said with a wink.

Bina threw a little clay pebble at him. "You know what I mean!" she said.

He caught the piece of clay and tossed it back at her. "Actually, not exactly. When you say 'like us', do you mean red hair and turquoise eyes like you and your family, or black hair and brown skin like Ben and I, or..."

"Okay, okay, fine. It's just that I heard that people from the south sometimes have, like, blue skin, or really white hair, or put, like, jewellery in their *noses*!"

He looked at her with his head tipped to the side, one eyebrow raised. "Where did you hear *that* rigmarole?" he asked. "You've been had again, Bee."

She huffed air out through her nose and looked down at her swinging feet in embarrassment. "Randy said so. And he lives in town, he knows more stuff! And he was really serious when he said it, too. I felt it."

Andy ruffled her hair in passing on his way back from depositing the wedged clay pieces on the board next to the pottery wheel. "Don't take it to heart, Bee. Randy likes to pull your leg, and he knows that if he can make himself feel serious when he says something you'll believe him. But he's never yet beat you at hide-and-seek because you can always feel him getting nervous when you get close. You can take that as a comfort."

"Yes, but that new game that Mumma and Aunt Nicky taught everyone, that chest game—nobody's beat him at that yet. He's really good at it. And really smug about it, too."

"It's called 'chess', not 'chest', isn't it? As for Randy, he'll get his come-uppance yet, don't worry. Pass me the cutting wire?" He slapped the first of the clay lumps down

25

in the centre of the wheelhead and kicked the flywheel into motion.

Bina let out a sigh. "I'm glad you're here, Andy," she said. "I can *tell* you stuff."

He raised his eyes from the spinning clay under his hands and smiled at her. "I'm glad you tell me stuff, too, Bee."

"Oh, oh, oh!" she said, and wriggled around so her feet hung off the other edge of the table and she was facing him. "I haven't told you about Rhitha yet!"

"No, not much, only that you met a new cousin. So what about her? How did you meet her, anyway?" Andy squeezed some water over the cup taking shape under his hands.

"I was going in the library to tell Mumma something, and you know I always go in the back, because—well, just because. And there was Rhitha, in the garden! You know, by the big walnut tree, the one Mumma and Master Nikor make ink from in the autumn. Nobody's ever in that garden. But Rhitha was, 'cause it's a place not a lot of people would look for you. She was hiding. And she was crying, at least I'm pretty sure she was—she felt really sad. And she was scared when she saw me. But not for very long, 'cause I said hi, and . . ...."

"Yes, that would do it," Andy said with a smile. "Why was she sad?"

"That's just it," Bina said, "she told me all about it. Well, once I'd said hi, and told her who I was and stuff, and she wasn't feeling scared any more and was feeling more, you know, like I liked her. Which I do. You know," she continued eagerly, "she's neat. I think she's my friend!"

"I'm not surprised. So what did she tell you? If you can tell me, that is." He cut the finished cup off the pottery wheel and put it to one side, then took up a new piece of clay and smacked it on the wheel.

"Oh!" Bina looked thoughtful for a moment. "Do you think I shouldn't tell you? But no, I think it's okay. And you're not going to tell anyone else anyway, are you?"

"I don't see why I would," he said.

"Okay, so, you know why she was sad? Because of her sister. Her sister, and her mother. But mostly her sister. Mumma said her name was Kash—Kashinka, I think."

"Kashinka?! She's back in town?" Andy's thumb went right through the wall of the cup he was shaping. "Oh *bother*." He pressed the whole lump back down into a rounded mound in the centre of the wheel and started over.

"There!" said Bina, "what is it about her? Mumma doesn't like her either, and she wouldn't tell me why."

"For one," Andy said, "she was after your Uncle Sepp, when he was still single. She wanted to marry the Septimissimus."

"But Papa's the Septimissimus!"

"They didn't know that then," Andy said. "Also, she spread rumours about your Papa. This was all before I was here; I only heard about it. And then, she is just not a very pleasant person. She left not too long after Ben and I got here, but in that little while, whenever she saw one of us, she looked right through us like we did not exist. Probably because we were only apprentices. Or came from a foreign place."

"That sounds like what Rhitha was telling me! And you're feeling really angry about it still."

"When you're fourteen and a boy, having a beautiful girl treat you like a piece of dirt stings. Remember that, Little Bee, when you're that age and boys give you sheep-eyed looks."

Bina giggled. "They wouldn't! And fourteen is *ages* away! Besides, I'm not going to be mean like Rhitha's sister."

Andy quirked up the corner of his mouth. "No, that you won't; I'd be prepared to bet on it. So your friend was upset because of her sister?"

"Yes," Bina said, swinging her legs. "They've only just come back to Ruph, her and her mother and her sister. Their father died, back in Ilim; I think he got sick, but Rhitha isn't really sad about it, so that's okay. I would be horribly sad if Papa died, wouldn't you? But Rhitha isn't. They came back here because they were going to live with her grandmother, but when they got here, it turned out that she didn't have room for them. And now they're living in a rented place, which isn't at all what they wanted, Rhitha's mother and her sister, I mean. Rhitha says she doesn't care, but she just wants them to not be so angry, because they take it out on her. Her sister says really unkind things, like that Rhitha is ugly—she's not! She's got such pretty hair, it's so fair it's almost white, and really long, longer than mine even. And her eyes are a soft colour, sort of grey. She looks—I don't know, nice, you know?"

"I think I do," said Andy. "Some people are beautiful because there's a lovely inside that shines out." He placed another cup on the drying board.

"Exactly!" said Bina eagerly. "Like Mumma."

"Yes, like Mistress Cat," Andy said.

"But Rhitha," Bina continued, "she doesn't know that. She says her sister is really beautiful, and she's always going on at Rhitha about being hideous. And they make her do the work they don't want to do, like emptying out the chamber pots, and scrubbing the floors. And then, she says, when she's tried her best, they still nag her and say she didn't do it right. She doesn't even know why they're so mean to her. And she is really sad about that. She didn't say so, but, well, I know."

"Of course you do."

"But she likes her grandmother. She didn't say that either, but when she talked of her, she felt warm. I like Mistress Urnhild, don't you? So I think me and Rhitha, we're going to be friends. And tomorrow, we're going to help Master Nikor at the library with the books; Mumma says there's a lot of books need sorting because people have been reading them and they never got put back on the shelves. Rhitha likes books. Are you making a really little cup out of that piece you've got left? Can I have it when it's done? I've got almost a dozen of them already, I just need one more. Can you make a tiny little handle on it, too?"

"Sure, Bee."

They went off into a discussion of the shape of Bina's collector's cup.

CHAPTER 5

C AT WALKED OVER TO the cupboard and took down the stack of brown pottery bowls. She'd have to ask Guy to make new ones; there were only enough for the eight of them, and two of those were already cracked, and one other badly chipped. Shoemaker's children go barefoot, and potter's children don't have a bowl to eat their soup out of? She smiled to herself. It wasn't like they needed fine china—although there were times when it would be nice to have a pretty teacup to drink her Sunday afternoon mintbrew out of.

She remembered her grandmother's Royal Doulton set, which she had always considered far too fussy for her tastes; all things being equal, she did prefer Guy's rustic pottery to the gold rim and dainty little rosebuds of Grandmother's dishes. And she had hated the extra work of having to hand-wash the fragile china, anyway, rather than sticking it in the dishwasher like the everyday dishes.

In Ruph, of course, handwashing dishes was all there was, china or no china. And she never seen anything resembling fine china here; the dishes people used were stoneware or earthenware, if not wood.

She stepped around Kell and Dyllie who were making a big block tower on the floor, and distributed the bowls on the long deal table. It still had the pale colour and smell of new pine wood; Sepp had built it for them a few weeks ago because the old table had become too small for the whole family, let alone visitors. The kitchen was getting quite snug as it was. Cat looked out the front window at the building of the pottery workshop, which stood across the clearing that was their front yard. It had been completed a few months before Kell was born—by then it had been obvious that they needed more space for the family, and moving the workshop across the yard allowed the family to expand into the old pottery room next door. But even that was starting to get rather tight: her and Guy's box bed, a smaller one like it for Bina, and the boys' bunk bed took up almost all of the space. They were talking about yet another extension to the house, either out back into the forest, or upwards, by raising the roof and adding another story.

Cat sighed. She was not looking forward to the racket of another construction project, but there were definite limits to how many people you could fit into a two-room cottage, especially if those people kept getting bigger. But she was grateful that Guy's income stretched far enough that they could even consider building.

"How soon is dinner?" Bina asked, coming through the door from the bedroom.

"As soon as you get the spoons on the table," Cat replied. "Where is Cory?"

"In the workshop, I think; Papa is mixing new clay and had him doing the stomping because he hangs around anyway," Bina said. "And it's his turn to help with the dishes today!"

"I know," Cat said, "and I'm sure he does too. How was book sorting at the library this morning?"

"Fine," Bina said a little unenthusiastically.

Cat smiled. "Getting a bit bored with it, are you?"

Bina grinned. "Yes, kind of. Rhitha still likes it though! She says she likes the way the books smell."

"I did say she was a girl after my own heart. Maybe you have to be born to love books. I don't think *you* are, and that's okay too. We can't all be bookworms."

"No..." said Bina, her voice trailing off. She fidgeted with the last two wooden spoons she had in her hand. "Mumma?" she started up again, "can I ask you something?"

"Of course, dear," said Cat, taking a couple of thick hot pads and lifting the heavy cast iron pot full of bean-and-bacon soup off the top of the stove.

"I'm just wondering—is tattling bad?"

"Yes, it is," said Cat. "You don't—ouch!" Some of the hot soup had splashed out of the pot when it thumped on the table a little too abruptly, and spilled on her hand. She shook her hand, blew on it, and quickly stepped over to the pump to stick it under the tap. A few minutes of holding her hand in cold water cooled down the burn.

"All right," she said, dabbing her hand with a dry towel, "time to eat. Wash your hands, boys. DINNER!" she hollered out the front door in the direction of the work-shop.

It was not until the afternoon when they were thinning the carrots in the kitchen garden that Cat remembered the conversation.

"By the way, Bina," she said, "was there any particular reason you were asking me about tattling earlier? I'm sorry we never got done talking, it went right out of my mind when that hot soup splashed on my hand."

"No, it's okay," Bina said in an unconvincing tone, "never mind."

Cat gave her daughter a look. "Come on, dear," she said, "you know better than that."

"Better than what?" said Bina, studiously keeping her eyes on the inch-high carrot seedlings she was pulling out of the rows.

"Better than trying to pull one over on me. I may not be an Unissima Maxima, but I *am* an Unissima. And what's more, I'm your mother and I've known you from the time you were two. Something's worrying you. So, out with it," Cat said, sitting back on her heels and dusting the soil off her fingers. "What prompted that question?"

"Well," Bina said reluctantly, "I don't want to be a tat-tle..."

"No, of course you don't. But if there's something you need to talk about, that's not the same as tattling."

"What's the difference then?"

"I would say tattling is where you're telling on someone to get them in trouble or to make yourself look good. But if it's about something that needs to be addressed, something that needs changing, that's not tattling, in my books. Sometimes we need to tell, so that a wrong can be made right."

"Oh." Bina pulled a few more carrot seedlings.

"Why don't you just tell me, dear," Cat suggested gently, "and let me decide? If it's something that's no business of either of us, I'll forget I ever heard it."

Bina raised her big turquoise eyes to Cat's face with a look of relief.

"It's about Cory," she said in a rush. "Him and Tor are being real brats in Master Nikor's reading lessons! They don't pay attention, and make fun of Master Nikor, and they make faces when his back is turned and make everyone else laugh and not listen, too. I saw it this morning! I know Cory doesn't like having lessons with Master Nikor, but I didn't know he's being like that in the library.

"And it's Cory, mostly; I think Tor wouldn't mind learning to read and write, but Cory makes him be a brat, too. Master Nikor didn't really notice that the kids were all laughing at him today, but nobody was paying any attention to the lesson. And then at the end, when they were all leaving, Cory switched out Master Nikor's slate chalk with a plain piece of stick he'd coloured white so that next time Master Nikor wanted to write it wouldn't make any mark; and him and Tor were snickering about it like anything. But me and Rhitha switched it back after they left. I don't know what to do, Mumma! That's not right what they're doing, is it?"

Cat had been steadily looking at Bina during this recital, and now she shook her head.

"No, that's very much not right. Thank you for telling me. I didn't know." She hadn't even known that her oldest son disliked his reading lessons with the little old librarian. What kind of mother was she? For that matter, what kind of Unissima was she? Shouldn't she have had an inkling of this herself? "But you don't need to do anything about it, Bina; that's for me and Papa to deal with. How long have you known Cory doesn't like his lessons?"

"Oh, all along," Bina said, in a much lighter tone of voice. Cat could tell that sharing her concerns had lifted a load off the girl's chest. "He hates it, because it makes him feel scattered."

"Does it now?" said Cat. "Yes, that's definitely a matter for Papa. And that was *not* tattling, just so you know. Now, we should get on with the beets, too; I want the thinnings for supper."

"But Master Nikor's lessons are so boring!" Cory protested, his lower lip stuck out in a pout. He looked up at his father from under his eyebrows, a dark brown lock of hair flopped over his forehead and shadowing his eyes. He looked half scared and half sulky; Cat really hoped they could get this worked out.

With his arms crossed and a scowl on his face, Guy stood over his son, who was perched on the kitchen bench. "Coryell Septimusson!" he said sternly, "there is no excuse, ever—do you hear me, not EVER!—for being rude and disrespectful to an elder, let alone your teacher. Do you understand me?"

Cory ducked his head.

"Coryell, look at me!" Guy demanded. *Do you understand me?"*

The boy raised his head and reluctantly met his father's gaze. His brown eyes filled with tears, and his chin trembled.

"Yes, Papa," he whispered.

Guy's look softened. He crouched down in front of Cory and took him by the shoulders.

"Come, son," he said, "come. What's all this about then?"

Cory gave a sob and threw himself into his father's arms. "Itslltoohar!" he sobbed into Guy's shoulder. "Idon'unnerstandit andeyjumaround!"

"What?" Guy said, an undertone of amusement swinging in his voice. "I didn't catch a word of that." He picked Cory up and sat on the bench, putting the boy on his lap.

Cat pulled out a handkerchief and sat beside them. "I think he said that it's all too hard and he doesn't understand it," she said. "Right, sweetie?"

Cory let go of his father's neck and pulled back a little. He nodded his head and sniffed. "It's so hard," he said tearfully, "Master Nikor's lessons, I don't understand it! It's boring!"

Guy took the handkerchief out of Cat's hands, dried the spot on his neck where the deluge of tears had hit, and wiped the boy's nose. "I have to admit you've got a point there, son. Master Nikor's lessons were boring when

I was your age, and that was thirty years ago. I always found it hard, too. But you've got to try your best, and be respectful, son, there's no way around that."

Cory scrubbed the backs of his fists across his cheeks. "They jump," he said, "the letters. I can't make them be the words that Master Nikor says they should be. I tried, honest I did! But I can't."

"Oh!" Guy looked at his wife. "Cat—he's got it too. That dys—dys—whatever-you-call-it, where the letters won't stand still, so you can't read them."

"Dyslexia," Cat said. "I guess it shouldn't be a surprise; it does run in families, from what I've heard." She should have known. She should have had an idea that her son struggled with learning to read just like his father had; that Nikor was getting past it and didn't do a good job teaching the kids any longer. But she had been so busy, and so tired, and there was always so much to do...

"Do I have to say sorry to Master Nikor for being rude?" said Cory in a small voice. "Is he going to give me a whupping?"

Cat and Guy exchanged a look.

"Master Nikor wouldn't give you a whupping," Guy said. "The only time I've ever seen him close to striking a boy was when Toria Woodcutterson tore a page out of a book on purpose, and even then he only *almost* hit him. But he certainly never let Toria into the library after that."

"Tearing a page out of a book is different," said Cat, "that's—well, I would get mad at that too!"

"Would you give a boy a whupping if you were the reading teacher, Mumma?" asked Cory in an interested tone.

Guy laughed. "I wouldn't care to put it to the test if I were you," he said, "Mumma would be a very strict reading teacher, and certainly wouldn't let young varmints like you and Tor pull any shenanigans!"

"I think I'd like Mumma to be the reading teacher," said Cory, "and me and Tor wouldn't pull any sh'naginans if she was. Do I have to say sorry to Master Nikor, Mumma?"

Cat considered. "No, dear, I don't think so. As long as you truly are sorry and don't do it again. But I do think you need to tell Tor, so he knows it was a wrong thing to do. Can you do that, do you think?"

"Okay," Cory said in a resigned voice. "Do I still have to have lessons with Master Nikor?"

Cat looked at Guy. "Well..."

"Yes, for now you do, son," Guy said decisively. "But not forever. Just do your best, all right?" He lifted the boy off his lap, stood him on the floor and gave him a slap on the rump. "Run along, rapscallion," he said, "I think Bina and Kell found a bullfrog out back; why don't you go see?"

Cory scampered out the door.

Guy gave Cat a sidelong glance, then reached out his forefinger and gently ran it over the faint crow's feet at the corner of her eye.

"You know, that brat of ours has a point, Karana," he said. "You'd make an excellent reading teacher. If I'd have had you to teach me, maybe I would have mastered those letters after all."

She flicked his finger away with her own. "You'd have just blinked your big turquoise eyes at me and got away with murder," she said. "Guy, I'd love to teach the kids, but you know I can't. Who would do all the work around here and look after the little ones?" Her eyes suddenly stung, and she blinked back tears. She was so tired...

Guy wrapped his arms around her and pulled her close. "Hmm," he murmured into her hair, "I wonder... Let me think on that, Karana."

CHAPTER 6

R HITHA SLIPPED THROUGH THE library garden gate. Mistress Catriona wasn't there today; she'd said she had washing to do at home. That meant Bina wouldn't be there either; she'd be helping at home, and besides, she never went to the library on her own, as Rhitha had found out over the last few weeks. But that was all right; Rhitha just wanted to be alone and enjoy the peace in the small walled garden for a little. Just a little while with nobody scolding her, or nagging her, or telling her she was a clumsy fool and an ugly twig. Rhitha sat down under the old walnut tree and hugged her knees.

If only she knew why Mother and Kashinka always were on at her. If only she knew what it was about her that set them off so much. Maybe if she knew, she could avoid doing it, whatever it was.

She sighed, and buried her face in her arms. It hadn't been much better in Ilim, when Father had still been alive—he had been alive, but hardly around. Off on business, Mother had told the neighbours. Rhitha thought that some of that business must have been done in taverns, over mugs of ale or cider—quite a lot of that business, she thought, because he had so often smelled of the alehouse when he did come home.

And then he fell ill, and died. Mother had scolded, and wept, and then she told Kashinka they would go back to Ruph. She hadn't told Rhitha, because Rhitha heard things anyway. Kashinka had pouted, and argued, and complained that she would never find a husband in the godforsaken backwater that Ruph was, but Mother was firm and said they had no money and needed to go where they would have a roof over their heads.

But what finally tipped the balance was 'the piece'—the chance to get a hold of 'the piece' after all this time. Rhitha had no idea what 'the piece' was, but when Mother mentioned it—in a hushed tone; Rhitha was fairly certain she had not been meant to hear—Kashinka had got a thoughtful look on her face. And the next day she had packed her trunk, the canvas-clad one which was painted to look like leather, with the tin buckles that pretended to be brass. She had taken Rhitha's small wooden chest, the one that had been a gift from Grandmother for her birth, and had put her strings of beads and hammered hairpins into it, and put it in the bottom of her trunk. Rhitha didn't need the box, Kashinka had said, because she had nothing to put into it. That was true enough, but Rhitha had still wanted to keep her own box—it was hers, and Grandmother had given it to her.

She had not even known Grandmother then, or at least hadn't remembered her from when she was small, but the box had still been special. Now she knew Grandmother, and it hurt even more to know that the box—her own box, with the carved rose on the lid—was in the bottom of Kashinka's trunk. Because now Grandmother was special.

Rhitha wished they could live with Grandmother. At least, she wished *she* could live with her; but for Grandmother's sake she was glad they were not all staying with her. Grandmother lived in a small cottage in Cobbler's Row, where all the houses were stuck to one other—that's why they called it a row. The cottage only had two rooms, one in front where you stepped in, which was the kitchen and sitting room, and another in back with Grandmother's bed and a chest of clothing. There was no room for all of them; they could barely sit in Grandmother's kitchen around her little table. And Mother and Kashinka hated sitting in Grandmother's kitchen.

In their house in Ilim they had had a dining parlour just for having meals in, where there had been only the table and some carved chairs; and a sitting room with a settle by a fire that was used for nothing but keeping people warm. The kitchen with the cooking fire had been a separate room, in the far back of the house, and for a while they had had a maid who lived there and cooked their food. But sometime before Father died, the maid had left. After that, there had been a few others, women who had come in for a few days at a time, but none of them stayed long. And then father died, and Rhitha heard Mother say to Kashinka that they could no longer afford a servant at all.

The house had only been rented, and none of the furniture was theirs; it had belonged with the house. Rhitha found that out, too, from overhearing Mother and Kashinka. So now they were in another rented place, the back part of a house a few doors down from Grandmother's cottage. The furniture there was nowhere near as fine as in the house in Ilim, and they only had three rooms—one for Mother to sleep in, one for Kashinka, and one for the kitchen and sitting room and Rhitha.

Grandmother owned her cottage, though; she had told Rhitha herself one day. Rhitha had come over to see if Grandmother had any sugar to borrow. Sugar! What had made Mother expect that Grandmother would have any such expensive luxury in the house, Rhitha could not guess. But there was no point in arguing with Mother—there never was. So Rhitha had gone over to ask Grandmother about sugar. As she thought, Grandmother had just looked astonished, and then laughed in her soft cracked little-old-woman's voice—not *at* Rhitha, but *with* her. And from that moment Rhitha and Grandmother had been friends.

Rhitha had never had anyone who understood how laughable some of Mother's ideas were, and nobody to share that laugh with her, but Grandmother knew *exactly* how it was. And then she had put the kettle on the fire and made them a pot of mintbrew, and had sat in her comfortable-looking carved wing chair beside the fire, and Rhitha sat on the little stool across from her, and they had shared mintbrew and Grandmother told her how she had sold the big, rich house by the market, and bought this lovely snug cottage, and how she was so much happier not needing to keep servants and being able to make her own decisions.

Rhitha did not bother to ask if Grandmother had any money saved from selling the big house—she did not care. Mother cared, though, very much, and Kashinka did too. Rhitha knew that they had expected to be able to move into the big house, and live a rich life, even though what counted as a big house in Ruph was only a small one by the standards of Ilim.

Kashinka grumbled about it a lot. She had spent all her childhood in Ruph and was already fifteen when they left for Ilim; she remembered the house by the market very well. Their own family had lived farther away from the centre of town, in a medium-sized house off Blue Street, which they had sold when they had left. Kashinka had pointed it out that day they had come to town; they had ridden right past it in the cart they travelled in. They had still expected to go to the market house then, but had soon learned better.

Mother was still quite angry with Grandmother. After a few weeks in Ruph, Mother had given up hinting for money; Rhitha supposed that she had finally come to believe that Grandmother was serious when she said she could not give her any. But Mother kept saying that she wished Grandfather Belock was still alive, because he would have treated her right; he would never have expected his daughter to live in such a cramped place with no comfortable things.

And even though Mother no longer asked Grandmother for money or talked about moving back to the big house, she nagged her at every turn, the same way she did with Rhitha. And she was just as unkind to her. She even took Grandmother's things, like Kashinka helped herself to Rhitha's; and Rhitha knew that Grandmother was hurt by it. She had seen the look on Grandmother's face when Mother had taken the pretty green pottery bowl off the mantelpiece, and said that it was just the size she needed to keep her cold cream in, and surely Grandmother would not mind as she was obviously not using it. Grandmother *did* mind, Rhitha knew she did. But she had said nothing.

Because Grandmother, Rhitha suspected, was scared of Mother and Kashinka, just like Rhitha was. So they said nothing, and let them take their things, and nag them and scold them. It was the unkindness that was the worst, the cold looks, the sneering lift of the corner of the mouth. Rhitha was afraid of those looks; they stabbed her right in the heart. She sometimes thought that she would not mind doing the dirty work, even the chamber pots although they made her gag, if only she would get a smile, or a kind word now and then.

For a long time she had thought that she was being unreasonable. She had thought that people who were poor were miserable, that was just the way it was. To be happy and cheerful you had to have comfort, and only rich living meant soft words and kindness. At least that's how it had seemed to her when she looked at the rich houses in Ilim; she was sure the people living in them were happy. Mother had always said that more money would make her happy, and Kashinka smiled whenever she had got a new gown or been given a gift. Rhitha had scolded herself for wishing for kindness, when they could not help having less than they needed for their happiness.

But lately, she was starting to wonder. Even before they had left Ilim, she had begun to doubt that it was only riches that made for happiness, but since they had come to Ruph, those doubts were become stronger and stronger. Grandmother lived in a small cottage, and she said she was happier there than in the big house. Grandmother's small house was warm, and comfortable; Rhitha thought her little table and chairs were very pretty, especially with that jug of wildflowers on it, even though Mother and Kashinka sneered at it. And the patchwork quilt on Grandmother's bed was beautiful; Rhitha loved the gently washed-out colours of the blanket and thought the pattern was the most clever thing ever—and Grandmother had made it herself! But above all, Grandmother was kind. She had a smile for Rhitha every time she saw her, and she called her 'dear child' and stroked her cheek with her paper-soft wrinkled hand. Grandmother had only little, just a small house and few things, but she had more kindness than Rhitha had ever met with before in her life.

And then there was Bina, and all of Bina's family. Bina's father was the Septimissimus! Rhitha had been told that after she had been with Bina quite a few times, and she had not known what the word meant when she first heard it. But then she learned that the Septimissimus was someone very special; that the whole Septimus family was something unusual, and very important in Ruph. Bina's grandfather, who had been a seventh son, had been able to build things, make them fit together so they worked, and all the people in town needed him. And Bina's father, who was *his* seventh son, had some extra-special powers. He was able to put his hands on people, and help them get well if they were sick, sometimes. And he was a potter, and could make special dishes which had unusual powers—apart from the things he normally made, which were very nice pieces of pottery; in fact, Rhitha was quite certain that the little green bowl Mother had taken away from Grandmother had been made by Master Dyniselm.

So Bina's father was special, and was important in Ruph. But when Rhitha first found out about it, she did not believe it, because that was after Bina had taken her to visit at her house in the woods (or the Wald, Bina said it was called), and her family did not look like rich people at all. They lived at the end of a forest road, in a cottage with two rooms with a garden beside it, and Bina's Mumma did all of the cooking and washing and everything herself.

Rhitha had found it hard to believe that they could be important people; she thought important people would be rich. And Bina's family was not rich. But they were kind. All of them. Rhitha was a little scared of Bina's father, because he was tall and she had heard him shouting at one of Bina's brothers who was throwing stones at the big kiln behind the house, where the potter fired his dishes. But Bina said that was because her brother was being a silly fool who should know better than to do something that was unsafe and could damage important stuff, and she hadn't seemed worried at all. And Master Dyniselm had laughed at some joke his apprentice made right afterwards, and he was so friendly and not angry at all when Bina had taken Rhitha into the pottery shop, so maybe Bina was right.

The apprentice, Andy, he was kind too. Rhitha had thought at first he was Bina's brother. He was about the same age as Kashinka, that was why, but also, Bina kept talking about him like he was—Andy this and Andy that, and if Andy said something then it was always true. He'd smiled at them, and called Bina 'Little Bee', and showed them a tiny cup he'd made for Bina which was almost finished. Until she met Grandmother, Rhitha had never known anyone who smiled at you as if they were happy just because you'd come into the room. Bina, it seemed, had a whole family like that.

Rhitha put her chin in her hands. They were even nice to *her*, all of Bina's family. Her mumma was the best of all. Rhitha sometimes went into the library when she knew Mistress Catriona was there just because she always seemed pleased when Rhitha came. Rhitha loved the books in there, but the warm smile she got from her friend's mother lit up the whole room. And Rhitha hadn't even done anything special. She tried to help out with putting away books, but Mistress Catriona seemed to think it was nice just to have her around, even if there was nothing to do.

They talked about stories, sometimes, and Bina's mumma always ended by going to a shelf, and pulling down a book, and finding a printed version of the tale, or of one like it, or one entirely different that talked about a similar thing or said the exact opposite—she always thought about things in stories and knew exactly where everything was in the library—just like Master Nikor.

Rhitha liked the little librarian, too; she thought he was funny. He hardly ever emerged from his books any more. Mistress Catriona said he used to be in the library more, when she first came, but now he spent most of the day in his back room, hidden behind stacks of books. He did still come out every morning to teach the children their letters, but sometimes the kids had to go fetch him, and tell him that it was lesson time, and afterwards he disappeared again as soon as the children left.

At least Bina's brother Cory and their cousin Tor were no longer rude to Master Nikor. Rhitha had hated it when they were like that. Even though Master Nikor had not seemed to notice their disrespect, it made her skin hurt to watch someone being teased and bullied. Bina said her father put a stop to it, and Rhitha believed it, easily. She could imagine that it would be very scary to have Master Dyniselm be angry at you. He had those bright turquoise eyes, like Bina and her uncle, Master Rysil Woodwright, which seemed like they could look right through you as if you were made of glass. Rhitha imagined being looked at by those eyes and told that she was in trouble, and it made her shiver so much she had to hug herself and rub her arms to make the goosebumps go away.

Bina would laugh at her if she knew it. She already laughed at her for calling her father Master Dyniselm—she said everyone just said Master Guy, and her uncle was Master Sepp. But Rhitha *couldn't*—you had to be polite to elders, or they got angry with you and looked at you with a frown. And Rhitha couldn't bear to be looked at like that. Bina didn't understand; Rhitha guessed that nobody had ever treated her with anything but kindness. You could tell by the way Bina was so kind herself. Even when she laughed at her, Rhitha didn't mind—it was a funny laugh that made you want to laugh too, not a you're-so-stupid laugh like Kashinka's that made you want to crawl into a corner and curl into a little ball.

Rhitha wished that Master Dyniselm would give Kashinka one of his looks. And cross his arms at her, and loom over her and shout at her, like Bina said he did to her brothers when they were naughty. Then maybe Kashinka would become small, too, and not sneer at and bully Rhitha and Grandmother any more.

Rhitha heaved a deep sigh. If only she knew what it was she had done that made Kashinka hate her so. She knew Mother was disappointed in her because she was not beautiful like Kashinka, and because Mother hadn't wanted another child in the first place—Kashinka was enough, and she was so much better than Rhitha. Mother had once said to Kashinka that it was a plague for a woman to get herself with child without meaning to; and she had looked right at Rhitha when she said it.

Kashinka had laughed and said something about how only fools would fall pregnant without promised marriage (which wasn't what Mother had been talking of), and Mother pinched her mouth shut and then changed the subject. But that was because she looked down on women who had children without a husband. To bear a child outside of wedlock was a terrible shame. Rhitha was glad that she knew who their own father was—even though she did not have Father's dark hair like Kashinka, they both had his funny shape of feet, with the second toe much longer than the others.

But why, even though they were sisters, did Kashinka hate her? Rhitha had never done anything to make Kashinka hate her. At least she could not remember having done anything. Perhaps she did when she was small? Or maybe—and Rhitha had suspected this for some time now—maybe Kashinka was angry just because Rhitha was *there*. Maybe it was being born that was the bad thing Rhitha had done. And there was nothing she could do about it.

But since they had come to Ruph, she had begun to wonder if there wasn't something else as well. Kashinka was giving her more of those looks now than ever, the kind with her eyes narrowed and the corner of her lip pulled up a little, like she had just seen something nasty. And she did it most of all when Rhitha had been at Grandmother's. Was it only because Kashinka hated Grandmother, too? Or was there something *at* Grandmother's, something Kashinka wanted? Was it that 'piece' she and Mother had spoken of?

Rhitha heard the big clock on the top of the town hall, on the other side of the marketplace from the library, strike the half hour. Oh no! She jumped to her feet. She was meant to have done the marketing, gone to the butcher's shop and brought home some chops for their dinner! And Mother wanted her dinner right on the stroke of noon. Now there would be no time to first go to Master Oldran's shop—he was another one of Bina's uncles—to see if he had any good prices today; she had to go straight to the butcher's in Nickel Alley because it was closer to home.

She ran around the corner and diagonally across the marketplace, her skirt flapping around her calves, and was just about to turn the corner into Seven Houses Street when she heard a high-pitched laugh that stopped her in her tracks and sent a cold tingle of unpleasant surprise skittering over her scalp and down her neck. Kashinka! Rhitha looked around, afraid of having been seen. Her sister would have nothing but scorn for her helter-skelter rush through town, and the fear of the cutting things she would say made Rhitha's stomach clench.

But luck was with her. Kashinka was turned away from her, standing between the tables which were set out in front of the town's inn on the other side of the marketplace, talking to two men. Or rather, she was talking and laughing with the one; the other she was half turned away from, showing him her shoulder. Rhitha did not even think of being surprised at that—the man Kashinka ignored was old, with white hair and a long white beard. It was his companion she was interested in, of course, a young, powerfully built man with hair as black as Kashinka's own, and a clean-shaven jaw that, together with the unusual patterns on his colourful cloak, proclaimed him a stranger in town. He bent closer to Kashinka and said something to her, and her shrill laugh rang out again.

Rhitha pulled herself out of her frozen state, raised her skirt a little, and lightly and quickly ran down the lane.

CHAPTER 7

I T WAS FRIDAY, MARKET day. Rhitha skipped down the steps of the library building. She liked it when the whole marketplace in Ruph was full of people, market stalls lining three sides of the square. The fourth side was occupied by the inn which was doing a booming trade in ale, and dinners that people could take away with them, rolled up in a paper cone, to eat while they walked among the stalls.

Rhitha stopped at the silversmith's stall and admired the ornaments on display. There were three new silver pendants meant for wedding chains—a rabbit, a bird, and one shaped like a lily—and in front of them, some enamel pins in bright blues, yellows, and reds.

Rhitha smiled shyly at the smith, an older woman with hair just the colour of those pendants. "They are very pretty," she said.

"Thank you, dear. I don't suppose you'll be looking to purchase one today, do you?" the smith said, looking over the top of her spectacles at Rhitha with a twinkle in her eye.

Rhitha regretfully shook her head. "Did someone buy the blue butterfly pin you had last week?" she asked.

The twinkle died out. "No, dear. Not so as I ever saw any coin for it. It was gone by the end of the day; but I couldn't have turned my back for more than a minute. Ah well. Thievery is one of the risks I have to put up with in my line of work."

Rhitha walked on, past the baker's stall which sent out delectable smells. Rhitha wished she had a coin to buy one of the apple cakes that were displayed prominently at the front of the stall, but all she had money for was a loaf of bread, some cheese from the dairyman's, and a few vegetables from the farmer's.

Chonyk Farmer's hair was mostly grey, but Rhitha could tell that it used to be red, probably as red as Bina's. She wondered if he was a relation.

"Hey, there you are, Rhee!" her friend said from behind her. "Hullo, Uncle Chonyk! What do you have that's good right now? Mumma wants to know if there's still any fresh kohlrabi; ours are either all eaten or went woody. Ooh, you've got strawberries!"

"Hi there, young'un!" the stocky farmer replied. "Yes, you may taste a strawberry. Your friend here, too—I don't think we've met?"

"This is Rhee, Uncle Chonyk! She's not just my friend, she's my *cousin*!" Bina linked her arm with Rhitha's, picked up a couple of strawberries, popped one into her mouth and gave the other to Rhita.

Rhitha bit a tiny piece off her berry and let the flavour wash over her tongue. A little sigh of pleasure escaped her.

Bina laughed at her. "They're yummy, aren't they?" she said, snatching another berry from Chonyk's display.

"Hold it there, young lady," the farmer laughed, "don't eat all my stock! Are you going to buy some, or not? Two coins for a pint. And yes, I still have kohlrabi, but this will be the end of them."

"All right, I'll have some strawberries. And some kohlrabi," said Bina. "But I don't know how much of that, for all of us."

"I'll give you three pounds," said the farmer, "that should do. And what about you, young lady?" He looked at Rhitha with an enquiring lift of his eyebrow.

Rhitha swallowed the last little piece of strawberry. "I need some vegetables, please," she said shyly. "But I'm not sure what kind to get."

"Why don't you have some kohlrabi, too?" said Bina. "They're really tasty; even my brothers like them!"

"I don't think I've ever had those," said Rhitha. "How do you eat them?"

"Well, they're the most yummy when you eat them raw right out of the garden," said Bina, "but Mumma slices them up and cooks them in salt water, and we eat them like that. They're a bit like cabbage, but nicer."

"Here, have a try," said Chonyk Farmer, passing Rhitha a sliver he had sliced off one of the pale green fist-sized round knobs.

"Ooh, me too!" said Bina, holding out a hand. Her uncle gave her a slice, then took a bite off the remaining piece of kohlrabi as if he was eating an apple.

Rhitha nibbled on her piece. It was crunchy and sweet, a nice taste.

"How many could I get for—for one coin?" she asked shyly. "There's three of us, and we'll have sausages as well."

"One coin would just about do it for what you need," said the farmer, choosing three smaller vegetables from his stack and handing them to Rhitha. "Anything else?"

"I don't think I have enough for strawberries," Rhitha said regretfully, looking into her coin purse. "I've only got two coins left, and I still need cheese."

"Tell you what," he said, "as those are the last kohlrabi and I don't know if they're not a little woody, I'll let you have some strawberries for one more coin."

Rhitha's eyes lit up. "Thank you, Master Chonyk!"

"Your uncle is nice," she said to Bina as they walked away from the stall. "Which number brother of your father is he?" She had begun to make a mental list of all Bina's relations; it was getting tricky to keep them all in her head.

"Oh, he's not Papa's brother," Bina said, snitching a strawberry from the little pint box in her market basket, "he's his cousin. You know, my Aunt Yldra's brother. You've met Aunt Yldra, right?"

"I think so," said Rhitha slowly. "She's got red hair like you, and has a little girl with blonde hair, and she lives on Radlor's Way? And she gave us pastries when we were there one day."

"Yes, that's the one! Aunty Yldra makes the best pastries," said Bina. "Her little girl is called Immy and her son is Randy."

"I don't think I've met him," said Rhitha, keeping herself with an effort from following Bina's example and snacking on her strawberries. She wanted to give some to Grandmother, and there would be none left if she ate them now.

"Randy is about our size," Bina said. "Actually, I think he's the same age as you. Eleven," she clarified. "Look! There he is right now!" She pointed across the market to the tables in front of the inn.

"Which one?"

"That one!" Bina kept pointing, "With Ben! They're playing a game. See, Andy is there too."

Rhitha looked over at the inn, and finally found among the crowd the two dark heads of the Shapers, Ben Carver and Bina's almost-brother Andy. She still could not tell which of them was which. She had been quite confused the first time Bina had taken her to her Uncle Sepp's house, and had found Andy, as she thought, working with him in the woodwork shop. But finally Bina had explained about them, how they had come from another world just like her Mumma had (except this was a different one), and how they both could make beautiful sculptures, but Andy—A'verelm, that was his full name—made them out of clay, and Ben—Br'oldyn—used wood, and so one of them worked with Bina's father, and the other with her uncle. And because they were twins, sometimes their sculptures were mirror images of each other, too, and then they had special powers.

At that moment, one of the two young men stood beside one of the inn tables, watching his brother who was facing a tow-headed young boy across a game board.

"Randy keeps dragging that Chest game around with him all the time," Bina said critically, weaving her way through the crowd. "He's always looking for someone to take him on."

"Chess," Rhitha said softly, trying to keep up with her. "No T, I think." Mistress Catriona had shown her how the moves of the game worked, one rainy afternoon in the library.

Bina didn't hear her.

"Andy, Andy, Andy," she called, "Uncle Chonyk has strawberries ripe on the farm already! Look, I got two whole pints!"

The standing young man looked up, and gave her a smile. "That's lovely, Bee," he said. "Do you think there will be any left for me by the time I get back to the pottery?"

His brother raised his head from the game and followed Andy's gaze. "Not if you don't take them away from her before she eats them all," he said. "At the rate she's going none of them are going to make it home."

Suddenly he caught sight of someone behind Bina and Rhitha, and his whole expression changed. "Liss!" he called, his black eyes shining, and he jumped up from his seat.

Rhitha turned her head. A slender young woman with red-gold hair worn in a coronet of braids was coming up behind them.

"Good day to you, too, Ben Carver," the girl said. "And where have you been these last however-many days? You haven't been near the fish farm in at least a fortnight!"

"That's my cousin Liss—Nygelis—" Bina said in an aside to Rhitha. "She's my Uncle Yokan's daughter; they have fish ponds. Ben likes her."

Rhitha smiled. She could have figured out both of those things for herself—the red hair seemed to be a badge of belonging to Bina's family, and the red face of the young man told its own story.

"I—I—I'm sorry, Liss," he stammered, "S-Sepp and I have b-been v-very busy!"

The young woman gave him a teasing smile, and he seemed to take courage from it. He ran his hand through his black hair, making it flop over his forehead. "Are you done your marketing," he asked, "or can I take your basket for you?"

"Well, if you must," she said with a little toss of her head, "I suppose you can carry it. I still need some flour from the miller's, and that's heavy." Ben took the basket out of her hand, and the two of them walked off together, the girl with a swing to her hips that Rhitha had seen on Kashinka when she wanted to impress a man—but Kashinka did it on purpose, while with Nygelis it seemed entirely natural—and Ben with a hint of a swagger.

Randy had missed the whole episode in his concentration on his game board. He moved one of his bishops three spaces forward, and looked up. "Hey!" he said, wrinkling his forehead. "Where did Ben go? I got him in check!"

Bina laughed at him.

"Liss showed up, and Ben took off," she said. "So much for check."

Randy huffed air out his nose. "Girls!" he said disgustedly. "Come on, Andy, finish the game! It's no fun to win if I'm not actually playing *against* someone."

"All right," Andy said good-naturedly, took his brother's seat and moved the black king out of check.

Suddenly Rhitha became aware that there was someone else watching the players at the chess board; in fact, he had been watching them for quite some time already. What had drawn her attention was the motion of his head when he turned back from watching Ben walk off with Liss.

It was the white-bearded foreigner, the one that Kashinka had so pointedly ignored the other day. He was alone this time, his companion nowhere in sight, and his deep-set brown eyes under the bushy white brows were fixed inscrutably on Andy who was focused on the chess board in front of him.

Rhitha studied the stranger carefully. He was not wearing the hat he had had on last time Rhitha had seen him, and she realized now that the dark tone of his face was not the shading from his head covering, but the natural colour of his skin, which contrasted sharply with the whiteness of his hair and beard. His nose was slightly hooked, and his moustache hid much of his mouth.

She wondered why he was staring at Andy so, when Bina interrupted her thoughts.

"There's Papa!" she called. "Andy, Papa's here!"

Master Dyniselm made his way through the crowd towards them, an empty crate under his arm. Rhitha saw him notice the white-bearded stranger, and he gave a slight bow. "Master Ekinoru," he said in greeting.

The stranger turned away from his scrutiny of the young man at the table, and inclined his head in response. "Master Guy," he replied, "a good morrow to you."

Bina's father laid his hand on his apprentice's shoulder. "Time to head home, son," he said. "My deliveries are made, and we have work to do."

Andy looked up at him, and readily rose from his seat. "Very well," he said. "Sorry, Randor. We'll finish the game some other time."

"Oh, come on!" Randy said, frustrated.

"We're going too," said Bina, "Rhee, you're coming to my house, right?"

"I have to drop off my shopping first," Rhitha said. "But wait a moment!"

She stepped over to the table and moved a black rook two squares to the left. "Check!"

Randy looked up from the chess board with his jaw dropped.

"What?!"

"Check!" Rhitha repeated.

"What? You can't—how—you're a girl!"

"So what?" Bina intervened. "Are you going to finish that game or not? Rhee and me are going."

He stared at the chess board in bewilderment, then moved his king one square over.

A black knight jumped. "Checkmate!" Rhitha said, picked up her basket, and walked after her cousin.

CHAPTER 8

"CORY NEEDS NEW CLOTHES—AGAIN!" Cat said that evening. "He's shooting up like a weed. And at the rate he's been wearing them out"—she held out the boy's pants to Guy to show him the hole she was mending in the knee—"they won't even be much good for Kell, let alone Dyllie when he gets to that size. This is getting expensive."

"Speaking of expense," Guy said, "you know that Ekinoru, the master from Rhanathon? He's been talking about the two of us doing business together, and from the hints he's dropped, there could be some decent coin in it for me. I'm not entirely sure yet what he's got in mind, but I invited him and his journeyman for dinner tomorrow to talk it over and to take a look around the workshop; then we'll see."

"What?!" yelped Cat. "You invited guests for dinner, and it didn't occur to you to mention it before now? Thank you very much! Oh dear, what am I going to feed them? I can hardly put the leftovers in front of them I was going to give *you*, mister! And this place is a mess..."

"Stop clucking, you're not a chicken," said Guy, and ducked out of the way of the swipe Cat directed at his head. "You can always feed them potatoes, those are good. And the house looks fine."

"Says you..." Cat said despairingly, looking around the kitchen which had laundry strung under the eaves in the corner and a box of wooden blocks, several stuffed animals, three odd socks, Dyllie's wooden drinking cup, and five jumbled pairs of children's shoes scattered on the floor, while underneath the baby's high chair were several sticky spots of unidentified origin. "How am I going to get this all done?"

"Another slice of pie, Master Ekinoru?" Cat asked in her most gracious hostess voice. Thank goodness Nicky had come to her rescue; between the two of them they had managed to beat the house into shape and put a decent dinner in front of Guy's potential new trades contacts. They still had not heard what this trade was supposed to be—but so far, the guests seemed to be enjoying the food.

"I thank you, Mistress," said the older man, and let Cat refill his plate. She put a slice of rhubarb pie and another spoonful of custard on his journeyman's plate, too, wrinkling her nose a little at the rather obtrusive scent the young man wore. Bel'ris'oem, that was his name—Cat had made an effort to remember it. He was a handsome fellow, somewhere in his mid-twenties, at a guess, with dark hair, curiously light green eyes, and a square jaw. Between Guy,

Sepp, and the journeyman, the conversation had ranged from the rigours of overland travel through the cuisine of the port city in which the two men did their trade to the latest political gossip of the capital city of Isachang.

Andy had contributed the odd comment to their talk, but the old master had been quite silent. Cat wondered about the subtle way the man's dark eyes during the meal were often fixed on Guy's apprentice at the other end of the table. She doubted that anyone else had noticed how he covertly studied the young man while he was ostensibly focused on the meat loaf and mashed potatoes she and Nicky had managed to produce just in time for the guests to arrive.

"Mumma!" Bina hissed from the door to the other room. "Can we have our pie now?" Cat picked up the second pie plate and took it next door where the kids had had a trestle table put up for them so they could eat by themselves and enjoy the company of their cousins without the interference of grownups—at least that was how Nicky had made the idea palatable to them when they protested about being excluded from the adults' dining table in the kitchen. Quite apart from the space problem, Cat did not want the guests to be subjected to the sight of her smaller offspring's eating habits. Bina was presiding over the kids' table with all the aplomb of a born hostess, so Cat left her to distribute the pie to her brothers and cousins and hoped that it would stay confined to the plates and not find its way onto the blankets of the boys' bunk beds.

When she returned to the kitchen, Andy and Nicky had started to clear the plates, and the kettle was on the stove for mintbrew. Cat went to take the mugs off their hooks in the cupboard.

"Oh dear," she said, "what's this doing here?" One of the turquoise-glazed Septimus cups was sitting at the back of the shelf. She showed it to Nicky. "That had better go into the box with the other ones before someone does themselves a harm," she said.

"Wait, Cat," called Guy from the table, "pass it here. I want to show Master Ekinoru and Bel'ris'oem. See, here, masters, this is one of those cups I told you of; my second run of this glaze from some seven years ago. This particular firing, with this clay, made reinforcer cups—these ones concentrate the powers of the contents."

"Hm," grunted Master Ekinoru. He took the cup in his hand and turned it over, scrutinizing it intently. Then he flicked his fingernail against it, setting it ringing, and tapped the bottom to test its thickness. "Hm," he said again, and passed the cup to his journeyman.

Bel'ris'oem copied his master's actions, turning the cup over and feeling the texture of the glaze. Then he held it close to his eyes and looked at it intently as if he was trying to see each particle of its makeup, and gazed into the depth of the vessel.

"So what does this do again?" he asked, handing the cup back to Guy.

"As I said, it concentrates the power of what it contains," Guy said. "One strong drink from this cup will put a large man under the table, and medicine taken from it has multiple times the effect it normally does. My wife thinks it is the combination of the clay body with the clay and ash that went into the making of the glaze, under the influence of my gift, that made it become like that."

A curious gleam came into the eyes of the journeyman. He looks odd, Cat thought—greedy, somehow! "Well," he said, looking at his master, "this might be what we are looking for. This glaze together with what we have to offer..."

"Forgive me, masters," Cat said, "but I still have not heard just what it is that is your trade. Do you deal in stoneware?"

"In a manner of speaking, Mistress," Bel'ris'oem replied. "We manufacture and trade in ceramic ware. As you know, no doubt,"—his look was slightly condescending—"Rhanathon is a port city which trades with all other countries around the Moon Sea. The market for specialty ware is great there. We have also sent wares to Isachang, the capital city, but our main trade is overseas."

Cat felt slightly irritated at his lecturing tone. She had read enough volumes of geography to be quite well versed in the layout of the country of Isachang without needing to be instructed by a sleek-haired foreigner, thank you very much. Then she mentally chuckled at herself—who was she calling a foreigner? Catriona Septimuswife, Bookwoman, of the Wald of Ruph, was hardly far enough removed from Catriona McMurphy of Greenward Falls, America, to feel superior to someone who had come into Ruph from elsewhere in Isachang, no matter how many geography and history books she had consumed over the last seven years.

Suddenly Master Ekinoru spoke up. "Show them," he said, curtly.

Bel'ris'oem looked at him in surprise. "Here, Master?"

"Here," said the old man, "let them all see."

There was a momentary flash of rebellion in the journeyman's eyes, but Cat hardly thought she had seen it before it had disappeared again.

"Very well, Master," he said, and reached below his seat. He pulled out the canvas bag he had worn over his shoulder when they had arrived and took from it a small box, perhaps eight inches square and six inches high, made of plain wood with the corners reinforced in brass. It had a small brass keyhole, for which he pulled the matching key, hanging on a leather string, from the collar of his tunic.

"A sample of our wares," he said with a practised grin that showed his extremely white teeth, and turned the key.

The first thing Cat saw when he lifted the lid was a thick layer of straw. He passed the open box to Guy. "There you are, Master Guy. Careful how you lift the contents."

Guy moved the straw layer aside, then Cat heard his quick intake of breath. "Look," he said, "look at this!" His long slender fingers lifted out of the straw a small, dainty cup. It was pure white, with a design drawn on it in a deep blue underglaze, and its walls were eggshell-thin. He held it up to the light. "This is practically translucent!" he said, awed. "I've never seen anything like it. Look at it, Cat!"

She carefully took the cup out of his hands. "That's beautiful," she said. "Look, Nicky, it's like bone china."

"It sure is!" Nicky agreed. "I didn't know it existed here!"

Master Ekinoru gave them a searching look from under his bristling white eyebrows. "Do you know it, Mistress?"

"Mistress Nicky and I came from—from another place to this country," Cat said. "We had many technologies there that are unknown here, and fine ceramics like this are not uncommon. We called it china or porcelain."

"Ah," the old man said.

"Is it valuable?" the journeyman asked, with a quickness to his tone that struck a slightly discordant note in Cat's mind.

"Some of it is," Nicky replied, "especially older pieces, or ones from particular sources."

"Yes, like my grandmother's Royal Doulton—that's a particular company which makes porcelain dishes and or-naments," Cat added. "Grandmother collected china, in-cluding figurines; there was a lot of money that went into it. My grandfather sold it when she died and used the money to help finance his stay in the retirement home."

"Huh," said Nicky, "I'm not surprised. Most china isn't that valuable now, but a complete collection..."

"Yes," Cat said. "Many years ago, when it was first dis-covered, porcelain used to be known as 'white gold'."

That oddly greedy look was back in Bel'ris'oem's eye, and he flashed his white teeth. "'White gold', eh?" he said. "Good word. These cups are worth good coin," he con-tinued, "and the southern lands by the Moon Sea have particular value for this white ware."

The cup had been passed from hand to hand, and had arrived with Andy. He was running his fingers over the elegantly curved handle of the dish with an absorbed look on his face. Cat looked from him to Master Ekinoru, and again noted the intent but secret look on the old man's face as he watched the young sculptor handle the piece.

Andy looked up. "Master Guy—do you think...?"

Guy had lifted a second cup from the wooden box and was testing the thin walls of the vessel with his fingers, as if he was picturing to himself how it would feel to make one like it on the wheel.

"I don't know if our tools and techniques would be up to the task," he said. "Where do you get the clay body to work this?"

At that moment a crashing sound came from the next room, and several small voices began to wail. Cat and Nicky jumped, and by the time the crisis had been dealt with, the men were gone from the kitchen.

Cat cast a look across the yard, and saw them moving around behind the windows of the workshop.

"I suppose they've gone to talk shop," she said to Nicky. "I wonder what exactly it is they want from Guy."

"The journeyman fellow was saying something about the glaze," Nicky said, reaching for a dish towel. "They seemed to be quite taken with the turquoise one on the Septimus cups."

"Well, I don't know if Guy can make that one again," Cat said, "but it could always be worth a try. And turquoise on that china, that could be amazing. By the way, thank you again for saving my butt today. I don't know what I would have done without you."

"No problem," Nicky said. "What's family for otherwise?"

"Well, maybe I can finally get it through Guy's head not to spring something like this on me without more warning. Especially when it's a trades dinner, where it matters. I do wonder about these two, though, Master Ekinoru and that journeyman of his. Something seems a bit odd there..."

———*ele*———

"Master Ekinoru wants to work out something between us about glazes," Guy said to Cat that evening, after the visitors had left. "I told him I can never guarantee the outcome, and have very limited resources of the materials for the Septimus glaze—there's only so much ash from the Septimus Tree branch, not much left now; and I'm not going to cannibalize that tree any further. But he seemed to think that I could give it a shot, and whatever comes out comes out. Not that he said so in so many words."

"He's not very talkative, is he?" said Cat, putting the last of the clean bowls back into the cupboard.

"No, but his journeyman makes up for it," said Guy with a grin.

"You mean that dark-haired man?" Bina passed Cat a stack of plates. "He's a bit weird; I don't know if I like him."

Cat looked at her in surprise. "What makes you say that?"

"Oh, *you* know..." Bina said. "Pass the cups, Papa."

"Hmm," Cat said, "I have to say I felt something too. Not strong, by any means, but it's there. Some funny looks that made me wonder..." For that matter, the looks the older man had given Andy—but she was even less sure about those. Besides, there had not been that undercurrent of something slightly off there with the master, as there had been with the journeyman; just something to make her curious. The journeyman, on the other hand, brought a hint of unease with him.

Guy looked from his wife to his daughter. "You two are feeling something about Bel'ris'oem, are you?" he said. "Interesting. I don't have the Knowing, of course, but I can't say I'm altogether inclined to make him my new bosom friend, either. He asks too many questions about 'power' and about how the Septimus dishes work and what else I might be able to do. For the first time I was rather glad I have no idea what makes the cups do what they do, that I don't have conscious control of it all."

"What was Master Ekinoru's reaction to this?" Cat asked.

"Not much that I could tell," Guy said. "He never says much, regardless. However, he seemed more inclined to look at the technical aspects of my work; he wanted to know the composition of my glazes. And he took a close look at the pieces Andy has drying on the shelf; that little portrait sculpture of Kell certainly had his attention."

Bina suddenly cried out sharply, as if she was in pain. "Mumma!"

"What? What is it, sweetie?"

The girl's face crumpled, and she hunched in on herself, her arms pressed to her chest. "Mumma, they're doing it again!"

Guy sprang over and took her by the shoulders. "What's wrong, Karana? Are you hurt?"

"No, not me! It's Rhee! They're being mean to Rhee again!"

_____ℓℓℓ_____

When Cat stepped back into the kitchen half an hour later, Guy was finishing the last of the cleanup.

"How is she?" he asked.

"Better now; she's asleep," Cat replied. "I held her for a while, that seemed to help, and she pretty much cried herself to sleep in my arms. Poor sweetie. Guy, this is getting bad. It used to be only us she could feel, but she and Rhitha have formed such a bond, she's picking up on _her_ feelings now, too, and it's hurting her. And Kashinka, that nasty, awful, bitchy ex-cousin-in-law of yours..."

"Steady on, woman," Guy said with a slight chuckle, putting his arms around her. "Don't blame me for what my ex-wife's cousin-once-removed is doing to her sister—who, incidentally, is just as much my whatever-grade-of-ex-wife's-relation, too." He laid his cheek on top of Cat's head. "It's got you all tied up in knots as well, doesn't it?"

Cat turned her face into his shoulder and nodded against him. "I don't know what to do about Rhitha—she's such a lovely girl, and I hate to see her hurt. But we can't interfere in another family; and so far there hasn't been any actual physical abuse that would give us proper cause to step in. I can only keep a wary eye out for her. But, actually, it's what this is doing to Bina that's getting to me. It's tearing her up. I can't feel Rhitha, not any more than any other person outside of the family, but I get a sense of Bibby—Bina, whatever. She's still my little girl, and she's hurting!"

He held her close. "Did I mention I love you, Karana?" he said into her hair. "Ashya had no idea of the favour she did us, me and Bina, when she took off the way she did and cleared the way for you to come into our lives. We will find a way through this, Karana. The best thing Bina has is you."

"Thank you." Cat wrapped her arms around his waist and held on tight. "What's hurting her the most is that she can't do anything—she feels the pain, and she's helpless. And she's never experienced anything like this in her life. All she's ever known is love—from you, from me, from Aunt and Uncle and Sepp and Nicky—everyone in her life... She has no idea what to do with the kind of nastiness that people like Kashinka can generate, and with the feelings that come from it. Rhitha, I think, has lived with it all her life; she's found ways to cope—maybe not good ones, but still—while Bina is completely unprotected. Is it bad of me to want to take fingernails to Kashinka's face?"

Guy laughed. "Yes, you bloodthirsty creature. Control yourself—I don't want to have to pay big fines to spring my wife free from the lockup where she's been imprisoned for assault. And how would I explain that to the boys? 'See you later, I have to go get Mumma from the round-house now. Stop hitting Kell, Cory; only grownups may injure people they're angry with.' Never mind the fact that it would hardly make Bina feel better."

Cat sighed. "I know. I just want to protect her from this... It's not fair that someone as small as her has to bear such a large burden."

"We'll find a way," he said again, rubbing his hand across her back. "Just love her, and we'll find a way."

CHAPTER 9

R HITHA HAD NOT MEANT to overhear. No matter what Kashinka said to her, how much she scolded her and called her names, it had *not* been on purpose that she listened to her sister and that black-haired man in whose company she was so often now. Rhitha had only sat in her favourite spot, her own private place in the library garden; she had *not* been sneaky and sly and secretive, like Kashinka said. How was she meant to have known that her sister and her boyfriend would stop right beside the gate, directly on the other side of the wall from the walnut tree? How was she supposed to have guessed that they would talk in voices loud enough to carry right across, about things they hadn't wanted anyone else to hear?

Rhitha had been awfully embarrassed, and wanted to sink into the ground when she realized that what she was hearing was her sister *and a man*, and the only parts worse than hearing what they were saying was what she was hearing when they *weren't* saying things. Rhitha's cheeks burned just thinking about it.

And that's how they had found out about her being there, in the garden. There had been some moaning noises, in between the kissing ones, and then Kashinka had gasped out, in a sort of breathy voice, "Here, in here, come on, darling, where no one can see us," and they had stumbled around the corner and through the gate, Kashinka wrapped around the man as if she was drowning, and he'd had—Rhitha's face flamed at the memory—he'd had his hand slipped right into her blouse, which had the laces at the front all undone and was pulled half-way off her shoulder.

And then Kashinka had seen Rhitha. And she had never, ever been so angry before, never. Her face had become all white, and her eyes had turned into little slits, and she had actually hissed at Rhitha—but Rhitha hadn't been able to hear what she said, because there was a high-pitched ringing in her ears and the skin on her face stung and tingled all over, she was so terrified. But she did hear what the man had said—Bel, was his name? That's what Kashinka had called him, before, on the other side of the wall. He had looked at Rhitha with eyes that were icy cold with contempt, and then he had asked in a voice that was so hard, Rhitha had thought it would splinter: "Did she hear us?"

And Rhitha had shaken her head, mutely, because she was too frightened to do anything else, and then she had found her feet, and jumped up and ducked around Kashinka and the man and run out the gate and down the lane, scared like the brown-eyed deer with its slender feet they had startled in the forest when they had come to Ruph in the cart from Ilim.

But it wasn't true that she hadn't heard. She did hear, almost every word. Everything the man had said. She did not understand all of what he meant, but she had heard the words. He had made promises to Kashinka, told her that once he had what he wanted, he would be rich. And buy Kashinka presents. All it took was to get the old man out of the way, and that was easy once he got a hold of what was rightfully his. He was the son of the man who had started the crafthouse, he said, and he had a right to—Rhitha hadn't caught the word of what he thought he had a right to.

Kashinka made agreeing noises. Rhitha was sure her sister had looked at the man with her eyes wide open and her mouth puckered in a pout; she had seen her do it often enough when she was talking to men, they seemed to like it. This one had liked it, too—he kept on talking.

"And then if I can get this potter master on my side," he'd said, "we'll have it made. Between what I have—what I will have—and what he can do . . . he'd have to be stupid not to come in with me. Although I'm not sure how bright he is,"—he'd made a scoffing sound—"he doesn't even seem to know what it is he's able to do."

Kashinka had giggled, in that tinkling way she had, and said: "Oh no, darling, they're not clever, those people. The whole family is pretty stupid, and so stuck-up—they think they're something special, and nobody else in this town counts for anything. They've always been that way, and that potter is the worst. But you'll show them all, won't you, darling? You're so clever..."

"But first I need to get an in with that family," the man had said. "The potter only sees me as the old man's drudge now. Haven't you got a connection there, gorgeous? The fellow at the inn said you have a cousin or such married there."

"Oh! No," Kashinka had said with another titter, "not now. I *had* a cousin, she was married to the potter himself—in fact, she was the mother of that red-headed brat of his, that girl—but she was smart and got out. They say she's living elsewhere now. I'm pretty sure he beat her!"

Then Rhitha had realized that who they were talking about so sneeringly was Bina's family. And she had gone hot all over, she was so angry at them for saying these things, especially about Bina's father who was brave and kind and clever and had smiled at Rhitha just the day before and thanked her for working so hard with Mistress Catriona in the library, as if it was something special she did just to be helpful and not something she enjoyed doing. It had made her feel warm inside, that smile. She hadn't been afraid of Master Guy for a long time now, at least two weeks, and instead she just felt a tiny bit jealous of Bina for having a family like that. So Kashinka and her companion had made her very angry with talking the way they did about them.

"I suppose I'll have to find another way to get to him then," the man had said, "perhaps through that apprentice of his."

"Who? Oh, that dark fellow," Kashinka had said, with a sneer in her voice. "I thought he was a servant."

"No, he is nearly a journeyman, and eats with the potter's family," he had replied. "In fact, he might know things himself, being on the inside of the craftshop. He doesn t have any powers, does he?"

"You mean special gifts? I doubt it. All those stories about them were probably just made up."

"What stories, about who?" the man had demanded in a voice that sounded a little harsh.

"Ooh, don't scowl at me so, you big brute!" Kashinka had fluted, and there had been more of those embarrassing noises, which abruptly broke off.

"What stories?" the man had repeated.

Kashinka had made a little pouting noise. "Aw, come on, darling," she had said, a little breathless, "what does it matter?"

"It matters to me." His voice had still sounded hard.

"Oh, well then," Kashinka had said, "from seven years ago, before we left. They said that he and his brother made things happen with the things they made, with their hands, I mean. I didn't listen to those stories; I have better things to do than paying attention to gossip about riffraff like them. But if you want," her voice had turned honey-sweet again, "I can try to find out more for you—for *you*, darling..."

"That would be fabulous, gorgeous." The man's voice had sounded all husky and soft then. "You do that, and we'll meet again and you'll tell me all about it, won't you, sweetheart?"

The noises got even worse, and then—then they had come through the garden gate, and found Rhitha.

And it had been terrible at home ever since, because not only was Kashinka still so very angry with her, she had got Mother on her side as well, and they both of them scolded Rhitha and said such unkind things at every turn that she could hardly bear it.

She could not even go to Grandmother's house to get away, because Grandmother was visiting a friend out in the valley for a few days. She was coming home tomorrow, she had promised Rhitha. If she weren't away, Rhitha would go and sleep in Grandmother's house anyway, even if there was nothing to eat there and no firewood to warm the house at night; being hungry and cold was better than what she got at home. But Grandmother had locked the door and taken the key with her, so Rhitha had no other option.

Oddly enough, Mother and Kashinka were unhappy about Grandmother's locked house, too. They hardly ever went to Grandmother's now when she was home; Rhitha thought that Mother was ashamed to be known as Grandmother's daughter because she was a simple woman—Kashinka even called her poor. So what they wanted in Grandmother's house while she was away Rhitha had no idea. But as soon as Mother had found out that Grandmother was away—she had stopped scolding long enough yesterday to ask Rhitha to go and fetch an egg from Grandmother's, and Rhitha had to tell her Grandmother wasn't there—she and Kashinka had gone over there.

Mother had made a show of not believing Rhitha about Grandmother being gone, as an excuse to go over which would hardly have convinced even Bina's little brother Dyllie, who believed anything. She had called Kashinka, and told her in a fake sort of voice that Rhitha said Grandmother was away, and that she couldn't be believed (and even though Rhitha knew she only said that for an excuse it still hurt to hear it); and then she said that they had better go and check for themselves, because Grandmother (mother called her 'the old woman') could be lying dead on the stone flags in the kitchen with no one to help her.

As if, Rhitha thought rebelliously. If Grandmother actually were dead, nobody could help her anyway. And if she were lying sick on the kitchen floor (which, by the by, was made of brown clay tiles, not flagstone), Mother and Kashinka would be the last people to do anything about it, because it would mean lifting a finger for someone other than themselves. Not that Grandmother would be lying sick or dead anywhere, because Rhitha wouldn't let that happen. But Mother and Kashinka knew nothing about that.

However, they had gone over to Grandmother's house, and tried the door, and when it wouldn't open even after they rattled the door latch a dozen times, they went around to the back entrance. It meant they had to go all the way around the row of cottages to the back alley and pick their way through the rubbish that Astani, Grandmother's neighbour, tossed out her back gate; Kashinka had put her heel right through the shell of a half-rotten little squash. Rhitha almost laughed out loud at that, but she knew better than to draw attention to the fact that she was there, watching all this. So then Mother and Kashinka rattled the door latch of the back door, and knocked on the window, and tried to peer in through the small window panes, but Grandmother had drawn the curtains, and there was nothing to see.

And then Kashinka had stomped her foot, and said in a loud, whiny voice, "We'll *never* get it now!" and Mother had shushed her, and looked around as if she was afraid someone might have heard. And unfortunately, she spotted Rhitha watching them then, and Rhitha had to tell them that Grandmother had taken the key, and there wasn't another one hidden anywhere. And the scolding and the name-calling had never stopped since, and Rhitha was so very, very weary of it. No matter how much she tried to put a shell around her heart, it still hurt so much. Every time.

One more day, and Grandmother would be home. Just one more day.

CHAPTER 10

"I told Rhee she should have come to our house, Mumma," Bina said, coughing. "She could have slept in my bed with me; I think there's enough room for one more. Don't you think?"

"Yes, there is, dear," said Cat, taking another shirt to fold out of the big basket of laundry that was sitting on the kitchen table. "But with you being sick, sharing the bed would not have been a good idea right now. Not that we couldn't have fit Rhitha in somewhere. I'm sorry we didn't know she was having such a miserable time."

"I did know," said Bina, grabbed a handkerchief out of the basket and blew her nose, which was still red from the receding cold, "but not exactly why. Or that Grandmother Urnhild wasn't home. She usually helps Rhee feel a little better, anyway. But it's okay now. Rhee isn't feeling so bad any more. And Grandmother Urnhild is back." She sneezed.

"Bless you," Cat said. "Drink up your sagebrew, dear. I'm glad Rhitha is feeling better. But there has got to be something we can do to help her. Make sure to tell her that she's always welcome here, won't you?"

"I already did, but I'm not sure she believes me. She's scared to come here by herself when I'm not bringing her; she doesn't want to im—impost."

"Impose, you mean. She doesn't; there is no need for her to be worried about that. We like having her. I'll make sure I tell her, too, next time I see her. I'm going in tomorrow morning for the kids' lessons; she's usually there to help out then."

"Mumma," said Bina slowly, "why are Rhee's mother and sister so mean to her?"

"I don't know, dear," said Cat. She so wished she had a better answer to help her little girl deal with this difficult situation. "I don't know Kashinka well at all, and I've only met Shamira once, a few weeks ago. But Kashinka was always—well, not content with her life. From the sounds of it, pretty much like..." She stopped herself just in time, but Bina had already caught her meaning.

"Like my born mother?" she said laconically. "I know, she didn't like it here with me and Papa. He told me."

"I'm sorry about that, sweetie," said Cat, contrite that she had brought up the subject, however inadvertently. "I'm sure he also told you that it very much wasn't your fault." It hadn't been his, either, and it had taken long enough to get that through his head. "Some people just aren't happy with what they've got. I guess they expect more from life." So had Cat herself, for that matter—just that the 'more' she had wanted she found in Ruph, with Guy.

"It's all right," said Bina in an oddly grown-up tone. "Maybe she just didn't like babies; some people don't. *We* all do, but even you get tired sometimes. Like when Kell and Dyllie were both throwing up, and Cory cut his finger and then Yaya's diaper blew apart. You didn't like that."

Cat laughed, partially to cover up her discomfort over the fact that her nine-year-old daughter had so much insight into her feelings. On that particular occasion she had, in fact, nearly lost her marbles, and Guy had found her out behind the house, crying helplessly into the hazelnut bushes.

"Yes, that was a bad day," she said. "But all told I'm really happy to have all of you; I wouldn't want to part with a single one of you."

"I know," said Bina calmly, "that's because you're our Mumma. Can I have some honey in my sagebrew? It makes my throat feel better."

The door latch rattled, and Andy stepped into the room.

"Here's the dried fish you asked for from town, Mistress," he said, laying a package on the table. "And this is for you, Little Bee." With a smile, he held out a small paper bag to Bina.

"Oh yummy, honey drops!" she said, peeking into the bag. "Thank you! I guess I better share with the boys, or they'll feel left out. Did you get that—whatever-it-was—that Papa wanted you to fetch from the old master?"

"Yes, although it took some searching to find Master Ekinoru. He wasn't at the inn, so I had to look halfway across town for him. I finally found him at Metz Stonecarver's, collecting the dust from Metz' granite project."

"So what did Guy want from him?" Cat asked.

"This," Andy said, pulling a rolled-up sheet of paper from his pouch, "a glaze recipe Master Ekinoru had talked about. He called it a hare's fur glaze, with streaks like a rabbit's fur. It sounds quite beautiful. Oh, and he also sent some of the white clay for us to try. I better take this over to Master Guy."

He was back in the cottage within a few minutes.

"Mistress," he said with a slightly embarrassed smile, "the master asks if you could come help."

"Oh," said Cat, "sure." She quickly finished folding the diaper she had in her hands and put it on the stack with the others, then followed Andy across the yard to the workshop.

Guy was sitting at the big work table, frowning at the sheet of paper in front of him.

"Is this even writing?" he said in a frustrated tone. "I can't make it out at all. And Andy doesn't read much better than I do."

"Yes, I know," Cat said. "Teaching young slave boys to read apparently wasn't high on the to-do list in Chaelia." She smiled at Andy, and looked over Guy's shoulder at the sheet of paper. "Let me see. Oh dear, you're right—this is hard to read! It's a really different style of handwriting." She squinted at the paper. "Okay, I think this says 'bone ash'," she said, "and this might be 'sand', and... something-stone powder?"

"Ah, probably grease stone," Guy said, "you know, the stuff you use on the babies' bottoms. I've heard of that being put in glazes before."

"What, talcum powder? Oh, right, that's a pulverized stone, isn't it. I would have called it soap stone, though, not grease stone. Okay, and then this is... l-something—wait, if that says 'grease', then this is an r—lr..."

"Iron," said Andy, looking over Guy's other shoulder.

Guy and Cat looked at him in amazement.

"You can read this?" Guy asked.

The young man shrugged. "Not very well," he said, "but that looks like an 'i' to me, the way someone would write it with a pen, not the way it's printed in a book. And iron rust, Master, would that not be the right thing to put into a glaze?"

The two of them went off into a technical discussion of glaze materials, forgetting all about Cat, and she let herself out of the shop and went back to the cottage. So Andy, who was not able to read much at all, could recognize the letters in that strangely convoluted piece of handwriting, could he? Letters Cat herself had never seen formed quite like that? Curious.

"Did you get that recipe all figured out?" she asked Guy at supper. "No, Kell, stop feeding the kitty. That cheese is for you, not for Johnny. He's already had a dish of milk this evening." The three-legged cat gave her a reproachful look, and hobbled around the table to try his luck under the baby's high chair.

"Yes, I think we can make that glaze," Guy said. "The ingredients are not too rare. I shall have to consult Master Ekinoru some more about the precise process; I have a feeling the glaze might run a lot in the kiln. Andy, when you go back to town tonight, could you stop in at the inn and mention it to him? Cory!" he rapped out. "Your brother's head is not a drum! However," he carried on as if nothing had happened, "if that glaze turns out, we could have a whole new line of dishes; I have several customers in mind who might be interested."

Cat spooned cereal into the baby's mouth. "That sounds great," she said. "Maybe you can do a test run for us; we need more bowls, and a few new mugs wouldn't come amiss. And I wouldn't object to a pretty glaze myself. How hard do you think it might be to make this turn out?"

Guy was cutting Dyllie's bread into pieces small enough for the little boy to pick up and put into his mouth one at a time. "I don't know," he said. "I sure hope it works. As a matter of fact, Andy," he turned to his apprentice, "if this is a good glaze, something out of the ordinary, it might well do for your journeyman's piece."

"What's a jur-man's piece?" asked Kell, stuffing cheese into his cheeks until he looked like a chipmunk. "Uncle Sepp 'n Ben was talking 'bout one, too."

"Don't talk with your mouth full," Cat said automatically. "A journeyman's piece is a final piece of workmanship an apprentice makes to complete his training," she explained. "It's a test of his skill, of all he has learned, so it has to be something quite special. And when he is finished, if he does well, then he becomes a journeyman. So is Ben working on his piece already? What did he decide on?"

"No, he has not started," Andy put in, "neither he nor I have decided on what to make yet."

"Ben saided he might maybe make a rocking chair like Mumma's one," Kell said importantly, "and Uncle Sepp saided he better start lookin' for the wood to make it from."

Cat looked at the black walnut rocker in the corner of the kitchen, a beautiful piece of workmanship her brother-in-law had made before she had even arrived in this place; it had since become hers by default. "That would be a great journeyman's piece," she said, "and I'm sure Ben will come up with something amazing; he's such a good carver. You know what would be neat, though,"—she turned to Andy—"if you two could make something that goes together—a vase and a stand, or something like that; your clay work with his wood work. That would be stunning."

"We have talked of it, Mistress," Andy said, "but we have yet to find a piece that calls us both."

Bina sneezed. "'Scuse me," she said. "Andy, if something's not calling you, you can't make it," she stated. "You've got to wait until something *makes* you make it."

Andy smiled at her. "I know, Bee, that's why we have not begun work yet."

"I hope you find something though," the girl said, "I can't wait. You haven't made anything, the two of you, since Mumma's birthday tree last year."

Cat's eye went to the twin sculptures of two small styl-
ized rose trees, one of wood, one of terracotta clay, which
sat next to each other on the mantelpiece above the stove,
and then to the blooming rose tree that had sprung up
right outside the window after the young men had given
her the sculptures for her birthday in April the previous
year. The tree was now a blaze of crimson blossoms for the
second year in a row.

"Well, they might not make anything together," she said,
"but I'm sure that whatever they'll make, it'll be beautiful.
Pass the butter, Guy."

CHAPTER 11

C AT HITCHED LITTLE YAYA up in his carrying cloth
so he sat more securely on her hip, took Dyllie firmly by the hand, and turned the corner to Ouska's house.
Guy had come home from the market that morning with
the message that Aunt wanted to see her, if it was convenient. Seeing as today was as good a day as any, Cat
thought she might as well. She reached the plank door that
was the entrance to Ouska's kitchen, and gave a knock.

"Come in!" Aunt's voice called and Cat pushed the door
open.

"You're right on time," Ouska said, "the kettle just
boiled. Here's someone I want you to meet!" On the
bench behind the kitchen table sat a stocky woman with
her grey hair pinned up on the back of her head and a
nice smile on her face. "This is Dola," Aunt said. "She's a
cousin. We haven't had a talk for a good long while, so I
asked her over after market today, her and her daughter.
Come on, little one, you sit here." She picked up Dyllie,
put him on the kitchen bench and handed him a slice of
dried-fruit cake.

Cat shook the woman's hand. "It's nice to meet you," she said. "What kind of cousin are you exactly? One of mine-by-marriage, too, or just Aunt's?"

Ouska laughed. "Actually, Dola is a Septimus, around a corner or two. So she's as much your cousin as mine, related to our husbands," she said.

"That's true enough—you're Guy's wife, aren't you?" Dola said. "I believe he's a second cousin, or some such. My mother was his father's cousin. Much older, of course, that's why Ouska here and I are nearly of an age."

"That's right," said Aunt. "Dola is Uncle's relation, but she and I grew up together." She turned to the other woman. "Where did that girl of yours get to?" she asked.

The door opened again, and a short round-faced young woman with slanted eyes and a slightly protruding tongue walked into the room. "Sorry, Cousin Ouska," she said, "I wanted to step out and look at that doggie out in the street!"

"Well, here you are then," said Ouska in a friendly tone, "and here's Cousin Catriona come to see us, too. Cat, this is Lahni, Dola's girl."

"Nice to meet you," said Cat again. She slipped Yaya out of his carrier and put him down on the blue-tiled kitchen floor.

"Oh, you've got a baby!" said the young woman. "Can I play with your baby, Cousin Cat?"

"By all means," said Cat.

Lahni had already plopped herself down on the kitchen floor.

"Hi baby!" she said. He gave her a solemn stare.

"His name is Iawar," Cat said, "but we call him Yaya. And this is Dyllie. Do you like babies?"

"Yes," Lahni said, "but we don't got any babies at home, do we, Mumma?"

"Well, we certainly have lots at our house," said Cat with a smile.

***

"Did you plan this?" Cat asked Guy a few hours later, pouring out a cup of mintbrew for him.

"Plan what, Madam Wife?" He reached for the honeycakes in the middle of the table.

"Dola and Lahni and I. Or was this all Aunt's doing?"

He threw up his hands in self-defence. "It's none of my fault! I was just thinking about how we'd talked a while back of getting you some help around here, and I mentioned it to Aunt, and she thought of Dola. I take it you hit it off?"

"You might say that. We talked for an hour straight, and still weren't done by the end of it. Lahni is quite nice, too."

"I wike Wahni," said Dyllie from the floor level where he was reconstructing his block tower, "she pwayed doggie wif me."

Cat laughed. "That's right, sweetie, Cousin Lahni was a great doggie, wasn't she? She was right on the floor with the boys within two minutes of meeting us," she said to Guy, "barking and growling louder than Dyllie."

"That'd be really loud!" put in Cory, who was sitting at the table drawing on his slate.

"Lahni is a bit slow, isn't she?" asked Guy.

"Not where the kids are concerned, that's for sure," said Cat. "And Dola says she's great with helping out in the kitchen."

"So would she come along then too?"

"Yes; from what I gather from Dola, she doesn't like leaving her at home alone, and besides, Lahni hasn't got anything to do there, no more than Dola. That's what makes this so perfect—Dola and Lahni are looking for something to do, and we're looking for someone to do things. But, Guy—could we afford to hire them? I'd love to have them, but they do need an income, that's the other part of the deal."

Guy scratched the back of his head. "I know; Aunt did say Dola's been hard up since her husband passed on, that's what made her think of her. Actually, with what Master Ekinoru is offering for our work together, I think we can make this work."

Cat let out a sigh. "That would be fantastic," she said. "To have someone that I could hand things over to for a bit..." She found herself blinking back tears.

Guy gave her a look. "Hey, hey, what's this?" He reached out an arm and pulled her onto his knees. "Don't cry, Karana. I'm sure it'll be all right; Lahni won't break the dishes."

Cat gave a watery chuckle and laid her head on his shoulder. "Maybe she can crack the rest of them and make them all into a matching set; that would be a good thing. I don't actually know why I'm crying..."

He gently wiped her tears from the corner of her eye with his thumb. "You probably hadn't realized how much it's been wearing you down. And I hadn't either—I'm sorry, Karana. We'll do better in future, yes? Make sure you get more rest. How about starting with an early bedtime tonight, hmm? I'll come help you rest..."

"Eew," Cory cried, "stop kissing! Yuck!"

ele

"We're making pretzels, Mumma!" Kell was kneeling on the bench in the kitchen, smooshing around a piece of bread dough.

Cat closed the cottage door behind herself and Cory, and put her basket on the floor beside it.

"That's great, dear," she said. "Did you have a nice time with Cousin Dola and Lahni this morning?"

"Woof!" said Dyllie, crawling through the door from the bedroom.

"Hello, Cousin Cat!" Lahni was crawling right after him.

"No!" Dyllie objected, "you're s'posed to say woof woof!"

"Well, woof woof to you, too," Cat said. "Would the doggies like a piece of sausage Cory and I brought from Uncle Oldran's shop?" She pulled a paper-wrapped package out of her basket and took out some dry smoked sausage sticks.

"Yes woof!" said Lahni and giggled, standing up and dusting her hands on her skirt. "We played doggie, Cousin Cat, and Mumma made bread, and we scrubbed the floor in the bedroom, and we're going to scrub the one in the kitchen too before we go home. And we used ashes to make lye for the scrubbing, and then Mumma said we'll make pretzels, too, because it's real nice lye. You've got clean ashes here, Cousin Cat! Ours aren't so clean, they got little dirty bits in it. Those are good sausages, Cousin Cat! We buy our sausages from Cousin Oldran, too, he makes good sausages. The butcher in Nickel Alley doesn't make them as good as that."

"Hush, you chatterbox," Dola said good-naturedly. "Cousin Cat doesn't want to hear all that when she's only just walked in the door. How was your morning, Catriona?"

"Good," said Cat, taking Yaya out of his carry cloth and putting him into the high chair. "The kids are getting used to me. And I sure like teaching them. They seemed to pay attention quite well."

"That's 'cause you read us a story at the end if we pay 'ttention," Cory put in. "Master Nikor never read us stories."

"Perhaps Master Nikor has forgotten what it was like being a child," Cat suggested, "he's been reading stories for himself for so long he might not remember not being able to."

"Nikor is around my age," Dola said. "I remember when he came to town; I think we were about as old as your Bina is now. That was a long time ago. Look, Kell, dear, make a snake with the dough, then we can make it into a pretzel." She demonstrated how to roll the soft bread dough into a long rope and twist it into the pretzel shape with its three holes, and laid it on the baking sheet to rise before it would be boiled in lye to give it its characteristic pretzel flavour.

Dyllie climbed on the bench. "Doggies make pwetzel, too!" he demanded. "Wahni, come!"

The young woman giggled and joined him on the bench. She pinched off a piece of bread dough and started to roll it; it was apparent from the speed with which she worked that she had done this many times before. When she had rolled it to pencil thickness, she laid it on the baking sheet in a squiggly shape.

The little boy, who had been watching her intently, frowned. "You're s'posed to make a pwetzel, wike dat!" He pointed at the piece Dola had made before.

"But I like it better like that," Lahni said, "it's a Sss for my name."

"What's a Sss?" Kell asked, a puzzled frown on his face.

Lahni giggled. "A Sss! It starts my name!"

"But it doesn't," said Kell. "Your name is Lahni!"

Cat gave her second-born a surprised look. Where had he picked up on the beginning sounds of words? Even after months of reading lessons, Cory, who was a year and a half older than Kell, still seemed to have no grasp of that concept.

"No, it isn't," Lahni said. "It's Sulahna!" She made another S to go on the sheet.

"Oh," said Kell, "like mine is Kelroda. And Dyllie's is Aldyl." He applied himself to his piece of bread dough, inexpertly squishing it into a snake.

The door creaked open, and Guy stuck his head in the kitchen. "Say, Dola, when my wife comes back, could you ask her—oh, there you are, Cat. Would you mind stepping over to the shop when you have a moment?"

CHAPTER 12

C AT AND GUY WALKED across the yard.

"How are things going with Cory?" Guy asked.

"Not as well as I'd like," Cat said. "Oh, he's well-behaved enough—good as gold, in fact—him and Tor both. I think he's so glad to not have to sit through Nikor's lessons any more, he's careful not to rock the boat. I know he's a bright boy, and learns quickly, but he just can't seem to remember the letters. I teach them to him once, on the slate, and he knows them, but the next time he sees them he doesn't recognize them at all, no matter how well he could do it the day before."

"Yes," said Guy, "that's how it is. They change, sort of shift around."

"I wish I could get into your heads," Cat said, "and figure out how that works. So, what did you need me for?"

Guy pulled open the workshop door.

"Another recipe from Master Ekinoru," he said. "We can't make it all out."

"Where did it come from?" Cat asked. "You didn't have this yesterday, did you?"

"No," Guy said, "the journeyman brought it. Bel'ris'oem. At least, that's what he said he came for. But actually, I think, he wanted to feel me out again. There is something he wants from me; it's like he is trying to talk me around to his side."

"So what *is* his side?" Cat asked, leaning against the table, absentmindedly watching Andy who was making clay coils to add to a large hand-built storage vessel.

"He seems to think he was rather hard done by when Master Ekinoru took over the crafthouse from Bel'ris'oem's kin. When the father—he founded the house—passed on, Bel'ris'oem was still away on his apprenticeship, and would at any rate have been too young to take over at that time.

"Once he became journeyman, he went back to Rhanathon to join the crafthouse; from the sounds of it, Master Ekinoru was glad enough to take him on. But that was about the only positive thing Bel'ris'oem said about his master. Oh, not in so many words—he talks of him in terms of respect, but there is always a 'but' underlying everything. 'My master is wise, but...'—that sort of thing. He resents not being the one in control of the shop, even though Ekinoru's purchase of it seems to have been all fair and above-board."

"That doesn't surprise me," Cat said, fiddling with a piece of clay, poking holes into it with her little finger. "Somehow there's something a bit off about that journeyman. Mind you, if he really is the son of the crafthouse's founder, I suppose he has a right to the shop. Or would he have inherited a share of the money that was given for it?"

"Probably. However, I think the crafthouse is worth a lot more now—the white ware they deal in is rare and valuable, and it was Master Ekinoru's doing to bring that into the crafthouse. And if Ekinoru bought the trade from Bel'ris'oem's father, he holds it by Right of Purchase."

"Isn't there some law that overrides Right of Purchase if a son has the skills to run the shop in his own right?"

"Yes, if there are no other heirs, then he could claim the Right of Last of His Line. But having the skills is crucial—he has to be at least journeyman, if not master, or have some kind of special trades knowledge. Perhaps that's what it is Bel'ris'oem is really after—knowledge and ability. He keeps asking me about my powers, wonders how many of the Septimus pieces I made, what their properties were, and so on, and doesn't seem to understand that I don't know how they work. He kept hinting for me to take him to the Arbour to see the Septimus Tree, but I played deaf to that one."

Andy looked up with a snort. "You almost made me feel sorry for him, Master," he said, "he tried so hard and you just would not understand." He cut the end off the rope of clay he was coiling on the rim of the vessel, dropped it on the table, and started to blend the coil into the smooth wall of the pot.

Guy laughed. "Poor him," he said. "Now, Cat, this recipe..."

But Cat was not listening. She looked at the clay coil on the canvas surface of the table, curled into the S-shape it had fallen into when Andy dropped it, and suddenly she knew what it was she needed to do.

"Guy," she said, "when you learned your letters—or didn't learn them, as it were—how did Nikor try to teach you?"

"With the slate, and then later pen and paper and books, of course. Why?"

"That's what I've been doing with the kids so far. But something just occurred to me... Do you mind if Cory and I take up a bit of space on the table here for a while?"

In the end it was Cory, Kell, and Bina as well, who stood around the pottery table while Cat made clay snakes and formed them into letters.

"See, there they are," she said. "Try it. This is an A." She laid it on the table. "You make one, Cory."

The boy had already made a fifteen-inch rope of clay. "Pass the knife, Andy," he said in a business-like tone.

Guy looked up from his work at the wheel and laughed. "You're looking at a future potter here, Cat," he said. "His coils are better than yours."

"I've made lots," Cory said. "Andy lets me make them when he hand-builds stuff. No, Kell, you don't squish them, you roll them! Like this." He showed his brother the proper coil-rolling technique, then took up the knife and sliced off a piece of his snake. "This big, Mumma?"

"Exactly. You've got the picture," she said. She started humming the alphabet song. The kids sang along; they had heard it often enough since they were little. Cat kept forming the letters as they sang.

"Okay," she said, "so now that we've got those, we can name them. See?" She pointed down the line as she sang.

Bina was already bored with making letters, and started to collect the letters of her name out of her alphabet lineup. "B—I—N—A," she sang to the tune of the 'Bingo' song.

"Stop it!" Cory yelled. "You're messing up my singing!" He was already as far as copying Cat's E.

"Sorry," Bina said, and started to make Kell's name. "Look, Kell—that's you!"

"Is not," said Kell, "that's just pretzels, like Lahni made."

"Actually, it is," said Bina, "that's the letters that make your name."

"Hmph," said Cory, "it doesn't look like Kell at all."

Andy had been watching these procedures with an interested look on his face. "Here," he said now, "how about this?" He pulled his little portrait sculpture of Kell off the drying shelf and stuck it beside Bina's clay letters. "There," he said, "that's Kell. And that, too." He pointed at the letters.

Cory looked between the two. "Kell?" he said. "That says 'Kell'?"

"Yup," said Bina. "And this," she moved over some more letters, "says 'Cory'."

"Hmph," said Cory. He tipped his head sideways. "Why?"

"C—O—R—Y," Bina said. "That makes 'Cory'."

"I don't get it," said Cory.

Suddenly Andy put a little clay head in front of him—a perfect little cartoon figure of the boy's head.

Cory's eyes lit up. "That's me!" he said.

"Yes. See, this *looks* like you," said Cat, "and this,"—she pointed at the letters—"this makes the *sounds* of your name."

"Oh," he said. "But you said *that* pretzel"—he pointed at the K of 'Kell'—"makes a 'kh' sound."

"Well, it does," said Cat, "sometimes there are two pretzels—I mean, letters—that make the same sound. This one can make that sound too. And when you put these ones all together, they make 'Cory'. See—'Cory' in letters in clay, and 'Cory' in a face in clay." She formed the letters CAT on the table. "There's another one, that's my name."

"But you just said the moon shape—"

"The letter C?"

"Yeah, that! You said it makes a 'kh' sound!"

"Yes, it does."

His face fell. "I don't get it."

"What don't you get?"

His lips silently formed a word, testing the sounds.

"No, silly," said Bina, "not 'Mumma'. It's 'Cat', that's Mumma's name!"

Suddenly the boys, who were sitting on Andy's side of the table, burst out into hysterical giggles.

"What?" Bina asked. "What're you laughing at?" She ran around the table and looked over Andy's shoulder, then gave a little shrieking snort, clapped her hand over her mouth and giggled through her fingers, her eyes laughing at Cat.

"All right, what's up now?" Cat said, and walked over to the other side of the table.

Bina pulled away Andy's hands from a little sculpture he had been hiding with his fingers. He laughed, and gave Cat a half-embarrassed, half-mischievous look. In front of him sat a small clay head with cat ears and a pointy little nose, which nevertheless was perfectly obviously a portrait of Cat herself.

"Cheeky!" she said with a laugh and gave him a little smack on the back of the head. "No respect for your elders!"

"What?" asked Guy, sliding off the wheel bench. "What's he done now?" He stepped over to look, and gave a guffaw when he saw the Cat-cat. He reached over Andy's shoulder. The young man ducked in fear of more retribution, his eyes brimming with laughter. But Guy reached out for the little sculpture, and gently lifted it up. He carried it across to the other side of the table, and put it next to the word 'Cat'. Then he looked from one to the other, back and forth, with the same gesture his son had employed earlier.

"Cat, C—A—T," he said, looking at the word. "Cat." His eyes turned to the sculpture. "Cat." There was a frown on his face. Abruptly he turned to his wife, his turquoise eyes blazing. "Why hasn't anyone shown me this before?"

CHAPTER 13

B INA SKIPPED ALONG THE forest path, trying to whistle because she felt happy. Papa was learning to read! And he was really, really pleased with that. Almost every day now, either she or Mumma spent some time in the workshop, making words for him and Cory and Andy, and Andy made the pictures to go with the words, and then Papa could remember them. And Andy too.

Andy didn't have the problem with the jumping letters that Papa and Cory had, where they felt all scattered, but when he tried to read, there was a big hole because he had never learned a lot of words (and not even all the letters) when he was a boy, back in that country he had come from where they had made him be a slave.

Sometimes he still thought about that place. Bina knew it because she could feel it—there was always a sharp little sadness in him, and a feeling of being scared, when he had told her about it. He didn't even know who his parents were, couldn't remember anything about them—there were only memories of people who were unkind to him, and forced him to do hard work. He had hardly ever talked about it, only once or twice that Bina could remember, but sometimes she could feel all that inside of him again.

But now there were more and more lights in that reading hole Andy felt, like someone lit a candle every time he learned to put together another word. And Papa, it was like the splinters that his mind had broken into when he tried to look at words before were coming together, like the picture Aunt Nicky had made last year on a tabletop Uncle Sepp had built, all out of coloured pieces of tile—she had called it a mow-say-ick. Cory's mind felt like that too, now. He was taking longer than Papa to learn the words because he still had to learn all the letters first. But he no longer felt scattered when he did it, like he had before every time he was having lessons with Master Nikor, and even with Mumma's lessons when she first started teaching the kids.

They were in the library right now, she knew. Mumma still made Cory come for lessons at the library with the other kids, and he didn't mind because she played games with them, and she always finished the lesson with a story. Cory liked stories a lot—they all did. Rhee did too, that's why she liked being in the library so much. Well, that, and now it was that she liked being there because Mumma was there, and Mumma was kind to her. Rhee was at the library right now, too. She was probably looking for something on the shelves for Mumma; her feelings were sort of calm and very awake at the same time.

When Bina got to the marketplace, the little kids were all running out of the big front doors of the library. Chetak and Saro Bakersons were pushing each other, and their cousin Elma was looking at them with a prim pout to her mouth. Bina knew that Mumma found Elma a little annoying because she was always so good and expected grownups to praise her for it. Goody-Two-Shoes, Mumma had called her when she was talking to Aunt Nicky—Bina didn't think she was supposed to have heard that, but she had, and she knew that Mumma hadn't meant it as a compliment.

She slipped past the kids through the doors; seeing as the doors were open, she didn't have to look at the scary carved face to get in.

Mumma was gathering up the slates and slate pencils and Yaya was standing up in the playpen, chewing on his hippo. "Bee-bee," he said when he saw her, and held out the slobbered-on toy to her.

"Hi Yappers," she said, "no, you can keep hippo, I don't want him. Mumma, is Rhee here?"

"You know very well she is," said Mumma with a smile, "or you wouldn't have come. Rhitha, Bina is here for you!"

Rhee came around the corner of the shelves with a stack of books.

"Oh hi, Bina," she said, "I just have to finish putting these away. Wanna help me?"

"Sure," Bina said, "where do they go?"

"They're about clay, so they should go over here," Rhitha said, going around to a shelf in the back corner. "We tried to find another story like the one about the rabbit who got stuck in the clay figure—"

"Oh, 'The Rabbit and the Clay Doll'! Mumma told us that one."

"Well, there doesn't seem to be one like it in this country; we couldn't find one. Just books about clay and pottery. And rabbits. So your mother told the kids the story without a book. She usually reads them one out of a book, because then they see that stories come from books and want to read for themselves." She put two of the books on the shelf above the pasted-on label that said, in Mumma's handwriting, 'Clay and Craft Lore'. "Miz Cat," she called out, "didn't you want to show this one to Master Guy? Here, hold these for a moment." She plopped a stack of three books in Bina's arms, and took a fourth around the corner to Mumma. Bina grinned—Rhee wasn't even using Mumma's full title any more, never mind her long name. It was neat how she wasn't feeling scared of Bina's family any longer.

Bina put the three books on the shelf.

"No, not there!" Rhee said, stepping back between the shelves—the stacks, Mumma called them."This one goes up here!"

Bina laughed at her. "Fine, bossy boots, you do it then!"

Rhee put the book in its proper place, and grinned back at her. "You've got to put them away right," she said. "It's important, or you can't find them next time you look. That one was about how to cook rabbit, that wouldn't be any good in between the clay books. The one we found over there, the one that your mother is taking to show Master Guy, I almost missed it when I was looking for clay books—it was over here by the stone carving books. But there is something in it about grease stone, putting it in glazes or clay or something; your mother thinks your father would be interested. It's what librarians do, find books for people that they think they would like..."

"Is that what you want to work at when you're older?" Bina asked. "I don't know what work I want to do yet."

"Rhitha's already working at it now," Mumma's voice came from around the corner of the book shelf. "She found me some great storybooks for reading to the kids last week, exactly what I needed. Are you girls going to stay for a while, or do you have other plans?"

Bina looked at Rhee and tipped her head in the direction of the back door.

"Do you need me any more, Miz Cat?" Rhee asked.

"No, I think I'm good," Mumma said. "Thanks a bunch, dear! You've been a great help today. See you soon!"

"'Bye, Mumma!" Bina called, took Rhee's hand and towed her out through the back room. "Hi, Master Nikor! 'Bye, Master Nikor!" she called on their rush through the room to the little librarian who was, as usual, ensconced in his worn leather armchair, reading by the light that fell in through the open back door. He raised his head briefly, gave them a slightly confused look, and went back to his book.

The girls collapsed against the walnut tree trunk, giggling.

"I don't even think he knows what just happened," Rhee said.

"Probably not," Bina said, "and what's more, he doesn't care!" For some reason, that was really funny, and set them off into another volley of giggles.

"I like Master Nikor," said Rhee when they finally stopped, "he's sweet. And he doesn't frown at me."

Bina could feel Rhee getting sad again when she said that. Which brought Bina to exactly the point she needed to discuss with her.

"All right," she said, pushing herself away from the tree trunk and looking her friend squarely in the face, "we gotta talk. What happened yesterday evening?"

"What? What do you mean?" Rhee pulled back against the tree trunk just a little bit.

"Something went on at your house," Bina said. "I felt it."

"Oh!" Rhee said. She was fighting against the sadness inside her. "Oh, that. It was nothing."

Bina crossed her arms at her friend, gave her a stern look, and said in the same tone Mumma always used when one of the kids was trying to wiggle out of telling her the truth: "That was not nothing! You were really, really upset! Come on, out with it!"

A wave of hurt washed back into Rhee's feelings, and her face crumpled. Bina sprang over and wrapped her arms around her friend's shoulders. "I'm so sorry, Rhee!" she said, "I'm really, really sorry! They were being mean to you again, weren't they? It's not fair!"

Rhee sniffled, and a tear rolled down her face.

"Here," said Bina, pulling a handkerchief out of her skirt pocket. Good thing Mumma always made her bring one. "Let's sit down." She got her friend to lean against the sun-warmed stones of the garden wall. A wild strawberry plant grew beside them, right where the base of the wall met the ground, and one tiny ripe fruit winked up at her,

111

scarlet between the green leaves. She picked it and popped it into Rhee's mouth. "There," she said, "come on, tell me."

Rhee chewed and swallowed the strawberry. "It's Kashinka," she said, her voice clogged with tears.

Bina nodded. "Of course it is," she said, rubbing her hand on Rhee's back. "What did she do?"

"Grandmother—I was at Grandmother's house, last night, and I only had my short-sleeved blouse on. And it was getting cool, and so Grandmother gave me her shawl for going home. It's beautiful, Bina, with red and green and blue weaving, and a long fringe, and so soft!" Rhee sniffed, and wiped her nose with Bina's handkerchief. "It came from a foreign place, a long time ago; Grandmother said it's made from a special wool from sheep that only live in very high mountains. That's why it's so soft. And when I came home with it, Kashinka just came in, too. I think she'd been at the tavern—she smelled just like father used to smell when he came back from the alehouse, sort of cidery, and she—well, she wasn't stumbling, exactly, but she—she..."

Bina's hands kept rubbing Rhee's shoulders, but what they really wanted to do was form into claws. That horrible Kashinka!

Rhee caught her breath in a little sob and tried again. "She was angry. Like father used to be sometimes after the tavern, for no reason. And when she saw Grandmother's shawl, she—she yanked it out of my hands, and—and starting yelling. And then Mother came out of her room, and asked what was the matter, and Ka—Kashinka shout-ed at her, too, and said that I was a snitch, and I had no right to have a pretty shawl and that it should be hers because she was the eldest daughter, and what would an—an—an—ugly d-dwarf like me want with..." Her voice drowned in sobs.

"You mean she took the shawl and *kept* it?!"

Rhee nodded.

"It wasn't even yours to keep!" Bina said. "And your mother did nothing?"

Her friend forlornly shook her head, her curtain of white-blonde hair swinging back and forth. "She—she—she agreed with Ka—Kashinka, and they pu—put it away in her r—room."

Bina discovered that her hands were formed into fists, and that everything around her looked as if she was seeing it through a red haze. She drew in a deep breath through her pinched nostrils.

"That's *it*!" she said through clenched teeth, and levered herself to her feet. "Come on. We're getting that shawl back."

Rhee looked at her with her eyes wide, and Bina could feel her friend's fear.

"But we can't!" she said. "They took it! It's in Kashinka's room!"

"I don't care," Bina said. "It's wrong, and we're going to make it right." She held her hand out to her friend. "Come on; I can't go into your house by myself!" She pulled Rhee to her feet, and kept hold of her hand. "Come on," she said again, "we can do this. It's Grandmother Urnhild's shawl, we can't let them take it."

That tipped the balance. Rhee pressed her lips together, and nodded. Bina could feel how her friend still felt scared, but now she was also just a tiny bit angry—she wouldn't stand up for herself, but Grandmother, that was a different matter.

They arrived in front of Rhee's house still holding each other's hands—it made them both feel braver. Bina took a deep breath, pushed down the door latch and opened the door.

"Is that you, Kashinka?" Rhee's mother's voice called from the back of the house.

"Hello, Aunt Shamira," Bina called, "it's me!"

Rhee's mother came out of one of the bedrooms. She had light hair that didn't have much colour in it—not like Rhee's, but more like it used to be blonde, and now it had all faded out. It was pinned up on the back of her head, but a lot of it was falling down again. Her blouse was cut quite low across the top, not like Mumma's, which was tied up higher, and the hem of her skirt was trodden down at the back.

"Oh," she said, and gave Bina a look with the corners of her mouth all pulled down like she didn't approve of her, "it's Ysbilla, isn't it." She turned to Rhee. "Did you get that cold cream I told you? I need it for my hands."

"Ysbina, Aunt Shamira," Bina said, "Rhee—Rhitha tried to get the cold cream, but my Aunt, the Wisewoman, is right out." That was a flat-out lie, all of it, but it was the first thing that had come into her head, and Bina thought that perhaps in this case it would be okay to not be entirely truthful. She'd have to ask Mumma about it later. "But

Rhitha said you have some lard, that would work for your hands. My Mumma uses it if she hasn't got any ointment. Can I see if I can find it?"

She gave Rhee a secret little shove and a quick nod in the direction of the other bedroom door, and stepped over to the cupboard beside the fireplace, intending to make a big show of looking for the lard.

But Rhee forestalled her. She gave a little shake of her head and twitched her index finger at the bedroom door her mother had come from, then said aloud, "No, the lard is in the other cupboard. Let me look." She began to clatter around in the dresser by the table, drawing her mother's attention to her. Bina could tell she was feeling really scared at what she was doing; she'd have to move quickly to get them back out of there before Rhee lost her nerve.

She sidled over to the open door, and slipped through it into the room. A bed stood against the wall with a rumpled blanket nearly sliding off the edge, and two bolsters tossed higgledy-piggledy across the untidy sheets. Under the window was a small table with a mirror leaning against the wall, and a comb, brush, several strands of beads, and a jar or two of creams proclaiming that this was Kashinka's dressing table.

If Kashinka had pots of cream sitting there, why did her mother need another one? Well, she had probably already been helping herself to her daughter's supplies, that's why she had been in that room. It certainly hadn't been to clean up; Bina wasn't a very tidy person herself, but even she noticed what a mess it was. Kashinka probably lost stuff all the time, like that pretty blue enamel pin shaped like a butterfly—Bina had seen one just like it at the silversmith's on the market—which was almost disappearing in the clutter on that dressing table.

There was Kashinka's trunk against the other wall, and—ah! Underneath the green gown that was lying half on the trunk, half on the floor, Bina could see something red, green and blue. The shawl!

She quickly pulled it out from under the dress, and slipped it into her blouse. It really was beautifully soft! Now, how to hide what she had done? Nothing easier. She picked up the two chemises and some of the stockings that were littering the floor, and tossed them on top of the trunk. Most likely Kashinka wouldn't remember exactly what kind of mess she had left her room in, and wouldn't even notice that the shawl was missing.

She slipped back out into the kitchen to hear Rhee stammering at her mother. "I'm—I'm—I'm sorry, Mother, I can't find the lard! We must be all out, after all!"

"You empty-headed fool," her mother scolded, "I might have known! Now you..."

"We'll go see if the butcher has some lard," Bina interrupted quickly, grabbed Rhee by the hand and pulled her to the door. "'Bye, Aunt Shamira!"

CHAPTER 14

T HEY SLAMMED THE DOOR shut behind them, ran out into the yard, ducked around a corner and flopped back against the wall, breathing hard.

"Did you get it?" Rhee asked, her eyes really big with scared excitement at what they had just done.

Bina reached into the neckline of her blouse and pulled the shawl out just far enough for Rhee to see. "Come on, let's go take it to Grandmother Urnhild!"

They were about to turn down the lane to get to Grandmother Urnhild's back door when they heard voices.

"It's Kashinka!" Rhee hissed.

There was a large bin against the wall of Astani's back yard, just big enough for two girls as slim as Bina and Rhee to duck behind.

"I hope she's not there right now," Kashinka said. Bina knew it was her because she had met her once or twice and recognized the whiny tone; but even if she hadn't, she would have known by the fear that came off Rhee.

"What? You only have two bed chambers?" said a man's voice. Bina knew that voice—where had she heard it before? Ah, she had it—it was that black-haired man who had come to their house with the old master, the one that she and Mumma hadn't liked much. Of course—Rhee had said that her sister was going around with him sometimes.

Their footsteps halted beside the bin. Bina flattened herself against the wall, and she could feel Rhee beside her, all her attention on trying not to breathe.

"That's what I'm telling you!" said Kashinka in a voice that sounded like she was stomping her foot. "My mother and sister take up all the space; I hardly have enough room to put my things! That's why I want her out!" Bina couldn't believe that a grown-up woman—why, Kashinka had to be at least twenty!—could sound as bratty as that. She was as bad as Ari when Aunt Nicky wouldn't let her have her way. Not enough room for her things? What a joke—when she had a whole room to herself and totally stuffed it with her clutter. "And besides," Kashinka went on, "if it wasn't for her, I could be an Unissima!"

"A what, gorgeous?"

"An Unissima? Don't you know, darling?" Kashinka giggled. "It's the only daughter of an only daughter. They have special powers. I was supposed to be one, like my cousin."

"Your cousin has special powers?"

"Well, she did—remember, darling, I told you she left. But when we were kids, she said that one of my family was going to be special—powerful, even. She told me that in the *strictest* confidence! But she *felt* it. We *knew* I was meant to be an Unissima, just like her. But then my mother had to give birth to that—that..."

"Wait," said that journeyman's voice, "are you saying that without your sister, you could have powers out of the ordinary?"

"Yes! That's why I want to be rid of her, so I can become an Unissima!"

What did Kashinka mean, she wanted to become an Unissima? Everyone knew you couldn't *become* one—you had to be born one. Not only did Kashinka sound like Ari, she made about as much sense, too. But then, she was probably just saying all that to impress that man.

"Really?" said the man thoughtfully, "really..." Their footsteps moved on, into the yard of Rhitha and Kashinka's house, and then the door opened and closed and they were gone.

Rhee drew a deep breath beside her, and the fear was slowly ebbing off her.

"Let's go!" Rhee whispered, "quick, before they come back!"

They ran the rest of the way to Grandmother Urnhild's house. Rhee tapped on the door, quickly, then pushed down the latch and slipped through. "Grandmother? It's me, and Bina. Can we come in?"

Bina followed her into the house, pulling the shawl out from under her blouse and shaking out the creases.

"Grandmother?" Rhee called, "where are you?"

"In here," Grandmother Urnhild's voice came from the kitchen, "come through!"

Rhee and Bina stepped into the tidy little kitchen and found Grandmother Urnhild just getting up from the wing chair by the fireplace.

"There you are, child!" Grandmother Urnhild said with her sweet smile that creased up her whole face like a very friendly wrinkled apple. She stroked Rhee's cheek with the outside of her fingers. "And Ysbina, too! Have you come to pay me a visit?"

Bina could feel how that lovingness was making Rhee's inside open up like a flower in the sunshine. Her friend smiled back at her grandmother with the exact same kind of smile, except without the wrinkles. "You've got a leaf on your head, Grandmother." She picked a little green bit out of Grandmother Urnhild's snow-white hair, which was pinned up on top of the little old woman's head in a wreath of braids like Aunt wore hers.

Grandmother Urnhild laughed, a soft friendly laugh that made her eyes twinkle. "There, child, I must have bumped my head against those mint bundles in the pantry again. What would I do without you to make me look respectable? Put the kettle on, there's a dear; we'll have us some mintbrew." She bustled over to the cupboard and opened a box. "See, I must have known you would bring Ysbina along today; I bought *three* tarts from the baker's!" She laid the little cakes on a small plate, and took them over to the table.

"We brought your shawl back, Grandmother," Rhee said, taking the folded cloth from Bina's hands and holding out to the little old woman.

"Oh, thank you, child!" Grandmother Urnhild said. "Did it keep you warm on the way?"

"Yes, it did, Grandmother; thank you again for letting me use it," Rhee said. "It's so beautiful and soft!"

The old woman stroked the rich material, and let the long fringes slide through her gnarled fingers.

"I've had this for a long time," she said, "a long, long time—since I was not much older than you, child. My brother sent it to me. He was a sailor and travelled all around the Moon Sea. One year, they went to Asbanar, that country where they grow fragrance wood, and he brought me back this shawl. I still remember opening the package—he had sent it especially with a trader's caravan as soon as they landed in Rhanathon, the port city, so I would have it for my birthday.

"I never saw him again to thank him in person—he never came home to Ruph before they sailed out again, and he drowned on their next voyage in a storm off Lipnang. When we got the news, I wrapped this around me and sat on his bed, for hours and hours... I felt that with this shawl, I had at least a tiny bit of him left to me; it was a small comfort. The colours are still as bright as they were that day." She held the soft shawl against her cheek for a moment, her eyes looking into the past, remembering.

Bina was fiercely glad they had taken the shawl back from Kashinka and Rhee's mother. Fiercely.

"Rhanathon?" she said. "That's where Master Ekinoru is from—him, and that journeyman of his—you know, Rhee."

"Your mother went there once, too," Grandmother Urnhild said to Rhee. "At least I think that's where she went—she was gone for more than four years when she was young, before she married your father and settled down here in Ruph again. She never did tell me what she had done those years, or why she came back. What master is this, child?" She poured two cups of mintbrew, and put one in front of each of the girls.

"You must have seen him around town, Grandmother," said Rhee, "he is old and brown—well, he has a long white beard, and white hair, but otherwise he's brown—his skin and eyes, I mean, like Master Nikor Archivist at the library, and Torgha Tailor."

"And Andy and Ben, too," said Bina. "He came to talk to my father about pottery work. He has a crafthouse down in the port city, making fancy wares to sell to those countries over the Moon Sea, and he wants Papa to help make glazes, or something." She took a bite from her raisin tart. "You should see those wares of his, Grandmother Urnhild," she said with her mouth full, "Papa said he's never seen anything like it." She swallowed. "Mumma and Aunt Nicky have, though; they called it por—porcelain, I think—that's the name for it in Outland. It's sparkly white, nothing like the clay work Papa and Andy do—you know, their most special clay is creamy-browny looking, but most of it is red, like this."

She lifted her mug and looked at the potter's mark on the unglazed underside where the red-brown clay showed through. It wasn't Papa's mark, the D and backwards S for Dyniselm Septimus; so it had probably been made a long time ago, by the potter who had been Papa's master, the one he had taken over his shop from. "And it's much more fine—you could almost look through the cups, they're so thin."

Grandmother Urnhild had a thoughtful look on her face. "White clay wares, did you say, child?" she said. "I wonder..."

"What, Grandmother?" Rhee asked.

But Grandmother Urnhild did not say any more. Bina could feel her being a bit scared, or maybe worried. It wasn't as clear as what she could feel about others, like Mumma or Papa or the boys, or even Rhee. Grandmother Urnhild drew in a deep breath, squared her shoulders a little as if she was shaking something off, and then took her raisin tart, of which she had only taken one or two bites, broke it in half and held out a piece to each of the girls. "Here, dears, you have it," she said.

"But Grandmother!"

"Take it," the old woman insisted, "I've had enough today. And I know you like those, child." She smiled her wrinkled-apple smile at Rhee, and Bina was glad to feel how warm it made her friend inside.

"Thank you, Grandmother Urnhild," she said. "You're the best!" She reached out for the tarts to pass one to Rhee, but a fly buzzed past her face and she jumped, bumping into Grandmother Urnhild's hands and making her almost drop the pastry pieces. She quickly caught the old woman's hand—"Good save," Andy would have said—but the moment her hands touched Grandmother

Urnhild's fingers, the old woman's feelings flooded into Bina.

She was so startled she snatched back her hands, and the cake fell to the table. It had only lasted for the blink of an eye, but she had felt a memory of something sad, and the need to keep a secret because of it, and disappointment and hurt—those were from a long time ago, but then again really new—and over top of it all, from right now, worrying and wondering about something the old woman had not thought of in a long time. And Bina had seen something—seen, and not only felt—that had never happened before! She had seen the shape of a little figure, really really fast, and then it was gone as quickly as she had pulled her hands back.

Bina blinked. "I'm—I'm sorry!" she stammered, "I didn't mean to..."

"It's all right," said Rhee with her Grandmother-smile, "they didn't break any more than before. And that was a fat fly!"

Fly? Oh yes, there had been a fly. Bina thoughtfully stuck the raisin cake in her mouth. That had been a really strange thing, what just happened. She would have to ask Mumma about that.

CHAPTER 15

C AT GATHERED UP THE plates with the last remaining crumbs of their dinner. "Once again, happy birthday, dear," she said, leaning over Guy's shoulder as she picked up his plate and giving him a kiss in passing. "Or as my grandfather used to say, many happy returns of the day."

"Quite," Sepp said. "I'm especially in favour of many happy returns of this kind of birthday dinner. Roast meat wrapped in flaky pastry—who would have thought such an outlander dish could be so delicious?"

"Sure, butter us up," said Nicky, digging her elbow into his ribs. She sat beside him on the bench at the long trestle table which they had set up in the courtyard between the cottage and the pottery shop. "For your information, darlin', it's called Beef Wellington. And Cat made the puff pastry—Yldra's recipe."

Sepp raised his cider cup to Cat. "Fine job, sis," he said. "I think we should have it for my birthday as well, and then we can call it Roast a la Rysil. Wasn't that a yummy dinner Mumma and Aunty Cat cooked, Ari Karana?"

His little girl had climbed onto the bench beside him. "I wiked the strawbewwies," she said, snuggling against his side.

Cat smiled at the picture they made, her dark-headed brother-in-law with his curly-haired blonde wife on one side and a perfect miniature version of her on the other. "Are you guys ready for the Solstice Fair?" she asked. "You know, Nicky, for the feast Ari might be able to wear that blue dress of Bibby's, from our first year here. She's smaller than Bibby was at three."

"I'm called *Bina*, Mumma!" the girl's outraged voice came from the other end of the table, where she was watching Randy battle Rhitha at yet another chess game. Cat was glad Bina had prevailed on her friend to join the family party; the kids seemed to be having a good time.

"Sorry, dear," she said, "but you've got to cut me some slack; when I talk about you as a little girl I forget. Do you remember that little blue gown you had? It was so cute."

"Oh yes!" said Bina, "I was really sad when I got too big for it! Is Ari going to wear it? That'll be great; her eyes are exactly the right colour! Rhee, you gotta see that dress; I had it when I was really tiny."

"Hmm?" Rhitha said, raising her eyes from the chess board.

Randy pounced on one of her white pawns. "Hah!"

"Oh no!" She groaned.

"That's not fair!" Bina protested. "That's the fifth pawn you've taken of hers!"

"It's not my fault if she's playing a lousy game," the boy said. "All's fair in chess and war."

126

"That's baloney," said Bina, "and you don't need to be so smug about it."

"What does 'baloney' mean?" Rhitha asked.

"I dunno," Bina said, "Mumma says it when something's really silly. Mumma, what's baloney?"

Cat laughed. "I guess real baloney doesn't exist here, does it," she said. "It's..."

Her reply was drowned out by the hollering of the horde of little boys racing through the yard, pursued by a roaring Andy wearing a hooded cloak. He captured Dyllie, who was the slowest, and swung him squealing over his shoulder. The other boys hooted their triumph at their escape, when Ben, similarly hooded and cloaked, burst out from around the corner of the house, heading them off, and caught Kell under one arm and Tor under the other. Cory nearly got away, but Guy flung out an arm and grabbed him as he tried to run by him.

"The grownups win!" Guy shouted, tossed his son across his lap and tickled him mercilessly. Cory shrieked and fought to get free, punching and kicking as hard as he could. His foot hit the trestle table and sent a shock wave through the board. It upset the cider jug, sending a gush of the last of the amber liquid running across the table cloth, made the remainder of the little nut cakes in the middle of the table jump off their plate, and tossed most of the forks and spoons to the ground.

"*Hey!*" yelled Randy from the other end of the table. "My game!"

The shock had tumbled about most of the chess pieces that were still left on the board.

"Oh no!" said Lahni, who came out of the cottage carrying the baby. "What happened to your toy people, Cousin Randy?" She squatted down, and picked up two of the chess pieces. They were simple, not much more than pieces of stick of various sizes crudely carved to symbolize chess figures; the board was a plank that they had drawn alternating squares on. Like the first set Cat and Nicky had put together when they had taught their husbands the game some months ago, the black pieces had been rubbed with charcoal, the white with chalk.

"They're not *toy people*!" Randy said, offended. "And that's not where that was! Here, give me that." He snatched a rook out of Lahni's hand, and pointedly moved the pawn she had put on a black square to a white one on the opposite side of the board.

"Don't be a rude jerk," Bina said. "Lahni is just trying to help! Thank you, Lahni," she said with a smile at the older girl, "that was nice of you."

"It's okay, Cousin Bina," said Lahni, "I know Cousin Randy is just grumpy because his toy people fell over." She serenely walked off with the baby, little Dyllie trailing in her wake.

Cat laughed. "And that's put him in his place," she said. "Lahni is priceless. I'm starting to wonder how we managed without her and Dola around here before. Rhitha, don't let Randy cheat you; I'm pretty sure that knight of yours hadn't been taken out of the game yet."

Rhitha gave her a shy smile, and put her piece back on the board.

Randy looked huffy. "That was an honest mistake," he grumbled, "I wasn't cheating!"

"Hah," Guy put in, "now I know how you always win! You've probably swapped out pieces on me, too."

The boy looked like he was ready to blow steam out of his ears, and Cat took pity on him.

"Don't listen to Uncle Guy," she said, "he's just teasing. He's jealous that he's only beat you—what, three times?"

"Twice," said Randy smugly, looking slightly more mollified, "and that was only when I first learned how to play it."

"Rhee's beat you lots more than that," said Bina, getting up from the bench to help Cat and Nicky get the cider-soaked cloth off the table. "And I think she's about to do it again. Move those pieces, Andy!"

The young man and his twin had released their captives and were standing by the end of the table, looking at the chess pieces that had been taken off the board before the upset. Andy swept them into his hand, while Randy and Rhitha carefully lifted the board with the replaced pieces so Bina could pull the tablecloth out from under it.

The chess board went back on the bare table, and the opponents resumed their battle. But Cat's attention was caught by the twins. Andy stood with the simple chess pieces in his outstretched hand, staring at them as if he had never seen them before. He picked up a white bishop and turned it over and over, then handed it to Ben. Ben swept his fingers through his hair, scratched his short black beard, and turned the piece over just like his brother had done, scrutinizing it intently. He put it back on the table, picked up two black pawns out of Andy's hand, held them side by side and stared at them. Andy's eyes had gone to the board. He stretched out his finger, and lightly ran it down the side of the board, tapping each of the squares as if he was counting them.

"Hey," Randy said absently with his eye on the board, pushing the young man's finger away, "stop it!"

Andy hardly seemed to listen. He was looking at Ben, who stared back at him with the same intent gaze. Barely looking at what they were doing, they dumped the pieces in their hands on the table, turned around, walked across the yard, and disappeared into the pottery workshop.

Cat looked at Guy and found that he had been watching the twins as well. He raised his eyebrows, and looked at his brother.

"Well!" he said, "if what just happened is what I think just happened, we might have a couple of journeymen on our hands in not too long a time!"

"It sure looked like a light bulb went on, to use outlander talk," said Sepp. He looked at his wife. "Getting on with his journeyman's piece might do Ben some good."

"No kidding," Nicky said, "take his mind off things. If he can concentrate, that is."

"What's going on with him, anyway?" Cat said, her voice lowered a bit so the kids on the other end of the table wouldn't hear. "He doesn't quite seem himself. Incidentally, why didn't Nygelis come today? I invited her."

"Got it in one," Nicky replied in the same tone, "that's exactly it. She's not been as, shall we say, available lately, when he wanted to spend time with her. And the other

130

day, on the market, we ran into her with that Bel'ris'oem fellow; they seemed mighty chummy. Or to put it more bluntly, the guy was flirting with her, piling on the flattery, and she didn't seem to mind. I haven't seen Ben so bent out of shape in a long time."

"Was that last Friday?" Bina said, sliding on the bench beside Cat. "Ben was really sad that day. And angry. And he's tried to not feel that way ever since. Was that because of Liss?"

Cat exchanged a look with Guy, and put an arm around the girl's shoulders. "Yes, dear, most likely. It looks like perhaps she found another man she likes more than Ben." Although Cat would have thought better of Nygelis than to hook up with that Bel'ris'oem; she seemed like a very sensible girl, and she and Ben had been fond of each other since they had been in their early teens.

Bina tipped her head to the side. "I dunno," she said, "I think Liss just likes it when that man says flattery things to her. It makes her feel special."

Cat was a bit startled that Bina seemed to have that much insight into an older girl's feelings—but then she remembered that Nygelis was her first cousin, a Septimus, and even though they were not particularly close with Yokan's family, Bina had known her all her life.

"You could well be right," she said, "let's just hope they work it out."

"Right now Ben's happy," Bina said, "and Andy too. They're thinking really hard, that's what they feel like; and they always like that. Uncle Sepp, can I have the last bit of your raspberry cake, or are you gonna finish it yourself?

And don't be sad, Rhee, you'll beat Randy again next time. Do you want to share my raspberry cake?"

CHAPTER 16

"I BETTER GET TO work," Guy said with a look out the kitchen window, getting up from his breakfast. "There's Andy coming along already—and look, he's got Master Ekinoru with him! I wonder what that's about?"

Ten minutes later he stuck his head back into the kitchen. "Need you for a minute, Cat."

Cat handed the boys their bread-and-jam. "Keep an eye on Yaya, Cory," she said, took off her apron and bundled it on the counter. "What's up?" she asked Guy, on their way over to the shop.

"It's Master Ekinoru, he came to discuss glaze and clay compositions," he said. "Well—that's what he says he is here for, anyway. And there was something in that last book you brought me from the library I need you to find for me so I can show him; I think it could be important."

"What do you mean, that's what he says?"

"I can't help feeling there's something else behind his visits," Guy said. "I mean, of course he wants to further our cooperation over the white ware, but I think he wants something else, as well. Something from Andy. He doesn't say much, but he looked extremely pleased when he found out that the boy is using that white clay he gave us for his journeyman's piece." He pulled open the workshop door.

"Here is my wife, Master," he said. "She can help us find the passage I was mentioning to you."

"Mistress," the old man said, bowing his head to her.

"So what is it we are looking for?" Cat asked, flipping open the cloth-bound volume Guy had in the middle of the table.

"There is a part about using bone ash in producing white ware," Guy said, "it suggested replacing a part of the composition of the clay with ash. But I can't find the section now."

Cat gave him a look. "I don't recall reading any of that to you," she said.

He smiled. "That would be because you didn't," he said, "Andy and I figured it out between us."

"Oh, well done," she said. "Here, is this the part?"

He took the book over and laid it in front of the old man, pointing out the passage in question.

Cat wandered over to where Andy was putting handles on mugs.

"How is your piece coming?" she asked.

"Well," he said. "They should be ready to fire soon."

"They?"

He smiled and turned around to the shelf behind him where some shapes were swathed in damp pieces of material. He removed one of the cloths to reveal two figures sitting on the shelf, shaped out of pale grey raw clay. The larger one stood about three inches high, a little taller than the other piece. It was a squat little bearded man, sitting on some kind of seat, wearing a loosely draped gown and holding a sword across his lap. On his head he had—

"Oh!" Cat said. "It's a crown! It's a king, and the other one's a queen! Look at her, with her hand held to her cheek—she looks a little worried; is the king going to do something she doesn't approve of? Those are brilliant, Andy."

He pulled the cloth off another lump that sat beside those two.

"That's one of the knights," he said. "He needs a bit more work."

"Chess pieces," said Cat, "that's great." The knight was a little soldier sitting on a diminutive horse; together with his mount he was no taller than the king. It looked like he was going to be holding a spear in one hand and a large shield in the other, and his squat little head was topped by a bullet-shaped helmet with cheek pieces. "Interesting colour, though, that pale grey."

"It'll be white when it's fired," said Guy. "At least we hope so."

"It will," put in the old master in his slow, deep voice, looking up from the text he had been absorbed in. "There is no need to fret."

"What did your man—Bel'ris'oem—what did he do for a journeyman's piece?" Cat asked.

"I do not know," Ekinoru replied. "When he joined the trade I had purchased from his father's kin, his time of apprenticing was already complete."

"Oh, right," Cat said. "Guy already told me that. Bel'ris'oem didn't come along today?"

"No."

"What has he been doing in town?" Guy wanted to know. "You're still staying at the inn, are you not?"

"He was heading off to the other side of town this morning," Andy said. "I met him on my way out here. At least he now greets me when he sees me; in the beginning he looked right past me."

"He does not have much truck with those who are below him in the trade," Master Ekinoru said. "His respect is for those of power or of wealth. It is them he seeks, and aims to make his friends."

Guy looked thoughtful. "I'm still not quite sure what he wants with me," he said. "He keeps talking as if he had something we could work out together. Does he make many of the decisions in the crafthouse?"

"To a certain measure. But his aim is for the mastership, he hopes to gain it all," said the old man. "He bears no love for me, that I know well. But so long as I hold the knowledge of our craft ways..." He laid a hand on the small leather pouch he wore on his belt, then abruptly turned back to the volume on the table. "Master Guy, the intelligence in this tome might well be the piece that was lacking for a new composition of the ware." His voice held an undercurrent of excitement. "I have been seeking a way to provide means for the increase of our trade without depleting the scant sources. This ash of bone, in what measure might it be needed?"

The door creaked open, and Kell's red head appeared in the crack. "Mumma, Yaya ate a 'tato peel from the scrap bucket and Dyllie satted on the cat and it scratcheded him and now he's crying and Cory says we have to cut off his hand with the scratch because it'll rot, but it won't, will it, Mumma?"

CHAPTER 17

NIKOR WAS FINALLY ASLEEP. Cat gently took the book he had been reading out of his slack hands, put in a bookmark and laid it down beside his bed. The old librarian had been very tired in the last few days. He had caught a summer cold (probably the same one Bina had been dealing with) and been sneezing and sniffling for a few days already. Now Cat had him tucked into his bed, a kettle of soup simmering on a little brazier for when he woke up, and she hoped he would get some rest. Cat folded up his clothes, hung his cloak on the hook behind the door, and gathered up the books she was certain he was finished with. There were always at least a dozen stacked in his room behind the library.

She picked up the chess board with its simple figures that she had been amusing Nikor with, and put the crude little wooden pieces into their cloth bag. Even after seven years of working with him, the little librarian still surprised her now and then. She and Nicky had only introduced chess to Ruph a few months ago, this past winter, in fact, but it turned out that Nikor had known about it all along—from a book, of course, some medieval volume with detailed gaming instructions from which he had taught himself, years ago, and then had put aside and forgot all about.

She heard the big double doors in the main library room creak open. Somebody come in for books? She had her hand on the door knob and was about to call out to whoever it was, when she heard voices.

"Shh! I don't think anyone is here. Come quick, we can be alone in here!" It was a woman.

Cat's hand stilled on the door handle.

"Are you sure, gorgeous? Why is the door open then?"

"Ah, it's only a bunch of dusty old books; nobody cares about them, so they leave it unlocked." The woman giggled, and Cat recognized Kashinka's voice. "All right, so what's your plan, darling?"

"It's like I told you, doll." Ah, Cat had it—it was Ekinoru's journeyman, Bel'ris'oem. "With this new piece of knowledge the old man got from the potter, the trade could be twice as valuable; I want it now." Yes—just as the old master had said. "But I need that recipe before the old fool spoils everything. He actually gave the potter a lump of the raw clay to try, and told him how to fire it. If the key to creating the white ware gets out, it will become commonplace and lose all worth. I know most of the secret, but I still need the parchment with the complete recipe. The old man carries it on him in a pouch on his belt; he never takes it off. Probably not even for sleeping—or for bathing, I suppose. Huh!" he scoffed, "that's why he smells—he never takes a bath."

Kashinka went off into a shrill giggle. "You're *so* funny, darling!"

Cat could have smacked them both. Accusing the old pottery master of being smelly? What nonsense. It was Bel'ris'oem himself who carried a scent cloud around with him, from some kind of hair oil or aftershave. The smell had lingered in her kitchen for hours after they had been to dinner and only dissipated when she had burnt the porridge the next morning and thrown open all the windows and doors to get rid of the smoke. But what was this plan they were hatching? She would have to tell Guy; this did not sound good.

"So I just need that recipe," the journeyman said, "then I can claim my right to the crafthouse. Then *I'll* be in charge, finally!"

"Of course you will be!" Kashinka said. "It's yours by right anyway, darling, you're the *son.* You should have had it *long* ago."

"I *will* have it," the man said. "And if I can convince the potter to use his gift to join with me..." *You wish!* thought Cat. If Guy didn't already dislike Bel'ris'oem, this would make sure of it. "I have a foot in the door there already," the man continued. "I should be able to work it to my advantage." Foot in the door? What did he mean?

"Our advantage, you mean," the girl said.

He gave a throaty laugh. "Of course, gorgeous, *our* advantage. Would I leave you out of this?"

"Well," she said, sounding as if she was pouting, "I saw you with that redhead the other day. I don't like it when you pay attention to other women, darling!"

He chuckled again. "That's the foot in the door I mentioned, doll. She's not only part of that family, the potter's apprentice walks out with her, so she's on the inside of the craftshop."

Potter's apprentice? What potter's apprentice? Andy was the only one in town—and he didn't have a girlfriend, redheaded or otherwise.

"Oh!" Kashinka seemed to be considering. "Yes..." she said slowly, "she's a cousin, I think. There are hundreds of them in town; I told you they're everywhere. Like rats. How did you find out about her and the apprentice?"

"I saw them, at the market and once in the tavern; it was obvious they were together. So, the parchment with the recipe, doll, that's where you come in. I can't get it myself, he'd notice me, but you with your nimble fingers, I need you to—"

The window in the room behind Cat slammed, and she jumped.

Nikor's voice came querulously from the bed. "Book, where is my book?"

When Cat finally had him settled again, sitting up in bed with a bowl of soup and his book propped on his knees, Kashinka and Bel'ris'oem had gone.

The afternoon had turned sultry, and Cat took a detour to Nicky and Sepp's house to stop for a cup of water and to cool off a little. She found her sister-in-law in the kitchen, papers spread all over the table. Fabric samples cluttered the surface, snippets of thread and swatches of cloth clipped to design sketches.

"Here, what do you think of this?" Nicky asked, showing Cat a deep green piece of fabric with small woven-in yellow spots. "I was thinking I could have little vines and leaves embroidered around the spots, in different shades of green, so the dots read like flowers." Her pencil travelled over a piece of paper. "See, this is what I was thinking of for the design. It's supposed to go on a wing chair Sepp is working on; he's going to do some inlay along the sides and back which could echo the design on the seat cushion. Come see; I think he's got it mostly finished."

Cat followed her through the door into the carpentry workshop. They were greeted by the smell of wood shavings and glue and the hissing of Sepp's plane over the planks of the table he was smoothing down. He looked up from his piece and grinned at them.

"Look, here's the arms of the chair," Nicky said, pointing out the pieces in a deep cherry wood. "What happened to that ebony you had, darlin'?" she asked her husband. "I was going to show Cat how it goes with the cherry. If you make the inlay with that, and little bits of, say, maple, it could be pretty amazing."

"Sure, it could be," Sepp said. "But only if genius carver over there"—he cocked an eyebrow at Ben, who was working the lathe in the corner of the shop—"leaves me any of the ebony to work with. No sooner did I bring that wood into the house and he got his hands on it than he got that look on his face—you know the one—and I haven't seen any of it since. And it's not like it was a particularly big piece to start with."

Ben looked up from the table leg he was shaping, and shrugged his shoulder.

"What are you doing with—oh!" said Nicky. "Are you using it for your journeyman's piece, Ben?"

The young man shrugged again, and went back to his turning.

"Talkative today, isn't he?" Cat said.

"He's sore about Nygelis," Nicky replied in a low voice. "He went all the way out to the fish farm yesterday with a little walnut wood carving he made for her, and she wasn't even there."

"Hmm," said Cat, thinking of what she had overheard that afternoon, "I hope she's not getting herself into some kind of trouble." She glanced out the window. "Good grief, look at that sky! That's a doozy of a storm blowing up, unless I miss my guess. I still have to pick up Yaya from Dola's; I better bustle or we'll get caught in this. 'Bye, guys!" She hurried out the door.

CHAPTER 18

RHITHA, KASHINKA AND MOTHER had only just finished supper when the kitchen got dark as if someone had drawn a curtain over the sun, and the first wind blast hit the house.

Mother jumped. "What was that?"

Rhitha put Mother's cup right side up again. "Wind, Mother," she said. "There has been a storm building all afternoon. When I was at the baker's, Ouska Wise-woman was there, and she said—"

"What does *she* know?" Kashinka said disagreeably.

Rhitha closed her mouth.

"She *is* an Unissima," said Mother. "She has the Knowing. Even though she keeps it close to her chest and lets no one but that family of hers benefit."

That was untrue. What Bina's aunt had, in fact, said was that this looked to be one of the worst storms coming that she could remember at this time of year, and everyone had best tighten down their shutters as well as they could and tie down or bring inside anything loose. Rhitha spoke up.

"Mistress Wisewoman came into the baker's shop especially to warn everyone," she said.

"What?" shrieked Mother. "Why did you not tell me before? What are we going to do? Where can we go? We aren't safe here! Kashinka, what are we going to do?" She stretched out a beseeching hand to her older daughter.

Rhitha quietly got up from the table. There had been no point in trying to close the shutters earlier; apart from the fact that it would make it far too dark in the kitchen, the latch on the kitchen window shutters was broken. The bedroom windows were permanently closed up, anyway; Mother preferred not having to bother with working the shutters when she wanted to rest during the day, and the curtains didn't make the room dark enough for her liking. Rhitha hoped the storm would not be too bad; at least not to break the kitchen window, but it would probably be a good idea to dampen the fire.

As soon as she had thought that, a wind blast howled down the chimney, sending a cloud of smoke and soot into the room. Kashinka jumped up with a shout, sending her chair crashing to the ground, and Mother gave a shriek. "We'll all be killed!" she wailed. "What are we going to do, what are we going to do? Oh, if only we were still in the big house, we would be safe! This flimsy cottage, all the shingles are going to be torn from the roof! What are we going to do?"

"Wait, Mother," Kashinka cried. "The inn has a tile roof, and much thicker walls than here! It'll be safe there! Where is my cloak, you?" she threw at Rhitha.

145

"On the hook in your room," Rhitha replied. "Mother, do you really think these cottages are unsafe?" Grandmother—she had to see to Grandmother!

"Of course they are! Kashinka, darling, wait for me!" Mother snatched a brown shawl from the top of the dresser, threw it around her shoulders, and ran after her older daughter out into the back lane, barely closing the door behind her.

Rhitha caught the door, which the wind had whipped open again, and was stung by the first massive raindrops that were hissing down onto the hard-packed dirt of the yard. She took a deep breath to calm herself—it was important that she keep her head. She pulled the door shut against the wind, then with shaking hands dampened the fire. There was nothing she could do about the broken shutters; she only hoped the window pane would hold. The rain had begun to drum on the roof like horses were galloping over the shingles.

She took her woollen blanket from the corner of the kitchen where she stored her bedding during the day and wrapped it around her head and shoulders. Another battle with the door—no point in locking it, Mother and Kashinka had gone without the key. She slammed it and pulled to make sure the latch was properly clicked in, then she ducked her head and ran for it. The rain had turned to hail; ice pebbles the size of children's marbles were bouncing off the roofs, striking Rhitha's head and shoulders.

"Grandmother, Grandmother," she called, bursting through the door, "Grandmother, are you all right?"

The old woman looked up, startled. "Why, child! What-ever is the matter?"

"It's not safe, Grandmother!" Rhitha ran over to her and took her by the hands to pull her out of her chair. "We have to go to the inn, it's stronger! The storm is going to rip the roof right off the cottage, and—"

"Child, child!" Grandmother said, "calm yourself!" She patted Rhitha's hand soothingly. "There is no need to fret; we are as safe here as anywhere else in town. Ouska Wise-woman brought the warning; we're quite prepared here. Come, sit! You're all wet—come, put away that blanket and sit yourself down."

Rhitha's thumping heart settled down a little, and as she looked around, she realized that Grandmother had the shutters firmly closed, the fire was out, and the room was lit by a lantern in the middle of the table. A brazier stood on the hearth, and a pot of water was just coming to the boil on it.

Grandmother smiled at her. "See, child? There's no need to fret. A pot of mintbrew, I think?"

Rhitha drew a deep breath. "I was worried, Grand-mother!" she said. "Mother said the cottages aren't safe; she and Kashinka have gone to the inn because it's got a tile roof and thicker walls." She laid her damp blanket on the bench by the table. "Are you sure you're going to be all right here?"

"Of course we will be all right, you and I," Grandmother said, putting some mint leaves in the brewpot and pouring hot water on it. "You just settle down here with me and keep me company, and we'll be all snug. I've seen many a storm in my lifetime, child, and though Ouska Wise-woman says it'll be a bad one—and I'll take her word for it, she has the Knowing—I doubt that it'll be so much worse that it will break us all to pieces. The shingles were new just a few years back, they'll stand up to a lot before they let the rain in. But listen to it coming down now, will you?"

The drumming of the hail on the roof had become so loud, Grandmother had to raise her voice to be heard over it.

"I'm glad you're here with me, child," Grandmother said with a smile for Rhitha. "It's more friendly with two." She settled back into her wing chair, and pulled her mending basket closer.

Rhitha pushed the footstool beside Grandmother's chair, and sat down, leaning back against the old woman's knee. She cupped her hands around her mug of mint-brew, drawing its warmth, and stared into the flame of the lantern.

They sat in peaceful companionship for what seemed like hours. The wind was pummelling the shutters, and howled over the roof with an eerie, shrieking moan; the rain pounded on the roof.

Once there was a loud crack outside in the street, and then a clatter as if something was being rattled along the cobbles of the lane.

"That's the ladder from three doors down, I reckon," said Grandmother. "They've let it sit outside for weeks on end!"

"Do you think there will be a lot of damage?" Rhitha asked. Now that she knew Grandmother was safe, the violence of the storm finally made an impression on her for its own sake, and it gave her the shivers to think of being out in that fury.

"There is no saying," Grandmother replied. "The worst storm I've seen was some twenty-five years ago, the Year of the Gale they called it because of that. Your grandfather had a to-do getting the house fixed up again after that, and he did not like it that he had to wait for the workmen to be finished with the houses that had worse damage than ours. Some did have their roofs ripped right off, and those who had no roof over their heads had to come first, of course, although he never could see why that should be so, when he had the money to pay for the work, and not all of them did."

"What was he like, Grandmother?" Rhitha took a warming sip of her mintbrew and tipped her head backwards to look into Grandmother's face. "I was too little when he died, I can't remember him at all."

"Who, your grandfather?" Grandmother was gazing into the flame of the lantern, and her eyes had taken on a faraway look. "Belock." The tone of her voice seemed sad. "He—well, you take after him in your colouring, child." She stroked Rhitha's hair. "He was as fair as you are, nearly white-headed. You get that from him. Your sister takes after your father, as dark as he was, but you have your grandfather's colouring. He was a very handsome man, and he knew it. His family was not poor; that's why we had that big house on the market. They traded with the cities on the Plains—your mother always liked getting first pick of the trade goods."

"Were they close, he and Mother?"

"Close? No. I do not know if Belock was ever close with anyone. He was proud of her for her looks, although she was not quite the beauty her cousin Ashya was later—your Ysbina's born mother. But still, Shamira was very pretty when she was young. She takes after him in many ways." There was something in Grandmother's tone of voice that touched Rhitha.

"Grandmother," she said, "was he—a kind man?"

"Kind?" Grandmother said slowly. Her stroking hand on Rhita's head stilled, and the girl felt it tremble a little. "Oh, child... I do not believe Belock knew what kindness is. He cared for money, that's what he liked. My family was well off; he would never have married a woman without a good dowry. And it still was not enough for him; there was less than he had expected. He let me know it often enough—he thought he had made a bad bargain when he married me."

"Oh Grandmother..." Rhitha rubbed her cheek against the old woman's hand resting on her shoulder.

"He could get very angry when things did not go his way," Grandmother continued. "Particularly when any money was spent. He never liked it when I had friends to visit, because he did not want me to spend coin on food to give them. So I stopped having them. And then I stopped going to their houses, because I felt I could not take their hospitality if I could give none in return. It was a lonely time...

"And then your mother came—she was a sweet baby, but as she grew, she became more and more like Belock.

150

She had little use for love if it did not come with things. She always liked pretty things, things that cost money—or things that could bring in money." The sadness in her voice was pronounced now.

"Just like Kashinka," Rhitha said.

"Yes, child. Your sister is one of that kind, too. She always was, even when she was only a little one..."

"Was she?" asked Rhitha, tipping her head back again to look at Grandmother. "I always thought—well, I wondered if it was because of me."

"No—no, not because of you. It started much earlier than that. She and I were close when she was a small girl, when I thought she was going to be my only grandchild. But there was one day..."

"What happened?"

"I made a mistake. I did not know it was a mistake then; I thought it was right to show her."

"Show her what? What was it, Grandmother?"

There was silence, and Rhitha could hear the drumming of the rain on the roof. The room was quite dark now except for the soft glow of the lantern.

"Grandmother?"

Suddenly Grandmother's hand gave Rhitha's shoulder a squeeze, and the old woman levered herself up from her chair.

"Wait here," she said, "I will show you."

She came back into the room with a plain wooden box in her hand—the kind that you could get candles in from the chandler's. It looked old and battered, and very, very ordinary. Grandmother put it on the table in the kitchen.

151

"I keep it hidden away now," she said. "I know they want it, your mother and sister. I've seen them look around, peek in the cupboards and under my bed. But they have not thought of looking for it in such an ugly box as this. I used to have it in a beautiful, carved box—one with a rose on the lid—"

"Oh!" said Rhitha, "the one you gave to me when I was a baby?"

"Yes, that's the one!" said Grandmother. "I did not think you would still have it."

There was a stab of sadness in Rhitha's heart. "I don't now," she said. "Kashinka took it for her ornaments. You know..."

"Yes, child," Grandmother said, "yes, I know." She rested her wrinkled hand for a moment on Rhitha's cheek. "That is why..." She laid her hands on the top of the plain old box.

"So, what is it, Grandmother?"

The old woman lifted the lid. A cloud of filmy cloth, yellowed with age, met Rhitha's eye. "This is silk," Grandmother said. "My grandmother told me that a long time ago, the silk that was in this box then came from the same place as what is in it, from Outland—but these pieces here are from our own southern lands, beyond the Moon Sea." Her gnarled fingers gently parted the folds. "This belongs to the women in my family. It has been passed down from mother to daughter, grandmother to granddaughter, for centuries." She lifted a small figurine out of the box.

Rhitha could not suppress a little gasp. The piece was beautiful. Sculpted out of pure white clay, it stood perhaps four inches high, and showed a girl in a dance. Her hair, glazed in black, was done in a curious style, piled high in a crescent on the back of her head; her little face with its slanted black eyes was tipped to look at her arm which was raised in a graceful dancer's gesture, the over-long sleeve trailing over the hand. The other hand lifted her long skirt, which was glazed a golden yellow, so it fell into smoothly elegant folds. The bodice of the gown was a deep red, echoing the colour of the dancer's rosebud mouth, pursed in a secret little smile; the neckline and hem of the skirt were trimmed with a thin rim of what looked like real gold. "Oh Grandmother..." Rhitha whispered, entranced.

Grandmother looked at her with a smile. "She is beautiful, is she not?" Her hand lightly cupped the small figure as it stood on the table.

"I have never seen anything so wonderful," Rhitha said, and she reached out a finger to very gently touch the little dancer's glossy head. "I love her."

"That is what I always felt," Grandmother said, "from the time my grandmother gave her to me when I was not much older than you are now, the day I became a woman." Then a shadow crossed her face. "There were two of them then, two of the little dancing girls."

Rhitha looked up at her, her eyes wide. "What happened?"

There was a deep sadness in Grandmother's eyes. "Your mother. She left, and she took the other dancer with her. She knew that it was the women in the family to whom the dancing girls belong, and when she was nineteen years old and left to go to Rhanathon, she took one of them. I did not know until after she had gone. I asked her once,

153

when she came back, what she had done with her, but she would not say. I am certain she sold our little dancer—for money."

Grandmother looked so sad that Rhitha could not help put her arms around the little old woman's shoulders. "But you still have the second one!" she said, "and look, look how beautiful she is! When you look at her, it seems as if her smile held a secret just for you."

Grandmother raised her hand gently to Rhitha's face, and she stroked the girl's cheek with the outside of her fingers. "You understand, child. You know how it is. I showed the little dancing lady to your sister, when she was five or six years old—and all she would say was that her hair was odd and the dress looked queer. And then, when your mother came to pick her up later, Kashinka told her that I had shown her an ugly little doll—and your mother told her to hush her mouth, because the piece was worth a lot of money, and that she would have it one day because she was the only girl in the family, so it was hers by right—I would have to give it to her. It was after that that the bond I had with your sister was broken. I never showed the dancing girl to her again, no matter how much she asked. She only wants it for the money... just like your mother did..."

The wind howling around the roof gave an eery moan, and something banged against the door. They gazed at the little figure, shining in the light of the lantern.

The hard knock on the door sounded again.

Rhitha looked at Grandmother, startled. "I think there's someone at the door!" She went over, drew back the latch, and pulled the door open.

A man stood outside. A sodden cloak was slung over a broad pair of shoulders, its hood pushed back from the man's head. The wind that shrieked down the alley whipped his pale hair, dripping with rain, across his face, and caught at his cloak, whirling it around his thighs.

"Is this where Urnhild lives?" he demanded in a rough voice.

Rhitha heard Grandmother give a gasp. Her head flew around. Grandmother was standing by the table, her face chalk-white in the light of the lantern, with both her hands pressed to her heart.

"Belock!"

CHAPTER 19

B INA'S HAIR HAD BEEN up in a ponytail when they
started out, but the wind had long pulled it loose and
was blowing it all over her face. Her hood wouldn't stay on,
even though she kept trying to tie it down, and if it wasn't
for Papa's cloak which he kept wrapped around her with
his arm around her shoulders, she would have been long
soaked to the bone. He had been holding her close to his
side the whole way, or holding her hand real tight where
there wasn't room to walk side-by-side, even though they
were trying to get on as fast as they could. She could feel
him being worried and afraid for her, and a little bit afraid
for himself in the fury of that storm—especially when that
big branch ripped loose from the oak tree and smashed
right across their path in the Wald. He had yanked her out
of the way just in time, and both of them had been really
frightened for a few minutes.

But then Bina could feel Mumma's worry and care for
them coming across the forest, and it had made them both
a little bit braver. Mumma had had to stay with the boys, of
course, and Kell was really scared of storms, even ones not

as wild as this one. Bina could feel his fear, but it had got less in the last little while; Mumma was probably singing to them or telling them stories. She could tell that it wasn't easy for Mumma to keep her mind on that with being worried about her and Papa at the same time. But now that they were out of the forest, it wasn't as dangerous, and Mumma knew it.

But above all Bina could feel Rhee's feelings, like a loud noise that drowns out all other sounds. She was unsure of what to call them—there was fear, and upset, and worry, and being muddled and mixed up and surprised, and something else that felt like curiosity, and some things Bina couldn't name; but it was all so strong, she knew they had to go and help. She had begged Papa, and he kept saying absolutely not, it was far too dangerous to go out into that storm, and he had scowled like he was very angry, but it was only that he was afraid for her and feeling the Papa-feelings of wanting to wrap his arms around them all and make himself be a wall between them and anything that could hurt them.

But then Mumma had said, quietly and strongly, "You have to go, Guy, you have to take her; this is stronger than anything she has ever felt before." She had been talking about Bina herself, of course; Mumma couldn't feel Rhee, because she was not part of her family, and because she didn't feel things as strongly as Bina herself. And she had looked Papa steadily in the eye, and had felt worried and afraid herself, but there were also the Mumma-feelings of needing to care for people, and the Unissima-feelings of knowing what had to be done. And Papa had looked back

157

at her for what seemed like a long time, and some of his fear had drained out of him—it usually did when Mumma looked at him like that—and then he hadn't said anything any more, but just taken his cloak from the hook behind the door, and Bina's too, and wrapped hers around her and tied the strings together really, really snugly. And he had wrapped Mumma in a tight hug and given her a hard kiss (Bina had looked away for a moment then, because their feelings were so strong), and then he and Bina had gone out into the storm.

The wind lashed the rain into their faces and yanked on their cloaks as they hurried through the streets. At least in town, there was less danger of having a tree crash down on them, but in Six Fishes' Lane, just before they got to the marketplace, a roof shingle would have hit them if Bina hadn't known a split second before that it was coming and stopped just in time, which stopped Papa too. The shingle smashed into splinters right in front of their feet.

"Good thing that was a shingle and not a tile," Papa shouted over the howling of the wind when they both started breathing again, "we'd have been sprayed with shards!" A huge wind blast ripped the shutters open on the baker's window, and one of them crashed against the wall beside them; and then the gale picked up even more and whirled and howled in a tremendous circle across the marketplace. It shrieked and crashed and boomed, and Bina saw, with her eyes staring wide open, how it stormed up against the big hall across the market square, climbed to the top, and ripped and blasted across the roof. The clock tower was torn loose, its bells clanging, until it hung half on, half off the roof; and then an enormous hail of red clay roof tiles came crashing and spattering down in a whirlpool onto the cobbles of the market, leaving a big hole where the roof of the hall used to be. Bina became aware that she was pressed against the rough plaster wall of the baker's house, Papa hunched over her, shielding her with his shoulder and arm from the pieces that were being driven down the lane. The huge blast only lasted a minute, although it seemed far longer than that. But then it died down a little.

"Come on, quick now!" shouted Papa over the wind, which was now only moaning instead of screaming, and they ran, and slipped, and dodged flying bits all the way across the market, down Red Alley and finally to Cobbler's Row.

Papa hammered with his knuckles on the door. "Mistress Urnhild!" he shouted, "Rhitha! It's Guy and Bina! Are you all right? Open up!"

With the jolt of alarm that Rhee felt at the noise of their knocking, Bina became sharply aware of her friend's feelings again.

"It's all right, Rhee," she called. "It's only us! Open the door!"

The latch scraped back, and Rhee's white face appeared in the opening of the door. Bina rushed in and threw her arms around her friend. "Are you all right?" she cried. "What's going on? Why are you feeling so, so..." She ran out of words.

"What are you doing here?" Rhee asked, her voice shaking.

"You needed us," Bina said, "me and Papa. So we came."

Rhee looked past her to Papa, who had pushed the door shut and was securely latching it again.

"You came through the storm?" she asked, her grey eyes big in her face, "for us?"

"We had to," Bina said, "but I don't know why. What's happened?"

Rhee gave a look over her shoulder at Grandmother Urnhild's bedroom door, which was half open, and Bina could feel her being worried and mixed up—confused, Mumma called it.

"I—I don't know if I should..." Rhee said.

"Yes, you should," Bina began, but Papa interrupted her.

"It's all right, Rhitha," he said gently, laying a hand on her friend's shoulder, "you don't need to tell us anything you don't want to, but Bina felt that you needed our help. And you know she is usually right about these things. Why don't you let us know as much as you can, and we'll go from there? Where is your grandmother?"

"Child?" Grandmother Urnhild's voice came softly from the back bedroom. "Who is it that just came?"

"It's Bina, Grandmother," Rhee called back, "Bina and her father!"

The little old woman appeared in the doorway of the bedroom. A few strands of her white hair were hanging loose around her face, and the shawl she wore pinned around her shoulder was crooked. There was a look of relief on her face.

"Master Dyniselm!" she said. "It's you! Can you help us?"

Papa smiled at her. "Don't call me that, Mistress Urn-hild," he said. "It makes me feel silly to be called that by you. I'm still just Guy Septimus; it's not all that long ago you brought me into your house and gave me quince sweets to cheer me up when I skinned my knee in front of your door. So what is it that happened here?"

Grandmother Urnhild pushed open the bedroom door a little further, and gestured into the room. "It's him," she said softly.

Bina looked through the open door. There was someone lying on the bed, quilts and blankets piled on top of him.

"He will not warm up," Grandmother Urnhild said, "and has not opened his eyes in almost an hour."

Bina gazed at Rhee.

"Who is it?" she asked.

Rhee looked back at her with her eyes wide, and Bina could feel the confused and worried feelings inside of her.

"He says he is my brother!"

CHAPTER 20

"H E CAME AN HOUR or two ago," Rhee continued, "and Grandmother was frightened, because he looks just like my grandfather. I thought she was going to have a heart shock!"

"I know," said Bina, "that's when you were really scared for her, wasn't it? And still afterwards. That's when I knew we had to come."

"I was afraid of him," Rhee said. "He said he was looking for Urnhild, and then he came in. And he—he had trouble standing up. He's come from a long ways away, right through that storm; he was so tired. I didn't see that at first, I was too scared of him. And then he saw Grandmother, and asked if she was Urnhild, and when she said yes, he—he said she was his grandmother."

"But—" Bina said, thinking fast, "your mother was an only child!"

"Yes," Grandmother Urnhild put in softly. "The only child I ever had. That's right, he is her son. Come, please, Master—Guy, come see if you can do anything for him."

They went into the back room. The man was lying on Grandmother Urnhild's bed, in the middle of the room, curled up on his side with his eyes closed, his pale hair, as fair as Rhee's, falling over his face with its lips that were so white they were nearly blue. It looked like Grandmother Urnhild and Rhitha had put every quilt and blanket they had in the house on top of him, but Bina could still see him shivering.

"He was telling us about—well, he was talking to us," Rhee said, "and he wasn't rough at all, but just so tired and wet and cold, and Grandmother was making some mintbrew to warm him up. And then he nearly fell off the chair! He couldn't even drink his brew, and couldn't keep sitting up; he kept slumping over. And so we got him in here, but we almost couldn't because he was too heavy and could barely walk." Bina could feel that her friend was no longer scared of the man on the bed, but now she was worried for him.

"He was out in the storm for hours," Grandmother Urnhild said, "and even before that, he was on a terribly long journey, out in the wilderness for a long time. He is utterly exhausted, and so very, very cold. Nothing helps, not the blankets, not the bed warming bottle, nothing."

Bina suddenly noticed that she had been feeling a fourth person in the room, aside from Rhee and Papa and the slight feelings she got from Grandmother Urnhild, who was not one of her family she was close to. There was darkness and sadness in these new feelings, but in the soft, sort of dulled way in which she felt people when they were asleep. It was the man on the bed!

"What was it he said, then?" Papa asked Grandmother Urnhild. "He really is your grandson?"

"He must be," the old woman said softly. "He is the spit of my late husband. You are too young to have known Belock in his prime, I think—"

"I only knew him as an older man," Papa said. "His hair was all white then. But even so, I can see the resemblance. Did he give you any proof?"

"No, I doubt he has any. He grew up in Rhanathon in an orphanage. My—my daughter—just left him, left that little child..." Her voice broke, and she covered her mouth with her gnarly fingers.

"Mother went there as a young woman," Rhee said. "She was there some years. Grandmother never knew what she did there; and certainly not that she was married there."

"I doubt that she was married," Grandmother Urnhild said quietly, her voice trembling. "One needs no marriage chain to get with child."

The feelings Bina was picking up from the man on the bed were changing, getting even duller than they had been, as if the life flame inside of him was growing colder. It felt like the little bird that had smashed against their kitchen window one day last spring whose neck had been broken. It had still been alive, but only a little, and then that tiny flame had gone out altogether.

"Papa!" she said, grabbing him by the sleeve and pulling, "Papa, you've got to do something!"

"What is it, dear?" he asked seriously. "What do I need to do?"

She listened to her inside, and to the feelings of the shivering man on the bed.

"It's the cold," she said. "It's what's making him sick! You've got to warm him." She pulled him over to the bed. "Put your hands on him," she said, "I think that's what you need to do."

Papa looked at her, then at the man on the bed. "I'll try," he said. "Tell me if it's right, Karana." He stepped up to the bed, then laid his big hands with their long fingers right on top of the heap of blankets. His eyes closed, and his face took on the focused look he always got when he was using his hands to do his Septimissimus work. Bina listened with all her might, and was now only dimly aware of Rhee and Grandmother Urnhild, who were looking at them from the side of the room with wondering expressions on their faces.

The man's feelings were becoming sharper, more alive.

"It's working, Papa," Bina said. "Keep on doing it!"

All at once she stretched out her hands, and laid them on top of the blankets between Papa's. The man's feelings rushed right at her, not only the sadness and darkness, but also the cold that was shaking him like Tor's terrier dog shook its chew bone, and that came from not just the stormy wind and the icy rain he had fought with so hard and so long today (she could *see* the fight, like she was watching it through a little window), but from being in a house with people who were of the same blood as him.

And then she felt the warmth that was flowing from Papa's hands, seeping right into the man's body the way the taste and the colour of the peppermint streamed out into a brew when you first poured the boiling water over the leaves. And at the same time, Papa's hands were drawing away the cold—the shivering iciness pulled out, and the warmth poured in. It went on for quite some time. Bina looked up at Papa, and saw that his forehead had beads of sweat standing along the hairline; his feelings were focused hard on the man on the bed, and he poured all his caring into his hands.

The shivering slowed right down, and then it stopped. The man's face went from chalky white to real face-colour again, and his lips stopped looking blue and started looking sort of pink, like a man's lips were supposed to be. He drew a deep breath, and then his eyes opened. They were a light grey, exactly like Rhee's. He just looked in front of him, then slowly closed his eyes again.

Papa took his hands off him. "Did we do it?" he asked Bina, in the same voice he sometimes used when he was talking with Mumma about serious things that had to do with the family—a real grown-up tone, not his Papa voice he used when he talked to the children.

"I don't know," Bina answered, in the same tone. "He isn't cold and frozen any more, but I think there's still something else we've got to do." She listened again, carefully. The coldness had gone out of the man, but the darkness and sadness were still there. And somehow, she needed to get at it. But how?

Then she knew.

"Can you make him sit up, Papa? Just a little, so I can hold his hand, and look at him."

Papa looked at her face.

"What are you trying to do, Karana?" he asked, still in that grown-up voice that said she wasn't his little girl now, but his partner in helping a person who was hurting and who needed them. But there was also inside him the Papa feeling that was worried about her, and wanted to keep her from being hurt.

"I think I need to—I'm not sure exactly—somehow read his heart," she said, just as seriously. "And I need to touch his hands and see his eyes for it."

Papa gave her another searching look, then he gave a quick nod. He stepped around her, and bent down to the man on the bed.

"Can you hear me?" he said, laying his hand on the man's shoulder. Then he looked up at Grandmother Urnhild and Rhitha. "Did he give you a name?"

"Ytahu," Grandmother Urnhild said, her voice shaking, "he said his name was Ytahu."

"Ytahu," Papa said, "can you hear me?" He gave the man's shoulder a very slight shake. Ytahu opened his eyes again. "I'm Guy," Papa said, his turquoise eyes looking into the man's grey ones, "I'm here to help you. But I need you to sit up." Ytahu's face gave no sign that he had heard, but he let Papa turn him, and raise him slightly against the pillow.

Papa folded back the top edge of the blanket, and looked at Bina. "Will this work?"

She nodded.

"Are you sure of this, Karana?" Papa said, and now she could feel his worry for her quite strongly.

"I—I think so," she said in a small voice, "I just know that I—I need to somehow..." She sat on the edge of the bed, and reached out for the man's hand which lay on top of the blankets now.

As soon as she touched his fingers, his hurt rushed at her like a black roaring beast. She cried out and snatched back her hand.

"No, Karana," Papa said in a low, stern voice that once again sounded like his Papa voice, the tone he used when he would not let the boys climb a tree with a cracked limb, "this is too hard for you. You cannot do this."

"But I have to, Papa!" Bina said, tears stinging her eyes. "He is hurting, and I have to help him!"

Papa cupped his hands around her shoulders, rubbing them. "I cannot let you do this if it hurts you too much yourself, Karana," he said quietly. "It wouldn't be right."

Bina felt a warm strength flowing into her from his big hands on her shoulders, and the fear that she felt of the roaring blackness inside the man shrank away from that warmth. She turned her head and looked up at Papa.

"If you help me, I can do it," she said, confidently now.

His face showed the worry for her he felt inside, but also another feeling, the one that went with the grown-up voice that said that he was the Septimissimus, and his task was to help and heal, and to strengthen others' gifts. And then the second feeling won out. He drew a deep breath, squared his shoulders, and gave hers a squeeze.

"Do it," he said simply.

Bina stretched out her hand, grasped that of the man on the bed and wrapped her fingers around it. She looked

168

up into his face, at his grey eyes that were like little blank windows. Once again the blackness and sadness rushed at her, but Papa's hands on her shoulders kept her from being whipped around by it like the wind had torn the shingles off the hall roof, and the feelings receded to the side of her vision. They formed a tunnel, a dark tube that she felt she was being sucked into, and at the end of it she saw a person. She drew closer, and gave a gasp.

Papa's hands were rubbing firm, warm little circles on her shoulders, making her strong, and she was able to keep looking and saw a small boy, not much bigger than Dyllie or at the most Kell, with a shock of very pale hair, so fair it was nearly white. He stood in a street—a city street, with dirty cobbles on the ground, and tall houses on either side—and there was a gash in his knee. The blood trickled down his shin, and he was crying like little boys do, with his mouth wide open, rubbing his fists in his eyes. And there was nobody. No one came to comfort him. He stood on that street, and cried and cried, alone.

Bina gave a sob, and the darkness flowed back into the tunnel, hiding the sight of the little boy, and she became aware of the room again and of the edge of the bed she sat on; and she let go of the man's fingers.

"Papa, you've got to do something," she sobbed, leaning back into his arms. "He was only a tiny boy, and he was all alone and he was hurt... You've got to put your hands on him, and..." Papa was still rubbing her shoulders, making soothing sounds in her ears, but now his hands stilled. "Will you, Papa?" she asked, turning her head to look up at him, tears streaming down her face, "Papa, please?"

169

But Papa wasn't looking at her. His eyes were on the man in the bed, whose face was no longer blank, but the eyebrows were drawn together and the bottom lip was trembling ever so slightly.

"No," Papa said, "this is not for me to do." He let go of Bina's shoulders, and turned around. "Mistress Urnhild," he said, stretching out a hand for the little old woman who stood at the side of the room, watching, "it is a mother who is needed here." He drew her to the bedside, and with his other arm guided Bina off the bed.

Bina understood. "He was just little," she said again, "and hurt, and all alone, and nobody loved him..."

Grandmother Urnhild sat down on the side of the bed. "Oh, my poor boy!" she said in a voice that was breaking, "my poor, poor child..." She reached out her wrinkled hand, and laid it on Ytahu's cheek, just like she always did with Rhee. And Bina felt something inside of the man break, a hard, brittle blackness that cracked open, and so much sadness poured out. He gave a sharp sob, and Grandmother Urnhild held out her arms. He lurched around on the bed, buried his face in her lap, and began to cry—and except for the deepness of his voice, it was the sound of a small boy's crying, like Dyllie or Kell. And just like Bina's little brothers were comforted when Mumma held them and rocked them, Grandmother Urnhild's hand stroked Ytahu's head, and her lovingness poured into him, and Bina could feel the big, deep, black hurts in his heart beginning to be soothed by it.

"Come, girls," Papa said, and with a hand on each of their backs he guided Bina and Rhee out of the room, closing the door behind them.

CHAPTER 21

R HITHA DREW A DEEP breath. Bina had told her about how her father could help people with his hands, but Rhitha had never seen it before. That was—that was amazing. And Bina herself...

"I saw him," Bina said, answering Rhitha's unspoken question. "When he was a tiny little boy. Probably in Rhan—Rhanathon—it was in the city. I felt his feelings, too. And he's starting to be all right now, because Grandmother Urnhild is caring for him."

"Well done, Karana," Master Guy said to Bina, put his arm around her shoulders and pulled her close. "Are *you* all right?" He tipped his head down and looked into her face, as if he was checking to see if she had got hurt.

"Yes, Papa," Bina said, looking up at him, "I'm fine. Quite well, actually. It was really hard at first, because he was hurting so badly, but because you used your hands, and Grandmother Urnhild is there now, he's going to get better. Because we helped him. And that's"—she broke into a brilliant smile—"that's great!" She looked at her father, and then at Rhitha, with her blue-green eyes shining.

"I'm so glad we came. And I think he'll keep getting better now, because he's found what he came for—he's got family. Although,"—she wrinkled her eyebrows and twisted her mouth sideways, which was her thinking face—"I'm not sure that he knew that that's what he came for."

"Yes, he did," Rhitha said. "He told us." She took the brewpot off the brazier, and put three cups on the table. "He still lives in Rhanathon, and a few months ago, he found out Mother's name—and Grandmother's and Grandfather's—and that they were from Ruph. He'd never known, only his own name. And even when he found out, he still didn't know anything about Ruph, just the name of the town. But then he was out in the mountains, searching for wood (he is a trader, he deals in things made of rare woods and other special materials), and he met someone who lived here for a while, and he—that other man, I mean—told him that Grandmother still lives in Ruph, and how to get here, and he realized that he wasn't all that far away and decided to come find her. So Yt—Ytahu came here."

She stumbled a little over the name. It was still too hard to believe she had a brother. She would never, in her whole life, forget how he had stepped into the cottage—he was so tall, he had seemed to fill it all out—and looked at Grandmother, and said in his voice that sounded so rough (but now Rhitha knew it was only because he had been so very tired), "If you are Urnhild, you are my grandmother. My mother was Shamira."

"How did he find out about your mother?" said Bina, who was sitting in the circle of her father's arm by the table, her chair drawn close to his. "Did someone remember?" She took the cup of mintbrew Rhitha gave her and took a sip.

"No—yes—no, not exactly." Rhitha filled another cup. She was pouring mintbrew for the Septimissimus! She, Rhitha, was passing Master Guy a cup of brew, and he took it from her like she was an adult who was to be taken seriously. Take *that*, Kashinka!

"This is excellent mintbrew, Rhitha," he said, and smiled at her with that smile he had that went up more on one side of the mouth than the other. "So what is it, yes or no? *Did* someone remember?"

"No—well, he remembered himself," Rhitha said, feeling warm inside from the smile and from the compliment. "He—he saw something that he remembered from when he was very small, when—before—when he was still with Mother. And—and that person who had it, *he* knew Mother's name, and Grandmother's and Grandfather's. He'd written it down when he got it."

"So what was it that he saw?" Bina asked curiously, and gave Rhitha a look that said that she knew Rhitha did not want to tell. "Or don't you know?"

Rhitha suddenly made up her mind. This was Bina, and Master Guy. They had come all the way through a terrifying storm only for her and Grandmother, and they had done amazing things right here in front of her eyes to help her—her brother, because Grandmother had asked them to. They had a right to know.

"Yes, I do know what it was," she said, and reached up on the mantelpiece. "He told us. When he came in, we had this on the table." She took down the candle box, lifted the lid, and took out the beautiful little dancer. "He saw it and said it was just like it—and that it was the final proof that Grandmother was really his grandmother."

Bina had drawn in her breath, and was looking at the little figure with her turquoise eyes big. "Oh, she's beautiful!" she said. "Isn't she, Papa?" She reached out a finger, just like Rhitha herself had done, and gently stroked it over the little dancer's sleeve.

"Yes, she is," said Master Guy, and there was a tone swinging in his voice that said he liked the figure for more than its graceful beauty. "May I...?" He looked a question at Rhitha, reaching out for the dancer.

"Oh!" He was asking *her* for permission to touch it? She nodded her head.

He picked up the little figure with gentle care, turned it over and over, inspecting it from all sides, then just let it rest on his hand while he gazed at it. "This is not only exquisitely beautiful," he said, "I would think it's worth a lot, too. It is very similar to the rare white ware Master Ekinoru deals in—but the glazes... This is the most marvellous piece I have seen in my whole career." He softly ran his finger tip over the dancer's golden skirts.

"It's Grandmother's," Rhitha said proudly, "it's been in her family for centuries."

"Lucky you," said Bina and smiled at her. "If we had a hair—hairloom like that, we would never ever ever give it up either, would we, Papa?"

"Heirloom, dear," her father corrected her. "And no, I should think not. But you said Ytahu saw another one, Rhitha, in Rhanathon?"

"There were two," Rhitha said, "and Mother took the other one when she went to Rhanathon. My—my brother says he remembers almost nothing from when he was still with her, but he remembers looking at the little figure, he remembers what it looked like. And then—I said he is a trader, right?—he saw it at another trader's, around winter solstice, I think he said. And he recognized it. And because it—well, because it is very valuable, in money, that trader had written down where he got it from, and where *that* person had got it from, the names of the seller and their family and the place they came from. Traders do that sort of thing, I think it's called provenance. I read that in a book once." She scratched her nose. "And when my—my brother saw Mother's name, Shamira, he said then he remembered hearing someone call her that when he was little, too. So then he knew who his mother was, and where she had come from, but not if she was even still alive, or where Ruph was. Until he met that man in the mountain, and then he came here."

"Why did he not look for your mother first instead of Mistress Urnhild?" Master Guy asked.

"That man who told him how to get here, he didn't know anything about Mother. He must have left here before we arrived from Ilim. My brother says that man only knew about Grandmother, and that she lived here in Cobbler's Row. And now—"

"Now he probably doesn't even care about seeing your mother," Bina said calmly. "When your mother leaves you when you're little and doesn't give a hoot, you don't give a hoot either." Master Guy gave her a look, and she shrugged. "It's true. You don't want to see her even if you could—at least when you've got real family to love you, you don't. And he's got you and Grandmother Urnhild now. So, then he brought the other little dancer back with him. Where is it?" She looked around the room as if she expected to see it on the mantelpiece.

Rhitha looked at her in surprise. "No, he didn't bring it back! There were two, but the one is in Rhanathon, with that trader."

"No, it's not," said Bina positively, "it's here somewhere. Can't you feel it, like this one?"

Her father looked at her just as astonished as Rhitha. "You know we don't feel things the way you do, Bina Karana! And what are you feeling about this sculpture, in the first place?"

"Oh," said Bina, looking from one of them to the other in surprise, "I thought you knew—that's why it's so special. Not just because it's so beautiful, but because it's got power. Kind of like some of the things you make, Papa. I think it protects the house, or the family, it belongs in."

"What's that you say, child?" Grandmother was coming out of the bedroom, quietly pulling the door to behind her. "He's asleep," she said softly, "poor boy. But quite warm now." She smiled at Bina and Master Guy, and her eye fell on the little figure in his hand.

"I—I thought it was all right to show them her, Grandmother," Rhitha began, "and..."

"Of course, child," Grandmother said, gently stroking Rhitha's hair, "don't fret. But what was it you said about my little dancer, Ysbina?"

"Didn't you know, either, Grandmother Urnhild? She has power—they both do. They keep your family safe. More so when they're together, but even the one on its own does. And now that they're both together again in the same house..."

"That's what Bina's been saying, Grandmother! She says the other one is here, she can feel it! But how could that be?"

Grandmother's eyes were wide open, and she had her fingers pressed to her mouth. "Is that what he meant?" she said to no one in particular. "Could it be true?"

"What, Grandmother? What is it?"

"Ytahu," said the old woman, still with this look of suppressed excitement on her face, "He said, 'I bought it back; I brought it,'—and then he dropped off to sleep, so I did not ask any further. Could he have...?"

Bina had her head ducked under the table, and now re-emerged. "Is this his?" she asked, holding up a black leather satchel.

Rhitha looked at Grandmother. "It must be," she said, "I've never seen it before! And that's where he sat at the table earlier."

Master Guy passed the pouch to Grandmother. "Here," he said, "it's yours to open."

Grandmother's fingers were shaking as she undid the buckles of the satchel. She reached in, and pulled out a bundle, wrapped in a coarse linen cloth, and when she pushed back the folds of the cloth, a carved wooden box was revealed. But now she put out a trembling hand to Rhitha, and pulled her to her side.

"You do it, child," she said in a shaking voice, "I—I can't..."

Rhitha's heart was pounding so hard, she thought it would jump right out of her throat. The box was kept shut with a slightly tarnished silver latch with a keyhole; a small matching key dangled on a little chain on the side. Rhitha put the key into the lock, and turned it. The latch sprang open. She lifted the lid, and there, under a layer of tightly packed straw and wool, lay the second dancing girl. Rhitha reached into the box, and lifted her out.

Grandmother was wiping her hands over her cheeks, trying to catch the tears that were flowing relentlessly from her soft blue eyes. "Oh child," she said, "oh, child..."

Rhitha gazed entranced at the two dancers side by side on the table. They were very different, but yet so much alike. The second dancer had her hair done up in two peaks on the sides of her head, like beautiful little rabbit ears. She was swaying to her left in a graceful motion, one long sleeve trailing over her raised hand, the other swinging by her hip, echoing the elegant folds of her gown, which was glazed in the same gold and scarlet as that of her sister. Rhitha could almost hear the pipes and zithers of the faraway land, the music to which the dancers had moved so sweetly for all this long time.

Bina's father heaved a deep sigh. "Thank you for letting us see them, Mistress," he said softly, "it is a great privilege."

"There," said Bina, "can you feel it now?" She looked from one of them to the other. "It's like they're humming. It's sort of a—a golden feeling."

Grandmother smiled at her through her tears. "No, child, I cannot say that I do," she said, "but I do not need to. Twenty-six years she was missing from my life, the little dancer—and today, there is a gap that has been filled in my heart. I have her back, and I have..." She laid her soft hand on Rhitha's cheek, and her eyes went to the door of her bedroom.

"That's part of what they do," Bina said wisely. "They keep your family, but it's got to be love-family. They dance a dance of love." She stacked her fists on each other on the table, rested her chin on the top one and gazed at the little dancing girls, gleaming in the flickering light of the lamp.

Then she looked at her father. "I think I want to go home now, Papa," she said in a small voice that sounded sleepy, and a little wistful, "I want Mumma and the boys."

He wrapped his arm around her shoulders. "Yes, Karana. You have done hard work today, and done it well. It's time to go home."

CHAPTER 22

"HE MUST HAVE A few coins to his name," Guy said to Cat, half-sitting on the kitchen table and chewing on a piece of bread, onto which he kept scooping strawberry-honey jam. The morning sun was streaming through the kitchen windows, and Cat looked out at the yard, littered with leaves, branches and debris from last night's storm.

"What makes you think that?" she asked, turning back into the kitchen, shifting Yaya on her hip.

"The dancer," said Guy. "Cat, you should see those pieces—looking at them, I've come nearer than I've ever been in my life to coveting someone else's possessions. They're exquisite. Maybe it's in part the power Bina says is in them, but for me, it's also the workmanship, the pieces as pieces—they're wonderful. And going by what I have learned from Master Ekinoru, they should be worth a small fortune. Ytahu would have to be very well off to have been able to buy the second dancer back from that other trader. Plus, when I went to get my cloak, I got a hold of his by mistake—and it's no poor man's piece of clothing.

Not that I know much of anything about cloaks, but even I could tell by the feel of the cloth and the cut that this was something a lot better than mine."

"So you're saying that Urnhild's grandson is rich?"

"That's about the size of it," Guy said.

Cat snorted. "That ought to be one in the eye for Kashinka and Co., if he won't want to have much to do with them, her and their mother." She put the baby on the floor and put a toy in his hands.

Guy chuckled. "Bina was pretty sure that he wouldn't—based on her own experience, I guess. And on what she felt of him. Speaking of which, where is she?"

"She hasn't even made an appearance yet today—I think the whole experience wiped her out pretty good. But just physically," Cat added, considering, "emotionally, she is quite well. She was utterly wrung out; it was very hard on her, but then—it must have been as soon as you and she between you were able to help him, when you turned the tide—she was fine. More than fine, in fact. There was a point when I could feel the pain she was in make way to—I'm not even sure what to call it—joy, perhaps, or even pleasure. It wasn't very clear—you know I don't get feelings as definite as hers—but I knew the exact moment when she went from hurting to happy. It was right around when the storm died down. I don't know if the same happened in town, but out here, all of a sudden things got calm, and then I noticed Bina was okay, too."

"Hmm," Guy said, chewing on his last bite of bread, "that could well be. I can't say I noticed exactly when the storm settled down; I was a little occupied at the time. So you're saying that this was a good thing for her, do you? She did say something along those lines herself."

"Yes. I think this might be the solution for her, Guy—we need to find a way for her to have an outlet for all those things she feels. If she can make a difference, can do something to help, she can cope with picking up on everyone's feelings. And I believe," she said thoughtfully, "that she is going to be exceptionally gifted in knowing what it is that needs to be done to help. A born diagnostician."

"A dia-whatsit? Don't go calling my daughter names!" He grinned at her, and she stuck out her tongue. "Yes, I know what the word means. I can't spell it, but that doesn't mean I don't understand it. And I think you could well be right; she told me exactly what to do."

"No surprise," said Cat, "she's done it ever since she was little—remember when Andy and Ben first came? But now her Knowing seems to be getting more precise, and it's expanding farther than just the immediate family. And even with family it's more focused when she touches people."

"Maybe it's time we started thinking of an apprenticeship for her so she can learn more healing skills," Guy said. He looked out the window and got to his feet. "I better go check how much damage the storm did to the shop and garden. I wonder how everyone fared in town. From what Bina and I saw, the poor hall roof has pretty much had it; it'll take quite a bit of coin to set that to rights."

A week later, Cat was walking behind Andy who carefully stepped along the forest path, clutching the box with the finished chess pieces which had just come out of the kiln that morning.

"So you and Ben are actually going to donate the chess set to the town to raise funds for repairing the hall roof and the clock tower?" Cat said. "That's great."

"It was Torgha Tailor's idea to have a contest of some kind," Guy said from behind her, "some game in which the winner would receive something valuable. He presented it at the town meeting the other day. And then the boys just looked at each other, and it was decided. The chess set certainly ought to be valuable—Ben's black ebony pieces no less than Andy's white-ware ones."

"So how is this going to work?" Cat asked.

"Everyone who wants to play pays some coin," Andy said over his shoulder. "Then their markers are drawn, and the two names that are picked play the game. The winner keeps the set."

"So not everyone who pays gets to play then?"

"No, there is not enough time," Guy said. "But we're counting on the competitiveness of the people of Ruph in trying their luck at getting a chance to play, and on everyone's local pride in wanting the hall to be restored. *And* on their good taste. I think once they see these pieces, they won't be able to resist the chance of owning the set."

"It's a shame to have it packed up and disappear in somebody's house," Cat said. "But, oh well—it's for a good cause. I hope we get lots of entries."

"Randy's been begging everyone for coin," Bina put in from the back of the line. "He thinks he's going to win if he can play, so he wants to get as many tickets as he can. He even mucked out the goat shed for Aunty Yldra 'cause she promised him a bit of extra coin."

Cat laughed. "He must be *really* determined—my goodness. These days he doesn't go near the goat shed with a ten-foot pole, especially when it needs mucking out. It would be great for him if he got a chance."

Guy snorted. "If he does get a stab at that game, I'd wager even odds that he'll win. I've not seen that boy lose more than a handful of times, even against his father, and Lozyb can think circles around most of us when it comes to games. Hmph. Uppity brat."

Cat grinned at him over her shoulder. "Still sore about losing all those games to a mere kid, are you? Aww, poor baby..."

He smacked her on the bottom. "Don't mock your husband, woman!"

"Papa!" scolded Bina from behind him. "Don't hit Mumma, especially not when she's right!"

Guy made a face at her. "Why did I have to get saddled with two of your kind? It's not fair; a man can't even feel his feelings in peace without being listened in on and bossed around by those Unissima-women."

"Stop complaining," said Cat. "You've got four sons and an apprentice to surround yourself with; they don't give a rip about how you feel, let alone tell you what to do. Anyway, I hope the kids haven't managed to completely trash their feast clothing yet. I'm glad Dola and Lahni took them on ahead, though, so we could finish up the cakes." She hitched the basket higher up on her arm.

They rounded the last few trees, and found themselves between the houses on the edge of town.

"Are we going straight to the market, Mumma?" Bina asked.

"No, we have to get to Uncle Sepp and Aunt Nicky's first and get the boys, and pick up Ben and the black chess pieces," Cat said. "And I think Aunt Nicky has some cakes to take along, too."

They were making their way along the lane that ran behind the inn, when Master Ekinoru emerged from the back door of the building.

"Ah, Master," said Guy after greetings were exchanged, "walk with us for a few steps."

The old man bent his head in agreement, and fell in with them. Cat saw him give a long look under his eyebrows at Andy and the box in his hands.

She stepped closer to Guy. "What are you up to?" she asked him quietly. "You're plotting something."

He gave her a slight smile. "Am I? I suppose I am. I want to stop in at Urnhild's and see if she will let the master see the dancers. And Andy as well."

"I've never yet seen them either," Cat said, "I hope she'll agree."

They barely managed to fit into the little kitchen at Urnhild's cottage. To no one's surprise, Rhitha was there as well as Urnhild and her grandson. Ytahu was staying with his grandmother and had not yet let himself be seen in the town; it had taken him some days to fully recover from his illness brought on by the exhaustion of his experience. Cat gave him a searching look—he seemed much better than even a few days ago when she had first met him.

He certainly was a handsome man. Cat could see the resemblance to Kashinka, who, even if not much else could be said for her, was a stunner, but his colouring was that of his younger sister. And that Rhitha was his sister, there was no doubt. Cat smiled inwardly at the hero-worship she saw in Rhitha's grey eyes, which were so much like his, whenever she looked at him, and she was pleased to see how comfortable the shy girl seemed to be around the man.

At the moment, they were all crowded around the kitchen table, and it was Andy's white chess men that had everyone's attention. The young man carefully unpacked them from the straw in his box, and set them out one by one.

The old master had the king in his hands, turning it over and tapping it with his finger nail. He ran a bony finger over the contours of the figure. "Yes," he murmured, "yes."

Ytahu reached out for one of the rooks, which was not the small castle tower Cat was used to, but a standing soldier with a beard and a round helmet, clutching a pointy sword and carrying an inverted-tear-drop shield just like the knights. He weighed the little sculpture in his hand, and looked across the table at the old master. "You work in wares like these, as well?" he asked.

"Yes," said Ekinoru. "There is demand for them, especially across the Moon Sea."

"I have heard of your dealings," Ytahu said. "Among Rhanathon's traders, your ware has good value. I am pleased to make your acquaintance." He turned to look at Andy. "This is exquisite work."

The young sculptor nodded in an acknowledgement of the compliment. "The first I made of this clay," he said. "It is a pleasure to work with."

"What material is it, what is it made up of?" Ytahu asked.

Ekinoru gave a slight chuckle, the first sound of that kind Cat had ever heard from him. "Its rarity is bound in its secrecy," he said. "My journeyman would give much to know the precise recipe."

Cat looked up. "Yes, he would!" she said. "Master Ekinoru, did my husband mention to you what I heard your journeyman say?"

The old man gave a brief nod. "Yes, thank you, Mistress. I have it secure." He touched his leather belt pouch.

"This is a lot like our dancers," Rhitha said. She had picked up the queen and was cupping it in her hands, and now looked up at Ytahu. "Isn't it?"

"Yes, they are quite similar," the man said. "Grandmother, may we...?"

"Yes, child, you may show them," the old woman said. "They will know to value them as they should."

This was the first time Cat had seen the figures of the little dancing girls, and she was quite as entranced as her husband and daughter had promised her. Something niggled at the back of her head. Suddenly it clicked.

"Did you say these came from Outland, Mistress Urn-hild?" she asked.

"Yes, that is what my grandmother told me," the old woman replied. "From Outland, many, many centuries ago."

"I think that would be my Outland," Cat said, "the place my sister-in-law and I came from."

"How do you know that?" Guy asked, "the Knowing?"

"No," Cat said, "plain old book knowledge, in this case. I told you my grandmother collected china—which is another name for this material—and she had a lot of books about it. These dancers look a lot like a picture in one of those books that I loved as a kid. If I'm right, they are more than a thousand years old, from the Tang period of a place called China—hence the name. Except that unlike the ones in the book these are perfectly preserved."

"They could have been brought here from there," Guy said, "back in those days. We know there was travel back and forth. And if Bina is right about their powers, that might account for the preservation. What do you think of them, Master Ekinoru?"

The old master appeared not to hear. He was still staring at the white chess king in his palm.

CHAPTER 23

T HE MARKET SQUARE WAS milling with a colourful crowd when they arrived at the fair. Most of the people of Ruph were dressed in their finery, though some liked to reserve their best clothing for the feast that was to be held in the evening. Booths were set up in a double row all around the perimeter of the market, many of them traders from the lower counties and even as far away as the coast.

Jugglers, musicians and acrobats strolled through the throng, advertising their shows; some had deals with merchants to do their performance next to a trader's stall to draw customers. In front of Ruph's town inn, a giant spit had been built for the occasion, and the smell of the ox which had already been roasting on it for the better part of the day was wafting all over the marketplace.

It was in front of the hall that the place for the chess set fundraiser had been set up. Between the target shooting booth and the cooper's stall, a large table was draped with a white linen cloth, green and scarlet paper banners hanging behind it and a large sign proclaiming, *Contest for the*

Shaper's Game Set, in Benefit of the Town Hall and Clock Tower of Ruph.

With great ceremony, Sepp deposited the chess board on the table. He had finished it that morning, made in alternating squares of ebony inlay and white ceramic tiles that Guy had made for the purpose. The wood was polished and oiled to the highest sheen, the glazed tiles gleamed in the warm summer solstice sunshine.

"All right, boys," he called, "let's get this set up!"

He picked up a large, locked metal coin bank and shook it. "Looks like we've got quite a bit already," he said to Atyrra Paperseller, who was sitting by the booth with a large sheet of paper on which she was taking down the names of people who had bought tickets and how many they got.

"Three-and-a-half dozen so far," she said, "and about a dozen of them bought three or more tickets." She showed him the list. "And then there's Yldra Pastrybaker's boy—one of your nephews, is he not?—he's already bought five. Here he comes again."

Randy was pushing his way through the crowd, his dark red feast vest with its purple embroidery unbuttoned, and his shirt hanging out of his breeches. "One more ticket!" he said to Atyrra, shoving a coin at her.

"Hello to you, too, nephew," said Guy, then supplied the response himself in a squeaky falsetto. "Hello, Uncle Guy and Uncle Sepp, I didn't see you there! How are you enjoying the fair?"

The boy looked up, and laughed. "Well, hello then," he said. "But look, Uncle Guy, I got six tickets!" He pulled

191

the paper stubs out of his pocket. "I'm gonna get as many tickets as I can, then I got the best chance of being in the game. I'm gonna ask grandfather for another coin. If I help him with the cider barrels, he ought to spring for one, or maybe two, or it wouldn't be fair!" He darted away through the throng of people.

Guy chuckled. "You have to wonder if Uncle expressed any desire whatsoever to get help with the cider barrels, or if it was strictly Randy's idea."

"I'll bet it's the latter," Cat said, "but Uncle is enough of a pushover for his grandkids, he's probably happy enough to go along." She brushed some linden blossoms off the cloth; they had drifted down from the big tree beside the hall, which had miraculously survived the ravages of the storm. The creamy-white blooms fell into the woven basket that sat beside the table; Atyrra had brought the table cloth and banner to the market in it. "So are we setting up the game here for people to look at right now?"

"That's the idea," said Sepp. "Here, you haven't even seen Ben's chess pieces, have you?"

Ben put a wooden box on the top of the table. It was a beautiful item, made of rose wood and inlaid in ebony and some creamy white material that looked like ivory or some sort of shell.

"Did you make the box?" Cat asked.

"Yes," the young man said, "quite some time ago, not specially for this. But it fit, so I thought I'd use it for these." He lifted the lid.

"Wow!" said Cat, "sure enough, you've done it again!" She looked back and forth between the carved black wooden pieces Ben was taking out of the box and the sculpted white porcelain ones Andy was setting up on the opposite sides of the chess board. Once again the twins' sculptures were perfect mirror images of each other.

Andy smiled at her and shrugged his shoulder. He was putting down the row of pawns, short squat little pieces half the size of the main chess figures, which looked like bareheaded farmers.

Ben suddenly looked up with an eager light in his eyes. There was Nygelis, making her way through the crowd arm in arm with her sister Kimira. She was laughing back over her shoulder at something behind them, her red-gold hair gleaming in the sunlight, set off by the bright green of her admirably fitting feast gown which emphasized her curves. Cat could certainly understand what Ben saw in the girl.

"H-hi Liss!" he stammered.

The girls turned their heads.

"Oh, hi, Ben," Kimira said. "I'll see you at the ribboner's, Liss. Bye!" She disappeared into the throng of shoppers.

"Hello," Nygelis said to no one in particular. Then her eye fell on the chess pieces, which were almost completely set up on the table now, and her face took on a more animated look. "Look at those! Those are neat," she said. "So that's what's being sold off for the hall roof?"

"Yes!" said Ben enthusiastically. "They're ebony; it's a very hard wood, not easy to carve at all! And..."

Nygelis pointedly picked up one of the white porcelain pawns, ignoring Ben's black pieces. "These are pretty," she said and smiled at Andy. "I like the colour, and the folds in his shirt. You're so good at this."

Cat looked from the girl to the slightly puzzled expression on Andy's face, and then to the hurt and baffled look in his twin's eyes. What was that minx up to?

Kimira came dashing back through the crowd. "Liss, Liss, you've got to come quick! He's got the exact colour ribbon of the blue cloth for your new gown, and if we don't get it quick, he'll sell it off! We'll never find one just like that again!"

Nygelis put the pawn back on the chess board and ran off after her sister.

"Now what was that all about?" Cat said in an undertone to Sepp.

"It looks like *she's* in a snit now," he replied just as quietly. "Ben got so absorbed in making the chess men, he had no attention to spare for anything or anyone, including Liss. She sat in our kitchen for a whole hour on Saturday, making conversation with Nicky, and he never even showed his face to say hello."

Cat shook her head. "Do you think knocking their heads together would help?"

He snorted. "Don't think I haven't been tempted. Oh, hello, Karana!" He turned to little Ari, who came skipping up to the table on Lahni's hand. The young woman had Dyllie on the other hand, and Cory and Tor were following behind, pretending they were too grown up to be with their small siblings but staying close to Lahni whose skirt pocket showed the promising top edge of a small paper bag, the kind that sweets came in.

"Hey, Pops," Tor said with a gap-toothed grin, "how's it goin'?"

"That's 'Papa' to you, young man!" Sepp said and caught his son's head under his arm, rubbing his knuckles in the boy's strawberry-blond hair and making him squeal. "What mischief have you been up to so far, hmm?"

"Nothing!" Tor protested. "We've just bin lookin' 'round, right, Cory?" He picked up a black pawn and made it do a fighting lunge at another. "Rraawr!"

"Ooh, look, pretty!" Ari called, stood on her tiptoes and reached for one of the white chess pieces, knocking another one to the ground. Dyllie followed suit, picking up a black pawn.

"Don't play with Cousin Andy's dollies!" admonished Lahni. She picked up the dropped white bishop and put it back on the chess board. "They're for the hall roof!"

"They're not called dollies, they're chess pieces," Tor said, replacing the black pawn. "And Andy's not our cousin."

"But he's Cousin Ben's brother, and Cousin Nicky is Cousin Ben's auntie," Lahni said. "Do you want a ginger sweet?" She held out the little paper bag from her pocket.

"Aunt Nicky is only Ben's aunt by 'doption, not for real," Cory said. "But yes please, Cousin Lahni, may I have a ginger sweet?" He gave a sidelong glance at Cat. "See, Mumma, I was being p'lite!"

Cat brushed his hair out of his forehead. "So you were, dear. But don't eat all of Lahni's sweets, your teeth are already sticking together. Ask Papa for a coin, then you and

Tor can buy a meat pastry from the pastry cook's. Thanks for looking after them, Lahni!"

"That's fine, Cousin Cat," said Lahni. "I'll go find Mumma now, she's got Baby Yaya. Bye, Cousin Andy and Cousin Ben and Cousin Sepp and Cousin Guy!" She walked off into the crowd.

"She has got to be the most good-natured person I've ever met," said Cat. She turned to Atyrra Paperseller. "You've been doing a booming trade over here while we weren't looking, haven't you?"

"Up to four dozen and ten," the woman said proudly, "wait, four dozen and eleven now." She gave a ticket to Elma Bakerschild, who carefully folded the paper into her frilly little purse, perfectly colour-coordinated with her preternaturally clean and uncreased feast frock.

"My grandmother gave me the coin," the child said. "I thought of spending it on sweets, but it's important to participate in activities for the common good. Did you know there is some dirt on this figure?" She picked up a white pawn and rubbed at the helmet.

"That's a discolouration in the glaze," Andy said with a smile. "There is a small spot somewhere on each of them; it makes the pieces unique."

"Oh." Elma set the pawn back on the board, her pursed mouth clearly indicating what she thought of such flawed workmanship. Cat shook her head—that kid was just a little over the top.

"Say, Catriona Bookwoman, would you take over for a moment?" Atyrra said. "I need to go get some sealing wax to seal up the list properly so nobody can add their name to it without paying."

Cat took her place behind the small sales table and sold another half dozen tickets for the chess contest.

Nikor wandered by the table, and absentmindedly looked up at the banner. "Clock tower?" he said. "Putting a clock tower on the hall. Good thought." He fished three coins out of his pocket and put them on the table. "Here, Catriona Bookwoman, some coin. Time for Ruph to have a clock." He shuffled on to the next booth. Cat smiled to herself, put Nikor on the list and wrote out three tickets with his name on it for the draw, although it was obvious he had been oblivious to the chess set or the contest for it.

Ben still stood by the chess table, fiddling with the pieces. Suddenly Cat saw him stiffen, and a scowl drew down his eyebrows. He turned his back and disappeared behind the booth. What on earth...? Cat followed the direction of his gaze. There was Kashinka, tripping through the crowd with her hips swinging, hanging on the arm of Bel'ris'oem, Ekinoru's journeyman—the latter was who Ben had been looking daggers at. Oh, yes—Nicky had said he'd been flirting with Nygelis. But now it was Kashinka who was clinging to the dark-haired man like a limpet, giggling. That woman had the most irritating laugh of anyone of Cat's acquaintance. It was hard to believe that she was Rhitha's sister—how could two siblings be so different from each other?

"Ah, the famous pieces," Bel'ris'oem said when they came up to the chess table, and he smirked at Andy with a flash of his white teeth. "Look, gorgeous." He picked up the black king and showed it to Kashinka.

She took the black queen and turned it over, then carelessly plopped it back on the board. "Ah, whatever. Oh, darling,"—she dropped her voice a little— "I still have to get you the you-know-what from the old man—I think now might be..."

"Shut up!" the journeyman hissed with a scowl, then noticed Cat's eyes on them and turned his frown into a smarmy grin. "Come on, doll," he said loudly, "I'll get you a gingerbread heart."

Kashinka batted her eyelashes at him, tucked her arm into his, and they vanished into the crowd.

Ben reappeared from behind the booth, shooting a resentful glance in the direction Bel'ris'oem and Kashinka had vanished in.

Cat was not impressed, either. It would be too much to expect a donation towards the hall roof from those two, wouldn't it? Two of a kind, that's what they were. Condescending, nasty, unpleasant...

"All right, finally got it," said Atyrra Paperseller, a little out of breath. She had a stick of sealing wax pushed behind her ear, and carried a pottery dish in both hands, which she was insulating with the outer skirt of her gown. As she got close, Cat could see why she was protecting her hands—the dish contained a glowing piece of charcoal. "Borrowed it from the meat man," Atyrra said, "the one who does those little sticks with roasted meats he grills right at his stall. I need something to melt my sealing wax with."

She put the dish with the hot coal on the table beside the chess set, on top of several more sheets of paper destined for further records of ticket buyers. Cat handed her the filled-out page. "We've made good progress," she said, pointing out the additional number of names on the list.

"Excellent," said Atyrra. She folded the sheet, held the stick of sealing wax over the glowing coal, and when it had softened to the right consistency, brought it over to the paper and let a drop fall on the folded edge. "One more," she said, and softened the wax again.

But at the very moment she was taking it to the sheet, a sudden cheer erupted from the target shooting booth next to them. She startled, and the hot wax dropped on her hand. With a cry of pain she jerked back her hand, struck the bowl with the burning coal, and tipped it over. The thin sheet of paper under it shot up in flame.

"No!" shouted Cat. But Andy and Ben had already sprung into action. Ben whipped the chess board off the table, Andy swiped the pieces off it into the basket that stood beside it, tore the table cloth off the surface and smothered the burning paper in the folds of the material while Ben used the chess board to knock the bowl with the burning coal onto the ground and stomped on the glowing lump to quench it.

The whole process had taken no more than a few seconds. Cat blew out a hard breath. "Phew! That was scary! Good thing you move fast."

"Sorry," Andy said, "I think the cloth is ruined."

"You saved the chess pieces, that's what matters," Cat said. "Yours would have been all right, but Ben's could have gone up in flame. Not to mention half the market with it—if the banner had caught, we'd have had a much larger Solstice bonfire than we bargained for this year. As is, we still only have the hall roof to fix, not the whole town, *and* we still have our fundraiser pieces to do it with." She looked into the basket, where the black and white chess pieces were jumbled together higgledy-piggledy. "I don't think they were even dinged," she said. "I guess the porcelain is pretty sturdy."

They began to set the pieces back on the chess board, but Cat noticed that Andy kept shaking his hands and blowing on them.

"Are you all right?"

"Only a little singed, nothing important," he said.

"That's no good!" said Cat. "Here, let's go fix you up; I think I saw an apothecary stall over by the library."

CHAPTER 24

T HE SUNLIGHT WAS TAKING on the golden quality that said the afternoon was getting on, and the time for the draw for the final chess game had come. Andy and Ben carried the table with the chess pieces into the centre of the marketplace, close to where the bonfire would be lit when it was fully dark; a crowd gathered around, pushing and shoving. The jokes flew thick and fast, and a cheer went up as Guy climbed up onto one of the heavy tables set out for the feast that was to come. Randy fought his way to the front of the throng, his tow-coloured hair standing on end and the freckles on his face stark against his pale skin. There was an intense light in the boy's eyes.

Torgha Tailor brought out a big drum, and stationed himself behind the table on which Guy was standing.

"People of Ruph!" Guy shouted. "You have given your coin freely for the benefit of our great hall! And now it is time to determine the two lucky players who will have the privilege to fight for the ownership of this game board and chess set!" Another loud cheer went up from the crowd. "May I have a drum roll, please!"

Torgha Tailor swirled the drumsticks, then sent up a tremendous rumble from the instrument, ending in one big bang.

"Atyrra Paperseller, bring the draw barrel!" Guy commanded.

Atyrra lifted up the bucket which held the draw tickets, all the slips of paper with the names of every contestant. Torgha made the drum do a low rolling thunder. Guy theatrically reached into the bucket, and stirred the contents with his hand, once, twice, three times...

The crowd began to shout. Someone started a countdown, and soon everyone was chanting: "Four! Three! Two! One..." Guy whipped out one of the pieces of paper.

"Aaaand the first winner is...." He stopped short, and squinted at the paper. "Uh..." He looked around for his wife, a laughing appeal in his eyes. "Help..."

Cat was standing right beside the table. She took a quick look at the paper he held out to her, and hissed up the answer to him. He gave a quick nod, then with hardly missing a beat he took up his theatrical announcement again, flourishing the ticket.

"The winner is—Nikor Archivist!"

"Nooo!" shouted Randy, who by now was pressed right up against the table.

"Hurrah!" yelled the crowd, "Nikor, Nikor!" The little librarian was nowhere in sight.

But Guy would not let that stop the proceedings. "We need another winner!" he shouted. "Shall we draw for our second winner?" Another cheer went up from the people. Atyrra Paperseller raised the bucket, Torgha rumbled out a long drum roll, Guy stirred the papers in the bucket. Randy was so pale with anticipation that his freckles looked like ink blotches across his nose, and he jumped from foot to foot with sheer nerves. The crowd counted down—"Three! Two! One!"—and Guy, this time, pulled out the ticket with extreme and exaggerated slowness. With a flourish, he held up the paper in front of his eyes, and stared at the writing as if he was trying to etch it into his mind.

Cat was ready to help out again, but this time he had it covered. He gave her a quick sideways glance and a wink, then drew a deep breath.

"And—the—second—player—is..." he shouted over the rousing crescendo of Torgha Tailor's drum roll, "the—second—player—iiiiiiiis..."—Torgha ended in a crashing boom—"RANDOR PASTRYBAKERSON!!!"

"YES!!!" Randy yelled, pumping his fists in the air and dancing in a circle. "Yes yes yes yes yes!!!"

Sepp slapped him hard on the back. "Well done, squirt! Defend the family honour!"

"I will, I will!" Randy crowed. "I'm gonna get the chess set, I'm gonna get the chess set!"

A group of people had finally located Nikor, and they were pushing the little librarian into the middle of the square.

"Chess game?" he said, looking confused. "Chess game. Ah, Game of Kings!"

"You won the draw," Cat explained. "You get to play a game with Randor, he's the other winner. And whichever one of you wins this game gets to keep the set."

"Set? Ah. Set." He looked at the ebony and porcelain pieces set out on the board, then to Randy, who was jiggling up and down on the balls of his feet with a faintly supercilious expression on his face. "Randor Pastrycookson."

"Does Master Nikor even know how to play?" Randy asked condescendingly.

"Game of Kings? Quite. Old volume, story of game. From Outland. Keep it with other game books. Which side?"

"What?" said Randy. "Oh, you mean which colour do we play? Uncle Guy..."

Guy jumped back up onto his table, and turned on his announcer's voice again.

"People of Ruph! This is where it is determined which colour the players will use!" He took one black pawn and one white, shuffled them around, hid the pieces in his hand, put his hands behind his back and made a big show of switching the pieces around behind him one more time. "The youngest player gets the choice!" he announced. "Randor Pastrybakerson, choose—left or right?"

Randy was still bouncing up and down on the balls of his feet. "Right!!" he shouted.

Guy pulled his left fist from behind his back.

"No!" yelled the boy, pointing, "the other right!"

"Sorry!" Guy laughed, put his left behind his back again and put out his right. He flourished his fist through the air, then dropped it in front of Randy's face and splayed open his fingers. On his palm lay the black pawn.

"Aww!" Randy groaned.

"You picked it," Guy said, then raised his voice again. "Randor Pastrybakerson will play black; Nikor Archivist takes white! Let the game begin!"

The crowd cheered and clapped, but many were already starting to wander off again. There was more shopping to do, and a considerable portion of the crowd was drifting to the north side of the square where Druce Innkeeper had started to roll the barrels of cider and ale out in front of the inn.

Nikor and Randy took their places across the table from each other, and the boy stared across at the little librarian. "I guess you get to start then," he said.

"Start? White, yes. Quite, quite," said Nikor, scratched his silver fringe of hair, and moved out his first pawn.

"Unca Guy, wanna sweetie!" little Ari said, tugging on Guy's shirt sleeve.

Randy took one of his black pawns and put it two squares further ahead.

"Me, too, Papa! Me sweetie too!" Dyllie pulled on Guy's other sleeve.

Guy laughed at Cat. "I'm beset on all sides!" he said. "Help, whatever shall I do?"

"On your head be it if they make themselves sick," said Cat. "Why don't you take them to see the Punch-and-Judy show instead? Oh, there's the girls!" Bina and Rhitha came through the crowd and stopped beside the table to watch the game. Guy took the two little ones by the hand and went off towards the library, where the puppet show was set up in front of the big doors.

Randy was already going for aggression. Only three moves into the game, he took his first piece, the pawn Nikor had moved out first.

Suddenly Cat heard a child screaming. Her head whipped around—she knew that voice! She took off at a run in the direction Guy had gone with the children and caught up with them to see little Ari frantically stomping her feet and shaking her left hand, howling in pain. "Owie, owie! Bee, bad bad bee!"

Nicky came pushing through the crowd from the other direction. Trust a mother to hear her child's cries from half-way across the market! She scooped her little girl into her arms and made soothing noises.

"Honestly, I couldn't help it!" Guy said. "That bee came and stung her out of nowhere!"

Nicky shook her head. "Don't worry about it," she said. "She'll be fine. Come on, honey, we'll go find Papa, and you can have a lemonade." She bore off her sobbing little girl.

Dyllie pulled on Guy's sleeve again. "Me have wemonade too!" he demanded.

Guy picked him up and put him on his hip. "You didn't get stung by a bee, did you?" he said. "We'll go see the puppet show."

Cat turned to go back to watching the chess game. As she passed the pastrycook's stall, she saw Elma Bakerschild with her grandmother, who had apparently sprung for another coin: Elma had a large turnover in her hand, the kind that was not unlike a jelly donut, filled to bursting with raspberry jam. And at that very moment, burst it did. The pastry practically exploded in Elma's hand, sending a spurt of bright red gloopy raspberry stickiness all down the front of the little girl's lime green dress. Elma let out a wail of distress, and Cat quickly hid her mouth behind her hand—it was a little rude to be laughing at the child, even though she knew that the girl was far more upset about getting messy than about losing her treat. It wouldn't harm her any, Cat thought; it was about time that kid learned to loosen up.

Another one of the white pawns had been taken off the game board—Randy was making inroads.

Cory and Tor had come along and were standing with the girls, watching the game. Bina gave her cousin a critical glance. "You don't look so good," she said. "Are you feeling sick?"

Tor shook his head, but he didn't say anything. Cat took a look at his face. Bina was right, he was quite pale.

"Pawn. Taking it," Nikor stated, and removed one of Randy's black pieces.

Tor's face suddenly turned a sickly shade of green, and he clutched his stomach. "Ow!"

"Oh dear," Cat said. "Too much candy?" She felt his forehead.

"Give him some mintbrew," Bina said, "that'll help."

"You're right," Cat said. "I wonder if anyone on the market has some?"

"There's a stall over by the poulterer's, they were selling some iced," Rhitha put in shyly.

"I want Mumma!" Tor said, his bottom lip wobbling.

"Of course you do," said Cat, taking him by the hand. "We'll go find her, and see if we can get a cup of that mintbrew for you on the way. Any idea where she is, Bina?"

Bina tipped her head to the side. "By the inn, I think," she said. "Uncle Sepp, too. Ari is happier now, because she's with her Papa, and I think he's happy because he got some cider."

Cat laughed. "I like your reasoning," she said, and took Tor to find his parents.

When she came back to the chess table, the girls had gone. The chess game had moved fairly little. Nikor was defending his position, but just as Cat stepped up to the table, the little librarian lost another piece to the aggressive play of his young opponent. With a gloat, Randy took one of the white bishops off the board.

A few minutes later, Bina was wending her way through the crowd, carrying Yaya.

"Here, Mumma," she said, handing Cat the baby. "He barfed on Lahni, so she had to go home and get changed."

"Oh dear," said Cat, "I'm sorry about that!"

"She didn't mind," said Bina. "You know, she's always smiling anyway. But he did literally hurl all over her, not just a little bit, so she couldn't keep wearing her dress."

"What did you have to do that for, hmm?" Cat said to the baby, who seemed to miraculously have escaped his own mess.

"Ba-ba," he said, pointing.

Guy was walking up to the table with Dyllie. The little boy tore loose from his hand, and ran towards Cat.

"Mumma, Mumma, we seed the puppets! And one of dem frowed the ovver down the steps!"

Just then, Nikor made a move. He leisurely stepped a pawn diagonally forward and removed one of Randy's matching black pieces.

"Mumma," called Dyllie, still running, "dere was..." He hit his foot on a protruding cobblestone. It seemed to Cat that she was seeing everything in slow motion. The little boy's headlong rush turned into a slow arc; his knees hit the pavement, then his belly, elbows, hands, finally his forehead.

Cat sucked in a sharp breath. "Ouch!"

Guy had already caught up with Dyllie, and scooped him up from the ground before the little boy even had time to realize what had happened. In keeping with Cat's strange sense of slow motion, it seemed to take Dyllie a second of stunned silence to collect himself, then he opened his mouth and let out a loud wail. His knee was bleeding, both hands were skinned, and there was a big graze across his forehead.

"Oh, sweetie!" Cat said, stepping over to look, "you poor baby!"

Guy had both the boy's hands in his, and was blowing on the scratches. Dyllie's sobs grew a little quieter. "You only fell down to get a lemonade, didn't you?" Guy said, blowing on the scrape across the forehead, then dug his handkerchief out of his pocket and dabbed at the cut on the little boy's knee.

"Wemonade?" said Dyllie tearfully.

"Well, we'll have to see now, won't we? And maybe there's even a honey sweet in it for you," Guy said, then gave Cat a look and rolled his eyes a little. "There goes another one..."

"You're right," said Cat, "this is weird. The kids are dropping like flies—and Lahni's been taken out of the game too! What's going on?"

CHAPTER 25

B INA LOOKED AT MUMMA, and Mumma looked back at her.

"That's exactly it, isn't it?" Bina said. "They've been taken out of the game."

Mumma gave a quick frown, the one she got on her face when she was thinking hard about something. Then she nodded.

"You're right, it's something to do with the game," she said. "But what?"

"Well, it is Andy and Ben's game," Bina said, "and it's one of their special things, not just any old sculptures—they made it exactly the same again. But the pieces were in separate boxes; they didn't really touch each other, did they?"

A spark came into Mumma's eyes. "Yes, they did!" she said. "They all landed in the basket together when the table caught on fire! Oh, good grief—they've activated something, haven't they?"

Bina scrunched her mouth sideways. She knew there was something about the chess set, and about the kids and Lahni—but what?

"There aren't any real kings and queens and knights here, so the chess pieces can't be calling them like the cats and owls did back when I was a baby," she said. "I wonder if the chess set *made* some, like the rose tree Andy and Ben made for your birthday."

"But why the kids?" Mumma said. "And only those few ones, not everyone? But wait, even with my rose tree, the sculptures didn't create it out of thin air—there was a little rose sapling the boys gave me with it; it was in the same box. It touched the sculptures. And then when I planted it, it grew almost overnight and bloomed right away. The boys' sculptures made something out of what was already there."

Bina looked at the chess board and thought about this. Master Nikor moved his bishop, and took one of Randy's black rooks. Mumma's head popped up, and she looked around the market. But the people just kept milling about, and Cory, who was sitting on the bench beside Randy, was perfectly fine.

"Hmm," Mumma said. "That's interesting—nothing that time. I wonder if it's only certain pieces."

"And certain people," Bina stated. She hadn't felt anything from those two pieces that had just been moved, and it made her realize that earlier, she kept feeling a little tug on her when some pieces were played, like something was happening to Dyllie and Ari and Tor—she just hadn't paid attention to it. She stepped over to the table, and looked at the pieces that were lying beside the chess board.

There, that was the last black pawn that had been taken off the board—right before Dyllie fell on his nose. She picked up the piece and weighed it in her hand. But now there was nothing that felt like Dyllie about it; it was only a funny little chess farmer. And Dyllie—Bina listened to his feelings inside of her—Dyllie was quite all right; Papa must have got him that lemonade or the sweet he'd promised him. There was no pull between her little brother and that chess piece now.

Randy moved one of his knights, and in response, Master Nikor took his queen a step to the side. And that's when Bina felt a sharp tug inside of her—and right at the same time, Rhee pulled her sleeve.

"I'm going to the book binder's stall," Rhee said. "Do you want to come?"

Bina whipped her head around and stared at her friend. "Why did you say that?"

Rhee looked at her with a slight frown. "I don't know," she said, "I just felt like going to the book binder's."

"But you love watching the chest game!"

"Chess," Rhee said automatically.

"Yeah, I know that," Bina said impatiently, "but why do you want to go elsewhere right now?"

Rhee shrugged her shoulders. "I don't know," she said again. "Actually, I don't want to go now. Let's stay here and watch."

Bina narrowed her eyes and gazed at the chess pieces. She let her eye travel over the board, piece by piece. There was definitely something about them, but only a few of them. There, the white queen, she was connected with Rhee. And that one—she reached out between the players and just touched the white king with her forefinger. The instant her skin made contact with the piece, the image of old Master Ekinoru flashed in her mind. And the black queen—she moved her finger over to touch it, but Randy smacked her hand out of the way.

"Cut it out!" he grumbled. "We're playing!"

"Sorry," Bina said, pulling her hand away from the chess board, but from having her hand so close to it she already knew who the black queen was: she was, after all, just as related to her as to Rhee, and being related by blood to someone, she'd realized, made her able to feel them much more easily. Even if she didn't like them—although that blocked most of their feelings from playing in her head, she could still pick up things about them that she couldn't feel about strangers.

Randy proved her right. His queen had still been on its original square, but now he pulled it several spaces forward. And Kashinka came around the corner of the cloth merchant's stall.

Bina looked at Mumma and tipped her head in Kashinka's direction. "See?"

"What?" Mumma said, drawing down her eyebrows a little.

"Kashinka!" Bina said quietly. "She's the black queen!"

"Oh! You think certain people are certain pieces? Yes, I think you're right! That's exactly how it is! But how, why?"

"You said your rose tree had to touch the sculptures. Maybe the people touched the pieces."

Mumma wrinkled her forehead again. "But then, shouldn't we all... No, we shouldn't, at that! I don't think I ever took one of those pieces in my hand. Andy cleared the kiln this morning, and packed up the pieces himself, and we didn't see Ben's pieces until he took them out of his box and set them up."

"And the things Andy and Ben make never do anything to them, themselves," added Bina, "so it doesn't matter that they touched them. They're the Shapers."

"But then, when did the kids... Oh, I remember! After the boys had set up the set, Lahni and the kids came, and they picked up some of the pieces!" Mumma looked into the air above Bina's head, pinching her eyes shut a bit like she was looking into the past. "I remember Ari and Dyllie handling one each, and Tor—oh, and Lahni picked one up that fell down. And Elma touched one, too! But not Cory. That's why he's still up on his feet without a skinned knee or a tummy ache."

"What about Yaya?" Bina wanted to know. "Is that why he threw up?"

"No, that was just a standard baby thing, I think," Mumma said, "but it was Lahni who had to leave because of it; it hit her. And she'd handled a chess piece."

"But, Kashinka?"

Mumma thought. "Wait a minute," she said, "she and that Bel'ris'oem came by the booth, and they each picked up a piece! I remember, because I was irritated that they didn't donate for the hall roof."

"Then that journeyman..."

"Yes, likely," said Mumma. "The black king, I think it was."

Bina had to test it. Quickly she nipped her finger in between the players, and touched it to the crown on the top of the piece's head.

"Hey!" snapped Randy, and flicked her hand away. He made her fingers bump right into the black king, and the piece toppled over.

Bel'ris'oem, the journeyman, stumbled out from between two of the stalls. He turned and snarled at someone in the aisle. "Watch where you're putting that!"

Randy put the black king upright again, but he let his fingers rest on the figure, lost in thought. Then he made a sudden decision, and moved the piece out.

The journeyman stepped over to the table, and Bina got a whiff of that weird smell that always hung around him.

"Ah, Mistress," he said to Mumma. "Is your husband nearby?" There was a gloating expression on his face that Bina didn't like. But then, she didn't like this fellow in the first place—and not only because he was keeping company with Kashinka, who was mean to Rhee.

"Here he comes right now," said Mumma and pointed to Papa, who carried Dyllie clutching a wooden doll.

"All better," Papa said, and put Dyllie down. "Aunt had a sticking plaster in her scrip, and the colourman over by the inn drew a doggie on it. So that made the skinned knee almost a good thing."

Dyllie pointed to his knee which was adorned with a big sticking plaster. "Wook, a doggie!" he said proudly. "My weg's aw better! And I got a dolly!" He held out his new toy.

"Master Potter," the black-haired journeyman inter-rupted—which was rude, even if Dyllie was just a little boy—"I have a proposal for you that I know you will find beneficial."

Papa gave him a look, kind of a slow one with one eye-brow up higher than the other. If that journeyman wasn't so stuck up, he'd know that Papa wasn't keen on what he had to say—you didn't need to know Papa all that well to figure it out, Bina thought, even if you couldn't read people's feelings.

"Beneficial for you, or for me?" Papa said, trying to smile a bit to make it sound less rude.

"Haha! Both, I trust, both, Master Potter. You see,"—he struck his hand against the leather satchel he wore slung around his shoulder—"I have obtained what I need to take up my inheritance." He drew himself up a little straighter. "I, Bel'ris'oem, will take the trade of my father's house."

"What about your master?" Papa asked, still trying to keep himself from letting the scowl show on his face that he was feeling inside. If Bina hadn't known that most peo-ple couldn't feel others' feelings, she'd have found it hard to believe that the journeyman didn't pick up on that—Papa feelings sounded like a loud angry rumble to her.

The journeyman laughed again. "We no longer need to concern ourselves with him," he said. "I hope for a long and fruitful association with your house." He slapped his leather pouch again, nodded his head as if their bargain had been concluded, and turned to walk away.

Just then, Master Nikor moved one of his white pawns, and Bina felt another tug. Who was it now? Someone else who was family, not really close, but... Oh! There she was! Liss was crossing the middle of the market, and passed by the chess table, right in front of the black-haired man.

"Ah, my lovely!" the journeyman said, giving her a smile that had, in Bina's opinion, way too many teeth in it. "Just who I was looking for! Let me buy you a drink! Or a sweet for the sweet! Our houses will be connected, we shall celebrate." He held out his arm to her.

Liss giggled, but Bina could tell she wasn't really happy. She would much rather have had Ben get her a drink or a sweet. Bina suddenly became aware of Ben himself, who was leaning his shoulders against the side of the poulterer's stall facing the chess table, and watching Liss with a scowl on his face. And then Liss saw him too, and Bina felt something inside her cousin snap a little. She tossed her head, giggled again, and hooked her arm through the journeyman's. "Lead away!" she said. "A cup of cider is exactly what I need!"

CHAPTER 26

C AT SHOOK HER HEAD at Nygelis' retreating back. Had she been that stupid herself at nineteen? She didn't think so, but then, she hadn't had a boyfriend who was dragging his feet about proposing. She hadn't had a boyfriend at all, come to think of it—so she didn't really know what was normal behaviour in that kind of situation. But regardless, at the moment she could have cheerfully given the girl a good shaking.

The expression on Ben's face was painful to see, and it looked like the hand he had shoved in his vest pocket was forming into a fist, as if he was clutching something he had stowed away there—or, possibly, wanting to punch someone. If those two didn't get their act together soon, someone would have to sit them both down and give them a serious talking-to; this couldn't go on like that.

"They'd better make up their minds one way or the other; I'm about fed up with that drama," Guy said quietly from beside her. Cat turned her head, and saw that he was looking in the same direction as herself.

"No kidding," she said. "This makes me appreciate how short our courtship was; at least we never had those issues."

He laughed. "No, we didn't—I asked you to marry me the moment I first set eyes on you, when I wasn't even conscious enough to have found out your name—that does cut down on courting conflict. Not that I'd recommend that method, though; not everyone gets as lucky as I in that kind of gamble."

"I'm a gamble, am I?" said Cat.

"I said I'd been *lucky*, woman! Focus on the important part, will you?" He grinned at Cat.

"Papa, there's Master Ekinoru," said Bina. "You wanted to talk to him, didn't you?"

"Yes, I did," said Guy. "How did you—? Oh, right, never mind." He turned to the old man, who had stepped out between the fairground stalls when Nikor moved the white king. "Master Ekinoru..."

And that was when Randy pulled his black queen clear across the board so it stood confronting Nikor's white one, and Kashinka—exploded. There was no other word for it. Kashinka, too, had seen Nygelis go off with Bel'ris'oem, and her jealous spite vented itself on the easiest target—her sister. She swooped down on Rhitha, her fingers literally curled into claws.

"You!" the young woman hissed, "what are you doing here? Why do you always have to be where you're not wanted? Ugly shrimp!"

Rhitha started back, her face going ashy pale and her grey eyes wide with fright. "I—I don't—"

"You're always getting in my way! Silly, stupid bitch!"

Beside Rhitha, Bina looked nearly as shocked as her friend at this eruption of vitriol. Cat could sense the utter bewilderment in her daughter, who had never in her life experienced such an outburst of nastiness. She tried to take a step forward to interfere, but it was as if something was holding her in place; and she heard Bina draw breath to speak out, but no sound came from the girl's mouth.

"You're such a weedy rag," Kashinka spat out, her face twisted into a snarl, "always fouling up the place! Get out of my way—get out of my *life*! You've spoiled everything!"

"What—what did I do?" Rhitha faltered.

"If it wasn't for you," Kashinka yelled, "I'd be an Unissima! I'd be something special! I wish you'd get lost!"

Nikor moved his white queen over a few squares to get out of the black queen's way.

Rhitha took a deep breath. "Even if I—if I left," she said, obviously trying to control her shaking voice, "you still wouldn't be an Unissima. You have to be born as your mother's only child ever, like Bina!"

Kashinka opened and closed her mouth a few times like a landed fish, accentuating the ugly curl of her lip. "Well, well—" she sputtered.

Randy pushed his queen several squares forward.

"Well, I still want you *gone*!" Kashinka screeched. "Why don't you just jump off a cliff! You're hideous, and dumb, and an ugly maggot, and you have no right to—to that piece the old woman has! It's mine, I tell you! It's worth good coin, I'll have it, it's MINE! Stupid ugly worms like you and her have *no right* to it! I wish you'd just *die*!"

The black queen moved all the way, and took the white. The piece dropped off the edge of the table and fell to the ground.

Cat saw Rhitha's face crumple, and tears poured down the girl's pale cheeks. She whirled around, ran sobbing between the fairground booths, and was gone.

Kashinka wore an expression of vicious triumph, and she looked around her, gloating. Her eyes fell on Ben, who still stood leaning against the corner of the poulterer's stall, staring at her, seemingly just as paralyzed as Cat felt herself.

"What are you looking at, slave boy?" the young woman said with a sharp-edged sneer. "I don't know why they even allow scum like you in this town! God, I hate this miserable hole!" She turned on her heels and walked off down the aisle between two of the booths.

Ben looked stunned, as if she had slapped him across the face.

Bina started to move again, and Cat could feel the anger radiating from the girl. She reached out her hand—apparently she was free to do so now—and caught her daughter by the upper arm.

"Don't, sweetie," she said, "it won't help anyone if you go after Kashinka!"

"But Mumma!"

"Yes, I know you want to scratch her eyes out, but it'll just feed the nastiness. We need to find Rhitha and see if we can help her!"

Bina tipped her head sideways. "She's gone to the library garden," she said. "And I think she—hey!" Her head whirled around, and she stared at the chess board.

Nikor had a white pawn in his hand, and walked it the last step to the end row on Randy's side of the board. "Pawn. Promoting it. Swap for queen."

Randy smacked his forehead with the heel of his hand and groaned. "I forgot about that!" he said. "Aw man!"

"That's Liss' piece!" said Bina excitedly. "What's happening?"

"Nikor reached the other side of the board with it, and now the pawn can become anything he wants," Cat explained. "But where is the white queen? He can trade them off." The white chess piece was nowhere in sight, and the players were becoming visibly annoyed at the delay in their game. "Just mark the pawn somehow, to show that it's the queen now," Cat suggested.

"Here," Bina said, pulling a piece of string out of her pocket, "give her that as a necklace." She reached out to drape the little loop over the pawn's head, but as soon as her fingers made contact she started back as if the piece had given her an electric shock. "Liss!" she cried, "we need her here!"

CHAPTER 27

B INA COULD FEEL THE hurt inside of Ben like a sharp jab as she ran past him. She had to get Liss! She wasn't sure why, exactly, but there was something she could do. And maybe she'd be able to make Ben feel better again, too; Bina kind of thought that Liss was about ready to.

She ducked through the gap between the two clothier's stalls, whipped around the corner by the meat man's, and just caught herself before she tripped over a stick that someone had left lying on the ground by the pastrycook's. Was she in time? She was. Liss was just getting up from one of the tables in front of the inn, right behind the big spit that had the ox roasting on it. And Liss—Liss was mad!

"Liss," she called, "Liss, come quick!" She reached the table, huffing for breath. "Liss, you gotta come!"

"Yeah, I'm coming." Liss said curtly, and Bina could feel the mad coming off her. "There's certainly nothing here worth sitting around for!" She picked up a piece of parchment from the ground. "He couldn't even stay long enough to make sure he had all his stuff with him!"

"Do you mean that journeyman fellow? Is that who you're mad at?"

"Yes, him," said Liss. "The nerve of the fellow!"

"What happened? Didn't he get you a drink?"

"Oh yeah, he got me a drink—and then he figured he could twist me round his finger for it! As if! He's not even smart enough to figure out that there's two of them!"

"Two of what?"

"Ben and Andy! He didn't know they're twins, or that Ben even exists! He said he was going to be rich, and he'd cut me in on it, and he showed me this thing." She waved the parchment. "But he said first he needed me to help him, and he wanted me to find out things for him from the 'potter's apprentice' because I'm 'friendly with him'—as if it's not totally obvious that it's *Ben* I li—am keeping comp—that Ben is totally different from Andy!" Liss gave an angry toss to her head.

Bina grinned. "So then what happened? Did you tell him?"

"I told him I wasn't going with the 'potter's apprentice'—and it's true!" she said in huffy tone. "I'm not going with him. *Or* with—" She broke off, and started again. "So then he—" She turned to Bina. "You know what, kid? That fellow is a snake! He only wanted to use me! He never cared for me at all—he only cared for what he could get from me!"

They had almost arrived at the centre of the marketplace. Bina thought quickly. Liss was ready to step in and tell off that journeyman, but it wasn't quite enough—she needed to be a little madder yet. "Liss, that's what Kashinka is like, too. She's so mean! You should have heard what she said to Ben just now! She called him a slave boy, and it hurt him so bad, he was totally knocked flat!"

That had done it. Bina could feel the mad boiling right up inside of Liss, just when they stepped out between the booths to the open area with the chess game.

And then she felt the tug of the chess pieces being moved, and Liss moved with them. Both of them walked over to the table. There weren't a whole lot of pieces left in the game. One of the ones Master Nikor still had was Liss' pawn-queen, and he had just stepped it over a couple of spaces. Randy, for his part, took his queen and made it slide right up so it was staring at Master Nikor's piece across the board—and Kashinka walked back into the square.

She saw Liss, and her face got that mean look again, with the eyes all squinty and the mouth curled down at the corners.

"If it isn't the fish girl!" Kashinka said. Then she looked from Liss to Ben. "Oh, and there's your fellow," she said. "You're well-matched. A servant should come in handy on the fish farm." She laughed a mean, tinkling laugh.

Liss looked back at her with the mad bubbling inside of her, and her eyes were taking on a really sparkly look. And then Master Nikor moved the pawn-queen, and Liss opened her mouth.

"That man," she said, pointing at Ben without even looking at him, "is worth a dozen of the one you've been stepping around with, Kashinka." She made the 'sh' in the name sound really hissy, like a water kettle on the boil.

"And if I were you, I'd not be quite so cocky about even him."

"Huh!" Kashinka tossed her head. "That's all you know! Bel'ris'oem is going to be worth a *lot*! He'll be rich, and we'll be together, and have a life that you people in this godforsaken hole can't even dream about!"

"Oh, really?" said Liss, and the mad inside her pulled back on its haunches, like Greyface the Cat stalking a mouse. Then she pounced. "Then why, Kashinka, may I ask, did Bel'ris'oem just ask *me* to marry him?"

The white queen on the chess board pushed the black one off its square.

Kashinka's mouth dropped open. "WHAT?!"

"If you don't believe me," Liss said, "ask him, next time you see him."

Master Nikor plopped the black queen by the side of the board, where it fell on its back and stared up into the evening sky.

"Oh!!" Kashinka stamped her foot, huffed air through her nose, pinched her mouth into a tight little parcel, glared at Liss, then swung around and ran out of the square.

The mad was settling down inside of Liss, and its growling was almost starting to sound like a purr.

"Did that man really ask you to marry him?" Bina said, although she knew by the way Liss had felt when she had said it that it was true.

"Oh yes," Liss said, and she gave a sideways look at Ben. "When I told him I wasn't going with 'the potter's apprentice', he said he wanted to marry me and make me rich, so our families would be connected."

Ben's feelings were scrunched up really, really tight inside of him, and when Bina looked over, she could see he was biting his teeth together so hard that the corners of his jaw were sticking right out. Well, he didn't know about Liss' mad—Bina had to help him out and make her say it. "So what did you answer?"

Liss snorted. "What do you think? Like I'd marry someone like *that*!"

The tightness inside of Ben shivered into a whole lot of little soft pieces, and he let the air slowly puff out of his mouth like he hadn't breathed out in a month. Liss gave him that sideways look again, and he looked back at her, and then they were both leaning side-by-side against the wall in the little passage between the poulterer's and the coppersmith's booths; just sort of leaning there and looking at each other and then away again.

And that was why the black-haired journeyman didn't see Liss when he came back into the square a minute later. Randy moved the black king, and the man came swaggering along as if he owned the town.

Master Nikor's white king moved a step sideways.

The old white-headed pottery master rose from the bench where he had been quietly resting, and his black-haired journeyman looked at him.

Then the younger man sketched a bow, and Bina could tell that it wasn't a bow of respect, but that he was mocking the old man. "Ah, *Master*," he said, "here we meet. I fancy there is something we need to discuss."

"Is there?" Old Master Ekinoru looked at his journey-man from under his bushy white eyebrows. "Well? What is it you want?"

The black chess king moved sideways to expose its rook, threatening the white king.

The journeyman stood in front of his old master and looked down on him.

"I want the craftshop," he said with a sneery twist to his mouth. "I have the recipe." He clapped his hand to his leather satchel.

The old master clutched at the small pouch on his belt, slid a finger under its flap to search inside, and then in spite of the dark colour of his skin Bina saw him turn pale.

"Check!" said Randy.

CHAPTER 28

C AT HEARD GUY DRAW a sharp breath beside her. The recipe? The instructions for the secret of the white clay? Master Ekinoru had said he had it safe! So Bel'ris'oem had got a hold of it after all? This sounded bad. It meant that Master Ekinoru was cornered—and the stricken look on the old man's face confirmed it.

But then the chess pieces moved again. Nikor picked up his pawn-queen with the string necklace, and drew it clear across the board, lightly trailing its foot along the diagonal he was moving it on, and placed it to protect his king.

Nygelis pushed herself away from the side wall of the poulterer's stall, and stepped back out into the open. She walked over to the two antagonists, let her eyes trail over Bel'ris'oem from head to toe, then reached into her pocket.

"Recipe?" she said. "Would that be *this* recipe?" She held out the piece of parchment to Master Ekinoru.

The journeyman's jaw dropped; he whipped open the flap of his satchel and stared inside, then a look of deep chagrin came over his face.

The relief that showed in the old master's eyes was profound. "Thank you, Mistress," he said to Nygelis as he took the parchment, bowing to her. "I am more obliged than I can express."

Once again the chess pieces shifted.

Bel'ris'oem looked furious, and he glared at Nygelis. "I offered you marriage!" he hissed. "Slut!"

The pawn-queen was withdrawn a little.

"I'm no longer 'lovely', am I?" Nygelis said. "Well, I do not care to be used for someone else's purpose." She made a little curtsy to the old master. "Master Ekinoru, it was my pleasure."

The black king moved again.

"I am *not* finished!" growled the journeyman. "The trade is mine by rights! I, Bel'ris'oem, claim the rights of the only-born, last of my line, and journeyman of the trade! By the laws of Isachang, you have no right to withhold my father's inheritance from me! Give me the mastership, give me what is mine!"

Master Ekinoru once again paled and turned away, staggering a little. Guy sprang over to grasp him by the arm, supporting him to a bench. "He is right," the old man said, his voice shaking. "I cannot withhold it if he claims the Right of the Last of His Line."

The black-haired journeyman stood with his legs astride, his arms crossed, his chest thrust out. On his face was a gloating, triumphant sneer.

Young Randy's face at the chess table bore a faint echo of the same aspect, only missing the malicious undertones of the man's, as he made his move. "Check!"

Cat and Guy looked at each other, and their expressions said the same: this was hopeless. The old master's game was lost.

But Bina tugged on Cat's sleeve. "It's not over!" she said in an urgent whisper. "Look, Mumma, Master Nikor still has one rook!"

And the little librarian, who had been lost in calm contemplation of the chess board, had seen it too. He grasped the white porcelain piece by its round helmet, and marched it straight down the board.

Into the square stepped a tall, broad-shouldered figure with a head of hair so fair it was nearly silver, Rhitha and Mistress Urnhild right behind him.

"Cousin Ytahu!" cried Bina, "I thought it might be you!"

Ytahu? All of a sudden Cat was in her memory back in Urnhild's kitchen, and she saw again the man's broad hand with its square-tipped fingers, the chess piece resting on the palm: Ytahu had been the one to handle the white rook.

The young man smiled at Bina, and inclined his head to Guy, Cat and Master Ekinoru in greeting. Then his eye travelled further, and he stopped short, his eyebrows rising in an expression of surprise.

Cat looked from him to the man his gaze was fixed on. Bel'ris'oem's face was a mask of fury as he glared back at Urnhild's grandson.

"Osera," Ytahu said. There was an undertone of distaste and scorn in his voice, but curiously also a slight suggestion of amusement. "An unlikely meeting place."

The journeyman looked as if he was struggling to make his expression into a bland one. "I do not know you, and I know no such person," he said haughtily. "I am Bel'ris'oem of Rhanathon, son of A'rakbel, to whose trade I lay my claim as journeyman."

Ytahu snorted. "You're from Rhanathon all right," he said, "but if you've forgotten the name you grew up with in the orphanage, your memory must have gone quite bad. Mine has not. I can assure you that it was not the name Bel'ris'oem which you forced me to carve on the plank behind the wash house and sign with my own blood, declaring myself your slave and swearing eternal fealty, when we were ten years old. You took good care I would remember your name, Osera."

"Check," said Nikor laconically. Randy looked flabbergasted. He moved his king a step back.

"I do not know this man," the black-haired journeyman cried out. "Who is he, anyway? He admits to coming from an orphanage! A foundling, without family or connections, no name!"

Nikor moved the white rook again. "Check!"

"I am Ytahu, trader of Rhanathon," the young man said. "Bastard son of Shamira, grandson of Urnhild." He drew the little old woman to his side. "*This* is my family."

The black chess king backed away another step.

"An old woman!" sneered the journeyman. "See, he has no one to vouch for him! He cannot be trusted!"

Guy spoke up. "Your face vouches for you, Ytahu," he said. "Any in this town who knew Urnhild's husband, Belock, will recognize him in his grandson."

Nikor's white king moved, and old Master Ekinoru rose to his feet. "*Not* Bel'ris'oem, you say? *Not* A'rakbel's son?"

He gazed at the tall figure of Ytahu, confronting his antagonist.

"Osera was used to boast of his father's having been a sailor, killed in a raid," Ytahu stated. "He grew up in the same orphans house in Rhanathon as I did."

"I came from Ancoth, where I apprenticed, to join the crafthouse! Ask him if I did not!"

"Ancoth, was it? I assume you returned when you heard of the vacancy for a son in A'rakbel's shop. So convenient that Bel'ris'oem died abroad, and that the change from boy to man is great enough that no one in Rhanathon would have recognized him had he returned—or you, for that matter, unless they had known you for more than a year or two."

One more attempt on Randy's part to get his king out of check.

"You cannot take the word of this foundling, this orphan, against an acknowledged journeyman of the trade!"

The white rook surged forward.

"Ah, yes," Ytahu said, leisurely crossing his arms over his chest, "journeyman of the trade. Which trade is this, Osera? It can hardly have been the potter's; you did not stay with Master A'rakbel above two years after he took you from the orphanage. So was it the tinsmith's, under whom you worked next? Oh, no, that was your third master, you only lasted a few months with him. The second one was the bricklayer, three years—*then* the tinsmith. And after that, the tanner. I recall stories of unpleasant smells being part of that particular trade, which is, no doubt, Osera, why Rhanathon saw nothing of you in the five years since you left that master, taking along his cash box for company. If you are a journeyman of any trade, Osera, it is that of bullying, thievery, and running from your masters."

Randy stared in shock at the chess board, and then from the board to the little librarian serenely smiling at him from across the table.

"Checkmate," the boy said with a stunned look on his face. "It's checkmate."

CHAPTER 29

R HITHA LOOKED UP AT her brother, sitting beside her on the bench at the feast table, and her fingers went to the little red and yellow enamelled butterfly pinned to her blouse, which he had bought her at the silversmith's.

Ytahu had a large mug of cider cupped in his hands, and he smiled down at Grandmother sitting on his other side. "Yes, Grandmother, I've had enough," he said.

"Are you certain?" Grandmother asked anxiously. "Are you not still a little bit hungry? I think there is some roast ox left; look, Druce Innkeeper is carving some more! You would like a little more meat, would you not?"

He laughed. "Grandmother, I had three helpings of the roast already!" he said. "*And* pork pies. *And* stewed eel, pickled carp, bread dumplings, cheese fritters, capon pasties, fried potato patties, pickled cucumbers, pickled beets, lettuce salad, cabbage salad, pear compote, plum stew... What am I forgetting?"

"Strawberries," said Rhitha with a blissful sigh, "and *ice cream*!" She had never tasted anything so delicious in her life. Bina's Aunt Yldra had made the ice cream, with great big blocks of ice that were brought in on wagons full of straw. Bina said her Uncle Chonyk had an ice house on the farm, where they stored the ice they cut from the big lake in the valley every winter.

"Yes, that," said Ytahu. "So you see, Grandmother, I absolutely cannot eat any more. But you didn't eat much yourself!"

Grandmother smiled her lovely smile at him. "Oh no, my boy," she said and patted his hand, "I'm an old woman, I do not need much food. But are you quite, quite sure you had enough? You and Rhitha?"

He laughed down at Rhitha. "Grandmother wants us to explode," he said. "I think she is already tired of having us in her house, so she wants to stuff us with food until we burst apart, so she can be rid of us!"

Grandmother laughed her soft little laugh. "Oh you!" she said and shook her head at them both. "But be sure you have enough drink! Do you want more cider?"

"*Grandmother*!" they both cried. Then Ytahu said with a twinkle in his eye, "I think Grandmother needs another cider, Rhee. She can think of nothing else!"

"Oh no, no," Grandmother protested, but Rhitha had already sprung up from the bench and leaned over to pluck Grandmother's cider cup from between her hands. She put a little kiss on her soft wrinkled cheek.

"That's what you get for fussing, Grandmother," she said. "Now you have to have another drink."

She ran over to the inn, where Sardor Brewmaster was drawing cider and beer from great big barrels. Randy was sitting beside his grandfather, looking glum. "One more pear cider for my grandmother, please," Rhitha said, handing over the small mug.

"One pear cider for Urnhild Tradersmother, coming up," Master Sardor boomed. "Come on, young'un, stop sulking and get to it!" He clapped Randor on the shoulder and put the mug in his hands. "Cheer up, boy," he said in a more kindly tone. "It's not the end of the world to have lost that game. I'll bet you gave Nikor a hard enough run for it."

"It's true," Rhitha said shyly to Randy, "you *nearly* won. Master Nikor almost didn't make it."

"That makes it worse," Randy grumbled. "I don't think I'll ever play chess again. For sure not with that set. Nikor won it."

"But didn't you hear? The set is going to be kept in the library—Master Nikor has no need for it himself, so it's going to be in with all the books, and anyone who wants to can go play it!"

"Hmph," mumbled Randy.

"Oh, hi, Rhee," said Bina, coming up to the cider barrels with a bouquet of three mugs in each hand. "What are you grumbling about, Randy?"

"He's unhappy about losing that chess game," Master Sardor said, taking the cups from her and filling them with cider, "even though your friend here says he can still play it anytime in the library." He held out two of the brimming cups to Bina, who slid her hand through the handles, and then two more which she took in her other hand.

"He's just scared that he'll lose again, especially if Rhee's playing him," said Bina casually. "Can you help me with the other two mugs, Rhee? Three in each hand is too heavy when they're full."

"Am *not*!" Randy said, incensed. "I'm not scared to take on anyone! I'll play her tomorrow if she wants!"

Bina grinned, and Rhitha realized that that was exactly the reaction her friend had been aiming for. "Deal!" she said quickly. "Tomorrow at the library!" She slipped her hand through the handles of the two big mugs like Bina had done, and hoisted them up. Bina was right; they were heavy! Grandmother's little mug in her other hand, she turned to Randy. "So are you game?"

"You bet I am!" he said with a combative sparkle in his eyes. "I'm going to beat you—see if I won't!"

"You got him," said Rhitha to Bina as they were making their way back between the tables. "That's cheered him right up!" She deposited Grandmother's cider in front of her and followed Bina to her family's table.

"Yes, I knew it would," Bina said. "Okay, this one's Papa's, and this is Uncle Sepp's, and, umm—which ones have you got, Rhee?" she said, passing along the cider cups.

"I have no idea," Rhitha said, "your uncle just handed them to me."

"Hmm, I think they were Mumma's and Aunt Nicky's," Bina said. "That means these ones are Andy's and Ben's. Here you are!"

"Enjoying the feast, Rhitha?" Mistress Cat said, smiling at her.

"Oh yes!" Rhitha said, smiling back. In fact, she couldn't remember ever enjoying herself this much. It wasn't only the strawberries and ice cream. Really, they were the least of it. The best was that she was with Grandmother, and with Ytahu, and with Bina and her family; and everyone was kind, and cheerful, and nobody gave her sneering looks and called her names—and she didn't even have to be afraid that anyone would, because Kashinka and Mother were *nowhere...to...be...seen*.

Bina had said that Kashinka had run away after her cousin Liss had told her off, and Bina could feel that she wasn't anywhere around. She couldn't exactly feel what Kashinka was doing, she said, but she could feel what she *wasn't* doing, and that was being anywhere near the feast on the market. It was wonderful.

Rhitha sighed contentedly. What a day it had been! First it had been so awful—so terribly, horribly awful, when Kashinka had screamed at her in front of all those people—Rhitha had thought she was going to die. And she had run, run to the library garden, and she wanted to hide until the hurt wasn't burning quite so badly—but then she had remembered the night of the storm, and how Grandmother had taken Ytahu in her arms and comforted him, and she had felt such a yearning for that comfort herself that she just kept running, right to Grandmother's house. And Grandmother put her arms around her, and wiped the tears from her cheeks, and stroked her hair, and it had felt like cool ointment on that hot burn, and so much of the hurt had been soothed away.

And then Ytahu, who had sat at the table that whole time with a frown on his face, got up and said, "Enough is enough!" He made them come with him to the market to confront Kashinka, and he was striding along like something was pulling on him—like Rhitha herself had been pulled earlier, when she was watching that chess game.

When they got out of the house, there had been Mother, at the end of the street. They all stopped and looked at each other. Mother had gone all white, and was staring at Ytahu like—well, like she had seen a ghost. And then she started to talk very fast—she was babbling, really—saying it hadn't been her fault, and everyone was going to know now, and how was she supposed to have taken care of a child when she had been so young, and one had to look out for oneself, and—But nobody was listening. Ytahu gave her a long stare.

Then he said, in a hard, indifferent voice, "Shamira." He gave Mother a short, jerky bow, and then kept striding on.

Rhitha and Grandmother had looked at each other and turned around to follow Ytahu; and they left Mother standing in the alley, and Rhitha knew from the look in Grandmother's eyes that they both felt a freedom they never had before.

"Come sit down, Rhee," Bina said. "I've got some more lemonade, do you want to share?"

Rhitha slid on the bench beside Bina and took a sip through the straw in her cup. That was such a clever idea, using straws for drinking through! It made the lemonade taste even better, Rhitha thought. Bina's little brothers had their own cups and straws, too, and so did her cousins, who were all sitting at the table together.

Just then there was a loud rumbling noise from Torgha Tailor's big drum, followed by a big *Boom*.

"Attention, attention!" a voice cried out somewhere from the middle of the marketplace. "Silence for the Town Chronicles!"

"What's going on?" Rhitha asked.

"It's the announcements," Bina said. "I forgot we haven't had those yet. Every year at Summer Solstice, they announce all the important stuff that happened in the town over the year. It used to be Master Nikor who did it, 'cause he writes the Chronicles, but his voice isn't strong enough any more. I think it's Atyrra Paperseller reading them now. Listen!"

It started kind of sad, Rhitha thought—first they listed all the people that had died. But then, as Atyrra went on, Rhitha realized it wasn't sad so much as solemn, and honouring. Every time Atyrra said a name, the whole town repeated it back, and everyone who had a cup or glass raised it, like a last toast to the person who was gone. And then, when they got through the list of all those who had died, and the last name spoken was that of Nyif Baker, who had only gone three days ago, all of the town raised their cups, and bowed their heads, and together they called out in one voice "We remember!"

But then the whole mood shifted. Atyrra Paperseller, who was standing on a table close to the bonfire pile—in fact, Rhitha thought it was the table the chess set had been on—now had a big smile on her face as she turned the page of the red-bound volume of the Chronicles of Ruph.

"The marriages of Ruph!" she called out. A raucous cheer went up from the crowd, and was repeated with every set of names of newly-married couples. Cups were banged on tables, and the newlyweds had their backs slapped and hands shaken and cheeks kissed.

From there it went—quite logically, Rhitha thought—to new babies. If the children were present—and most of them were—they got lifted into the air for all to see, and cups were raised and cheers went up. Rhitha cheered extra loudly when the announcement came: "August 20th: son of Catriona Bookwoman and Dyniselm Septimissimus: Iawar!" and Master Guy hoisted Yaya high up over their heads, where the baby squealed and waved his arms at everybody.

After the announcement of the babies, the Chronicles still were not finished. There were just a few more announcements: the trades news, telling everyone of the important events that had taken place in the business of the trades- and craftspeople in Ruph.

All of a sudden Rhitha caught a look from Master Guy to Master Sepp—a guarded glance and a nod, like they were passing a secret between them. The announcements came closer and closer to today's date. They had reached June 18th, with Metz Stonecarver taking to apprentice Byzora Blackdaughter, and the master was shaking the girl's hand. Surely this was the last one?

But no! Atyrra Paperseller drew one more deep breath, and let her voice ring out. "June 21st, Summer Solstice

Day: Dyniselm Potter and Rysil Woodwright declare their apprentices, A'verelm and B'roldyn Shaper, to be Journeymen of their Trades, on the strength of their Journeyman's Piece, an excellently crafted chess set!"

Andy and Ben sat for a moment with identical expressions of jaw-dropping surprise on their faces. But then a big cheer went up, and Master Guy and Master Sepp were on their feet, shaking the young craftsmen's hands and clapping them on the shoulders, and Mistress Cat and Mistress Nicky and Bina were hugging them, and then they had their hands shaken again by everyone and their health toasted.

Eventually the happy mayhem was over, and everyone settled back down on their benches with their mugs of cider or ale or lemonade. Andy and Ben seemed to be unable to wipe the smiles off their faces—they had not expected to gain their journeymanship quite so soon, Rhitha thought. Although, why wouldn't they have? That chess set was wonderful. Rhitha was glad it would be housed in the library, so everyone could look at it and play it whenever they liked.

More of Bina's cousins were sitting at the next table, the one over from them. Rhitha smiled across at Liss, who had taken down Kashinka. She hadn't seen it herself, but Bina had told her. Rhitha really liked Liss. The young woman was looking over at their table quite a lot.

Andy, who was sitting right on Bina's other side, seemed to have noticed it too.

"So," he said quietly to his brother across the table, "did you get it?"

Ben raked his fingers through his hair, and crammed his other hand into his vest pocket. "Yeah," he said, going a little red in the face, "yeah, I did."

"Let's see then!"

"Nah, some other time."

"What?" said Master Sepp, who sat across from Rhitha. "What's going on?"

"He got it," said Andy, "and I want to see it."

"He did, eh? Yes, come on, son, show it already!"

"Oh, all right." His face a shade darker yet, Ben pulled a little wooden box out of his pocket—it had beautiful carvings on the lid, he must have made it himself. He snapped open the lid. Inside the little case, on a soft bed of wool, lay a silver necklace, the pendant in the shape of a lithe jumping fish, its scales glimmering in the last fading light of the Solstice Day.

Andy gave a little whistle. "Nice choice," he said. Then he leaned his elbows on the table and put his face closer to that of his brother. "So?" he said softly with a raise of his eyebrows, "are you going to ask her?"

"What, now? No!" Ben recoiled a little. "No, no—I'll do it some other time."

Andy exchanged a look with Master Sepp and scoffed. "He's running shy," he said, with a suggestion of a smirk. "Thought he might be chicken."

"No! I'm not!" said Ben. "I just don't think right now is a good time!" His face was getting redder and redder.

Master Sepp looked like he was having a hard time keeping himself from breaking into a big grin. "Bawk, bok bok!" he clucked softly, "bawk bawk!"

Ben, his face looking like a beet root, narrowed his eyes and pressed his lips together. Then he pinched his nostrils down and huffed air out of his nose, hard.

"FINE!" he exploded. He scrambled to his feet, stepped on the bench, and then jumped right up onto the middle of the table. Andy and Master Sepp hooted, and Rhitha giggled from sheer excitement.

"NYGELIS FISHMANSDAUGHTER!" Ben hollered. Everyone turned to look at him.

Liss gasped loudly and stared up at him, her eyes wide. Then she gave a little scream and clapped her hands to her mouth. "Ben Carver! What are you doing?!"

Her sisters and friends seemed to know exactly what. They jumped up, pulled Liss to her feet, and pushed her over to the table. Master Sepp had sprung up from his seat. He gave Liss his hand so she could step up on the bench; she raised her skirt with the other hand and her sisters pushed her from behind.

Then Ben took her hand and pulled her all the way up to the top of the table, where she stumbled a little and landed right in his arms, amidst a chorus of hooting and wolf-whistles from the watchers. Ben steadied Liss, then held her away from him just a bit. The rowdy crowd got quiet, holding its breath.

"*Nygelis Fishmansdaughter*!" Ben said again, his voice unnaturally loud, a bit scratchy, and shaking with nervousness, "Nygelis, marry me!"

Liss made a little squeaking noise, then she drew in a big breath. "Of course I do!! B'roldyn Carver, I marry you!"

She threw her arms around his neck, and he drew her to him and gave her a hard kiss.

The crowd erupted into cheering, hollering, whistling, foot-stomping and table-slapping. Ben and Liss emerged from their kiss with big smiles, their faces flushed and their eyes shining. Ben took his carved box, opened the lid and held it out to Liss. "Your marriage chain, my sweet?"

"Ooh, it's beautiful, Ben!" Liss said, and let him put it around her neck, then gave him another long kiss.

"At last! I thought you'd never get around to proposing!" Mistress Nicky said, and when Liss and Ben finally climbed down from the table, she gave them both a big hug. Everyone else followed suit, and amidst all the congratulations, while Mistress Cat brought over the big red-bound Chronicles book to enter their marriage, and Atyrra Paperseller made another, belated announcement, Rhitha slipped away, back to Grandmother and Ytahu.

The two moved apart a little, and Rhitha wiggled herself in between them. Ytahu looked down at her with a smile, and Grandmother, too, smiled at her and stroked her cheek with her fingers. Rhitha leaned her head on Grandmother's shoulder and gave a contented sigh.

Through the crowd she could see Bina's family, and a little further over, there was the old pottery master sitting at one of the tables. He, too, was looking at the Septimus family, almost staring at them, the way Rhitha had first seen him back on the market when they had first come to Ruph. Why was he looking like that?

247

CHAPTER 30

I T WAS IN THE middle of all the hubbub of congratulations that Cat became aware of Ekinoru's stare. No,
not a stare exactly—he was giving them a long, steady look,
watching the excitement with a curious expression in his
eyes. Cat followed his gaze to see at whom he was looking
so fixedly, and found that it was Ben—Ben and Nygelis. The young carver had his arm around his new-made
wife, beaming from ear to ear, good-naturedly taking all
the teasing that was heaped on his head and periodically
getting lost for a few seconds at a time gazing at Nygelis by
his side, as if he could not believe his luck in finally having
got her for his own.

Cat thoroughly enjoyed seeing their happiness, particularly after the bumpy road the couple had lately had in
getting to this point. But, oddly enough, she had a strong
feeling that the old master felt the same. There was a look
of satisfaction on his face, a smile of pleasure, as if it was
a son or grandson of his own who was so patently happy
in having secured the girl he loved. And then Ekinoru's
gaze shifted over to Andy, who was sitting backwards on

the bench, leaning his elbows on the table and grinning broadly at his brother, and the old man's expression took on a look that seemed to Cat almost speculative. What was the connection?

It was getting to be difficult to see clearly; the summer solstice dusk was rapidly shifting to night. Cat's eyes turned to the dusk indicator in the middle of the square. Close beside the bonfire wood pile was a small lantern on a pole, which had been lit some time ago, when it was still full daylight. Beside it, on the second arm of the T-shaped pole, a curved mirror was mounted, reflecting the sky.

"Look!" she said to Kell, who was sitting snuggled into her side, "it's almost time!" She pointed at the dusk indicator. "When the light from the lantern is brighter than the light in the mirror, Summer Solstice Day is done, and the shortest night is here."

Kell sat up straight. "And then Uncle Chelm and Uncle Oldran and Cousin Yerina light the fireworks!"

"That's right. And then the bonfire."

"I want them to light it now!" the little boy demanded. He turned to Guy, who sat beside them with Dyllie on his lap. "Papa, I want them to start the fireworks!"

"We have to wait until the time is right and the stars are out," Guy said. "You can't start the fireworks if it's not night yet, or you shoot all the unlit stars out of the sky for the remainder of the year."

Kell's eyes grew round. "Really?"

Guy tilted his head. "Well, that's what they say. And I think we better not put it to the test, don't you?"

The little boy pursed his mouth. "All right, I s'pose. But what if there's lots of clouds? Would the stars still be shooted from the sky?"

"Yes," said Guy firmly. "That's what the dusk lantern is for. A long time ago, they used to wait until they could see the evening star when it first came into the sky, and then they lit the fireworks. But there was one summer solstice when it was so cloudy, they could not see the evening star at all, and they just guessed and lit the fireworks too soon."

"What happened?"

"I don't know," said Guy with a wink, "ask Mumma, I'm sure she has the story in a book in the library."

"Aww!" groaned Kell, "you just maded that up!"

"Maybe I did, and maybe I didn't," said Guy. "But that's why we have the dusk lantern. That's what our Papa told us when we were little, right, Sepp?"

"Yes," his brother confirmed. "That's what Father said. So it must be true. I could never wait for the fireworks, either, when I was your size, Kell. In fact, I still can't wait! That has got to be the evening star right there, hasn't it?" He pointed at the horizon that was visible between the library and the hall. "Come on, squirt, let's go find Uncle Chelm and tell him to get going!" He held out his hand to Kell, and the little boy eagerly hopped off the bench to go with him to hustle along the start of the fireworks.

Cat watched them go. "At least that'll keep him busy for a few more minutes," she said.

"Yes, that's a good thing," Guy said. "Sepp is a real pest when he gets antsy."

She laughed. "I meant Kell!"

He grinned his lopsided grin at her. "No, did you?" Suddenly he turned his head. "Master Ekinoru!"

The old man inclined his head. "Master Guy. Mistress," he said. His gaze travelled on. "Journeyman A'verelm." He gave his small bow again.

Even in the dim dusk light Cat could see that Andy went quite pink in the face with gratification at being addressed with his new title for the first time.

"Master," he said, bowing in response, rather more deeply.

"Might I...?" Ekinoru asked, gesturing at the bench beside the young man.

"Yes, of course!" Andy sat up straighter, and scooted sideways to make room for the old man.

"Thank you," the old master said, settling himself down across from Guy and Cat. He pulled his large-brimmed hat from his head, put it on the bench beside him, then placed one hand on the edge of the tabletop in front of him and folded the other over it. "Master Guy," he said, "Journeyman,"—again the slight bow of the head—"there is a matter I wish to have speech with you on."

Not for the first time Cat noticed his style of talking. It sounded very formal, and quite old-fashioned—she couldn't quite put her finger on it what—or whom?—it reminded her of.

"Certainly," said Guy, shifting Dyllie a little on his lap. The little boy had fallen asleep; his head drooped against his father's arm and his toy slipped from his slack grasp. Guy caught the doll and put it on the table. "It's been an eventful day, hasn't it? You've lost a journeyman—although he was not much of a loss, was he?—and I've gained one..."

"Yes, that is what I wish to—"

The sizzle and bang of the first fireworks rocket shooting into the air, sending a shower of sparks exploding over the wood pile in the middle of the marketplace, cut off the old man's speech.

"Oooh!" The crowd cheered and clapped, and Cat knew there was no more conversation to be had until the fireworks display was over.

She leaned across the table to make herself heard over the banging of the pyrotechnics. "We'll talk later!" she shouted. "This doesn't last all that long. Sorry about that!"

Ekinoru threw up his hand in a gesture of understanding, and he smiled through his white beard in a way that looked like he found the interruption quite amusing. Another smile—interesting. It was as if getting rid of his fake journeyman had loosened something right up in the old man.

So they sat back and enjoyed the fireworks. Chelm and Oldran had outdone themselves this time. The display had several additions that Cat suspected were the brainchild of Yerina, Oldran's teenage daughter, the family firebug, who, apart from being able to create a blaze out of even the most damp sticks of firewood, had a knack for creating spectacular effects with flammables. Cat was fully certain that they were watching Yerina's handiwork when they reached the grand finale of the show. From three sides of the centre of the marketplace three rockets shot up, hovered in the air above the big wood stack for a second, then exploded into chrysanthemums of red, green and blue stars.

A second explosion followed, creating Catherine wheels of yellow sparks, then a series of popping noises—and suddenly the rockets reversed direction, pointed nose-downward, and shot right into the centre of the ten-foot-high stack of wood in the middle of the marketplace. A sizzling from the core of the wood stack, white sparks spitting out like someone had upended a giant birthday cake sparkler into the wood pile, and then with a tremendous *WHOOSH* the bonfire burst into flame.

"Aaaaaaah!" the spectators shouted, cheered and clapped, and through a gap in the mass of people Cat could see the fire masters, their faces illuminated by the flames, beaming and bowing to their audience.

"That was a great one!" Sepp called out, making his way back through the crowd with Kell riding on his shoulders. "Did you see that finale?"

"Papa, Papa, the fire essploded!" cried Kell, when Sepp swung him off his shoulders. "Did you see the fire essplode?"

"I sure did, son," Guy said. "Uncle Chelm will have a hard time topping that one next year!"

"Cousin Yerina, you mean," Cat said. "That was definitely her doing."

"True, true," said Guy. "Now, Master Ekinoru, sorry for that interruption, entertaining though it was. What was it...?"

Kell gave a jaw-cracking, eye-watering yawn. He quickly clapped his hand over his mouth. "I'm not sleepy!" he said, opening his eyes as widely as he could to prove his point.

Cat looked at Guy. "I think we need to get the kids to bed," she said. "It's really late!"

"Nooo!" Kell protested.

Guy ruffled the boy's hair. "Mumma's right," he said. "Even feast days have to end sometime." He gave an apologetic glance at the old man across the table. "I'm sorry, Master—-if you are willing to wait—"

Ekinoru once again waved an understanding hand. "Your family," he said. "Might we have speech in the morning? The journey to your home is too long to ask for your return tonight."

"We're not going all the way back to our house now," Cat interjected. "We're staying in town, at my brother-in-law's. In fact,"—she turned to Guy—"instead of you coming back here, why doesn't Master Ekinoru come with us to Sepp and Nicky's? Just because the kids need to get to bed doesn't mean we can't be up a while longer."

Guy directed an enquiring look at the old man.

Ekinoru shook his head. "There is no need. The morrow will be sufficient. In my eagerness, I—But the morrow will suffice. Good night." He once again inclined his head to Guy and Cat, then gave a direct look at Andy, and it seemed to Cat that his little bow for him was even more particular. What was it the old man wanted to discuss with them?

CHAPTER 31

T HEY WERE JUST FINISHING up a late breakfast, all of them crammed around the table in Nicky's kitchen, when the newlyweds walked in the door.

"Oh no, the lovebirds!" Sepp made a face, trying to suppress a lopsided grin. "I don't know if I can bear it—Nicky's pastry rolls are so sweet already I'm going to get sick having to watch you two on top of it." He'd stood up and was enthusiastically wringing Ben's hand during this speech. Then, in spite of being several inches shorter than the younger man, he caught him in a headlock and rumpled his hair. "If it wasn't for your brother and me you'd still be making lovesick sheep's eyes at Liss instead of her wearing that wedding chain of yours, boy! I hope you appreciate it!"

Ben laughingly fought free from the arm of his master, mentor and uncle-by-adoption, and raked his fingers through his mussed hair. "I do, I do!" he said. "Doesn't it look wonderful on her?" He proudly beamed at Nygelis by his side, who truly looked radiant, then put his arm around her waist and gave her a kiss, which she eagerly returned.

Sepp made retching noises, instantly copied by his son and his nephew.

"That's enough, you guys!" Cat said, laughing, and Nicky smacked Sepp and Tor on the backs of their heads.

"Don't mind them, honey," she said to Nygelis.

"Oh, I don't," the young woman said, smiling up at Ben with such a glow on her face that Cat couldn't help smiling along with her.

"Mumma, can we go play now?" Tor asked Nicky, already halfway out the kitchen door, his cousin hard on his heels.

"Hold it, young man," Cat said, catching Cory by the back of his shirt. "You're so sticky from those cinnamon buns, you'll glue yourself to your fort. Hands and faces washed, first."

The boys held their fingers under the tap for a moment, quickly swiped them over their mouths, then rushed out the door. In another two seconds Tor whipped his head back around the door frame. "Uncle Guy, that pottery master is here!" His red shock of hair vanished again as fast as it had appeared.

"Ah!" Guy got to his feet. "That talk he wanted to have with us yesterday." He went out the door.

Cat and Nicky had finished wiping the kids' sticky fingers and sent them out to play by the time Guy returned with Master Ekinoru.

The old master bowed politely to each of them. Then he turned to Ben and Nygelis, who were sitting close together on the end of one of the benches. He caught up one of each of their hands in his, and gave the young couple an intense look from under his bushy white eyebrows.

"Journeyman B'roldyn, Mistress." His voice shook as if he was having trouble controlling it. "The blessing of the elements, the warmth of the sun, the washing of the rain, the blossoming of children upon your union." His eyes filled with tears. He laid their two hands on top of each other as if he was sealing their bond, gave them a squeeze, and released them again.

The young couple looked up at him, their faces showing how deeply moved they were by this blessing. But then Cat noticed Andy, at the other end of the table. His dark eyes were wide and his mouth slack, his look one of shock—and recognition.

"Master!" he said in a hoarse voice, "Master Ekinoru—the words spoken by your lips—I mind their tone—what meaning bear they?"

And it burst in on Cat what the old master's language had so naggingly reminded her of: it was Andy's style of talking when he had first come from Chaelia as a young teen, a cadence he had fallen into again with this question.

Ekinoru turned to the young man, his eyes awash in tears. "You mind these words because you have heard them spoken in rites to seal the bond of marriage, Journeyman," he said. "I once spoke them, more than two-and-twenty years since, for your mother and your father."

Cat dropped down onto a chair. "You—what?!"

Every face around the table held the same stunned look that she knew was on her own at that moment.

The old master turned to her. "Che'anth was my journeyman, Mistress. I trained him from a boy." He raised a hand to wipe away the tear that had spilled down his brown cheek. "He was a man of great gifting, and when he wed Caladh, daughter of Drefan the Carver, I hoped great things for the offspring of their union." He looked from Andy to Ben, and a tremulous smile spread over his face. "Your countenance is much like hers."

"So, wait," said Guy, finding his voice, "you are telling us you come from the same land the boys were taken from? How can that be, Master? We destroyed the last means of travel between that world and ours; those blue stones are gone."

Cat interrupted. "We destroyed all the ones *we* knew of and could get a hold of, Guy. That's not to say there weren't more."

Ekinoru inclined his head slightly. "Indeed, Mistress. The Slave Masters of Chaelia pride themselves on their reach and penetration, yet there is much they do not know."

Bina, who had been silent throughout, her turquoise eyes fixed on the old master, suddenly spoke up, and Cat could feel that the girl was not reacting for herself, but on behalf of the twins who were still sitting stunned and speechless. "Master Ekinoru—excuse me, but—Andy and Ben's father? And mother? What happened to them?"

A shadow passed over the old man's dark eyes. "The plague took them, swiftly and cruelly, when their little sons were but infants. I mourned them much. The babes were removed, taken by the Masters for their own aims. My search was long; years barren of hope."

"And then you found them," Bina stated, "right here!"

The old man's face became suffused with an expression of deep joy. "I find them prospering far beyond my hopes." His gaze dwelt on Nygelis, and it took on a paternal warmth. "And promises of more to come." The girl blushed and lowered her eyelashes with a little smile, and Cat saw that under the edge of the table she slipped her hand into Ben's and gave it a squeeze.

Ekinoru turned and looked at Andy, then at Guy. "It was denied me to guide Che'anth to mastership," he said, and he fell silent, letting the sentence hang in the room.

Cat looked from him to her husband, then to Andy, whose black eyes had a look in them Cat found hard to interpret. There was wonder, surprise, a little confusion, but also something Cat had not noticed until then had been missing from the young man's expression—a look that his twin had always had for as long as Cat had known him but that had not been in Andy's eyes. Ben belonged, she realized—he had a sense of who he was and who his people were. Ben was part of Nicky's and Sepp's family; the adoption had formed a solid bond, and with his marriage to Nygelis, his roots had become complete.

But Andy had grown up in Chaelia, separated from his twin, an orphan slave boy with no past and no future. He had been taken from that world and thrown into theirs as a teenager, and while he had become an integral part of their family in the years since, there had always been the tiniest suggestion of a look of sadness, of being lost, in the young man's eyes—a look that now, as she gazed at him, had transformed into one of self-knowledge and belonging.

Guy reached out a hand and gripped Andy's shoulder. Cat looked at her husband, and she knew that he had seen the transformation in his apprentice's face just as she had.

"Andy, son," Guy said, his turquoise eyes steady on the young man's face, "I'll let you go, if that is what you wish." The black eyes turned to him, the question in them so clear that it might as well have been spoken aloud. Guy's mouth twisted in a rueful smile. "I won't say that I won't sorely miss you, son," he said, "and not for the sake of the added work load, either. But if you must go, you must."

Andy's eyes blazed up in an expression of hope and excitement, and he turned from his master to the old man. "Will you guide me in my father's stead, Master Ekinoru?"

Suddenly Cat became sharply aware of Bina at her elbow. The girl was staring at Andy, her eyes like saucers in her face, and Cat could feel the emotional turmoil radiating off her. With a harsh sob, Bina whirled around in her chair, sprang to her feet and ran out of the room.

"I'll go after her," Cat said with a look at Guy and Andy, getting to her feet. "It'll be all right."

She found Bina in the back corner of Nicky's kitchen garden, hidden behind some gooseberry bushes against the garden wall.

"Oh sweetie," she said and folded the girls into her arms. A flood of tears drenched her blouse, and Bina's thin little shoulders shook with the storm of her weeping. Cat stroked her hair, rubbed her back and let her cry herself out.

"We'll miss him terribly, won't we," she said when the sobs finally subsided.

"I don't want him to go, Mumma," Bina said in a tear-choked voice, "but I do want him to go because he wants it so much!"

"I know, sweetie," Cat said, tucking a strand of copper hair behind the girl's ear. "It's the hardest thing in the world when you love someone, and that love makes you let them go to do what they need to do."

"He's so happy that he found his master who was his father's," Bina said, "it's almost like he found his parents. But Mumma,"—she lifted her turquoise eyes, still glazed with tears, to Cat—"I thought you and Papa—well, you're not really his parents, but—well, I thought—and he belongs with us!"

"He does," said Cat. "He's part of our family, and he always will be. And I'm sure that's exactly how he feels, too. But he also belongs with the people he came from. Master Ekinoru has spent most of Andy and Ben's lives searching for them—we have to let him have his share of them, too. Ben is staying here, because he's got Nygelis, but Andy can go. You know," she said thoughtfully, "I think it's a little bit like when someone you love gets married—you're so happy for them, and want more than anything for them to get what they want, but you're also sad for yourself. And that's what love is all about. Don't you think?"

Bina sniffed. "Why does it have to be so hard?"

Cat put her arms around her. "I know, sweetie, I know ..."

A firm tread sounded on the garden path between the beds. "Little Bee?"

Bina gave another little sob, then seemed to make up her mind. "Over here, Andy."

CHAPTER 32

B INA WAS SQUATTING DOWN in front of the bed of lettuces in their garden, pulling chickweed out from between the plants. Mumma said it was a weed and she wanted it gone, but you could actually eat it in salads, and Bina was fairly certain that you could use it to make people get better if they had something wrong with their skin—she could feel it in her fingers as she pulled the plants out. She'd have to ask Aunt about it. But she also enjoyed cleaning up around the lettuces; they looked happier with nice clean dirt around their feet, when they didn't have to fight with the chickweed for space to grow in.

Kind of like Rhee—she was so much happier because Kashinka wasn't taking away her breathing space any more. 'Cause that's exactly what Kashinka had done to Rhee, she'd squished her over until Rhee got hardly any air. And Rhee had let her because she didn't think she deserved any space to breathe in. But not any more!

Bina pursed her lips and tried to whistle—and all of sudden there was a sound! There was a whistley tune coming from—oh. It wasn't her that was doing the whistling at all, it was Papa. He was coming around the back of the house, from the privy.

"Bib-bib-bina!" he called.

Bina made a face at him. "Don't call me Bibby!" she said.

"I wasn't," he said and grinned at her, looking just like Cory sometimes did. And feeling like him when he was teasing her, too. "Can you interrupt your ravaging of the garden beds for a moment, Karana? Andy's got something to show you."

"Okay," Bina said, and rubbed her fingers together to get the dirt off. "When's he and Master Ekinoru leaving?"

"Next week," Papa said and gave her a look, sort of with his head tipped sideways, because he was trying to figure out if she was still upset about Andy going. She wasn't—well, not really really much. Just, sort of—well, yes, she was. But it was going to be okay. Mumma said the hurt would get a little less, and they'd get used to not having Andy around. And it wasn't forever, any-way—at least Bina really hoped it wasn't. Maybe Andy would even come back to visit sometimes before he got his mastership. Except Rhanathon was terribly far...

"Where is he?" she asked.

"In the workshop," Papa said. "Come on, Bib-bib-bi—"

"*Papa*!!"

He grinned at her to cover up his worried feelings, then opened the workshop door to let her in. And then he closed it again, with him on the outside.

"Hey, Little Bee," said Andy, looking around from where he was standing by the drying shelf.

"Hi," she said. "Papa said you got something to show me."

"Come here," he said, stretching out his hand towards her.

She walked over and put her hand into his big one, looking up at him. "What is it?"

The feelings inside of him were all jumbled, like they had been since yesterday when Master Ekinoru had told him about his father and mother and they had decided Andy would go with him to become a master himself, in his trade in Rhanathon. He was really happy that he had found Master Ekinoru, and very excited about going, and about learning more—but he was really sad to be leaving, too. It was because he was feeling sad himself that Bina was trying as hard as she could not to feel too sad herself, because she knew that made it worse for him.

"Ben and I talked," he said. "And we—we had an idea. Look."

On the drying shelf, right at Bina's eye level, sat two small sculptures. They were portrait heads, made out of the greyish clay that was going to become the beautiful white ware when it was fired.

"I wanted you to see it now," said Andy, "instead of waiting until they're all finished. I'm not sure I'll get it fired before—before we leave; your Papa might have to put them in the kiln for me. But I sure hope they get done in time, because this one"—he pointed to the smaller one of the heads—"I'm taking with me. I want to keep you in my mind when I'm at the coast, so I don't forget what you look like." It was a portrait of Bina herself.

She smiled at him. "And what about the one of Ben?"

"That one is for Liss. Can you tell that it's Ben and not me?"

She gave him a scornful look and scoffed. "'Course I can!" she said. "You're totally different!"

He laughed. "Master Guy couldn't tell," he said, "and you have to admit, we're a lot alike!"

"Well, yeah, you *look* alike, but you're really different people!"

He looked at her in a sort of searching way. "Can you feel that in the sculpture?"

Bina tipped her head and scrunched her mouth sideways, then she reached out a finger and very lightly, so as not to dent the wet clay, touched the little Ben figure. "Yup," she said. "It feels like him."

He breathed a little sigh of relief. "That's what we were hoping," he said. "Do you want to come to town with me to see what Ben is doing? I think his are a bit different."

It turned out that one of Ben's carvings was a counterpart to Andy's sculptures—he, too, had made a portrait of his brother, which he was just giving a final coating of finishing oil. But his other piece was of Nygelis. Bina closely looked at the smooth rosewood carving, and ran her finger over the wavy hair that was spilling over the little wooden Liss' shoulders.

"She's really, really beautiful," she said.

Ben looked up. "Yes," he said, "she is!"

"No, I mean this one," Bina explained. "Liss is really pretty, of course, but when I put my finger on the carving, I can feel how *you* feel about her—and even, how you make *her* feel. It's kind of real, like there's a little bit of Liss in this, but it's *your* Liss."

Ben went sort of pink in the face. "Really?"

"Yup. That's what you were trying to do, wasn't it?"

"Yes," said Andy, "that's exactly what we wanted. And we're thinking that when we put those sculptures together, they'll form a bond. They'll help us stay connected. I'll take the one of you with me, and you"—he took the portrait carving of himself out of Ben's hand—"you keep this." He put the little figure in Bina's hand and closed her fingers over it. She could feel a tingle from it, and all of a sudden the hole that the thought of Andy's leaving made in her heart felt much smaller.

"And the ones of Ben and Liss, when you put them together, are going to make the both of them hook together even more tight," she said.

"Yes, that's the idea, Little Bee."

"Like Mumma and Papa, they're hooked tight, too." Bina said, and put the little Andy carving into her pocket. But she kept her hand in the pocket with it, for now. "Are we going over to Rhee's place before we're going home? You were going to talk to Cousin Ytahu about the trip."

Cousin Ytahu was going to go with Andy and Master Ekinoru, because they were all going to Rhanathon, so they had decided to travel together. Besides, Cousin Ytahu was already making deals with Master Ekinoru for letting him handle the trading of his wares. It would be a proff-it-tible biss-uness part-nurship, he'd said.

Bina had said that it was family dealings, so it was only right, and when Andy had pointed out that Master

Ekinoru and Ytahu weren't related, Bina said that they were so—Master Ekinoru's journeyman's brother's wife's cousin, which was her, was Ytahu's cousin too, so that made them family. And Andy had laughed and said she sounded like Mistress Ouska, who knew all about everyone in town and who was related to whom and how. And that had made Bina happy, because she wanted to be like Aunt. Mumma had said that they were going to talk to Aunt about Bina coming to learn from her about herbs and plants and how to use them to make people better when they were unwell. Bina was excited about that, and that was another thing that made the hole in her heart a little smaller, because it helped her understand a bit more about Andy being excited to go with Master Ekinoru to learn, so it made her more happy for him and less sad for herself.

Bina put her lips into an "oo" shape and blew air out—and there was a squeaking noise! She stopped in surprise, then tried again. And there it was—a whistling sound!

"Andy, Andy, Andy, listen!" She whistled again, just one little squeaky note, but it was the real thing. "I did it! I can whistle!"

Rhee was at Grandmother Urnhild's, with Ytahu, of course. She was really happy, which was great.

"Bina," she said in a rush as soon as they got there, and dragged Bina by the arm out through the back door, "I'm so glad you've come! You've got to help me."

Bina laughed. "Where's the fire?" she said, which was something Mumma always said when they were in a hurry.

Rhee grinned back at her. "There isn't one," she said, "but if we don't go now, they might pack up my stuff and leave with it!"

"What—Aunt Shamira and Kashinka? Are they going?"

"Yes, first thing tomorrow! With the caravan of the traders that were here for the Solstice Fair. There's one group that's going to Ilim, and Mother decided they might as well go back there."

"But you're staying here," stated Bina.

"Yes, of course," said Rhitha. "Grandmother needs me, especially because Ytahu isn't going to stay—he can't, he's got business in Rhanathon. But he'll come back to see us when he can, he said; and—oh! Did you hear what he's going to do?"

Rhee was just bubbling inside with excitement and with being happy, and Bina loved feeling that.

"No, what?"

"He's talking to Astani, next door, about buying her cottage from her, and then, he said, we can punch a door through the wall from our kitchen to that one, and fix up the other half and make it all nice, and we'll have a house twice as big with a room for me to sleep in and one for him when he comes to visit! And you know what else he said?" Her voice got kind of quiet, in a happy way. "He said Grandmother and I won't ever have to worry about money. He's going to take care of us."

Bina grinned at her, just because she was so happy for Rhee, and then threw her arms around her friend and hugged her right off the pavement. When they were done squealing and giggling, they had arrived at the back door of Aunt Shamira's house.

Rhee drew a deep breath, and Bina could feel her getting a bit shaky inside. She grabbed her hand. "It's okay!" she whispered. "Let's do it!"

They pushed open the door and walked into the kitchen.

Rhee's mother was sitting at the table, which was cluttered with dirty dishes, the end of a loaf of bread, a jam pot, a pile of stockings, another of handkerchiefs, and the mug of something from which she had just finished taking a deep drink. A big trunk stood open in the middle of the floor, skirts, blouses and chemises jumbled inside it.

Kashinka came out of the bedroom.

"What do *you* want?" she said with a scowl on her face.

"I've come to pack my things," Rhee said, her voice a little wobbly. Bina squeezed her hand.

"Oh," said Aunt Shamira in kind of a blank voice. "I don't think there's room on the trader's cart for one more. The man only barely let me have two tickets."

"I'm not going to Ilim," said Rhee, getting a bit braver. "I just want my things so I can take them over to Grandmother's. I'm going to live with her." She walked over to the corner, where her small box of clothing was sitting. It had a blouse draped over top of it; she took it off and stood for a moment with it in her hands, looking around for where to put it.

"That's mine," said Kashinka in a disagreeable voice.

And that was when something snapped inside of Rhee.

"Yes, it's yours!" she said, marched right over to Kashinka and dumped it into her arms. "And so is this,"—she pulled an armful of clothing out of the trunk and piled it on top of the blouse—"and this, and this!" She kept loading Kashinka with her stuff, until she got to the bottom of the trunk. "But *this*," she said with a fierce sparkle in her eyes, holding up a small carved wooden box, "is *mine*."

She opened the box, upended it on top of the pile of clothes in Kashinka's arms, spilling out the trinkets inside, then clapped the lid shut again. "And *this*," she continued, still in the same angry voice, "is *Grandmother's*." She picked up a pretty green pottery bowl from the middle of the mess on the table. Then she marched back to the corner, stuck both those things inside her little trunk, picked it up, and turned on her heel with such a toss of her head that her pale hair whipped right across her shoulders. "Goodbye, Mother and Kashinka. Have a nice life! Let's go, Bina." She stalked out of the door.

Bina looked back at Kashinka and Aunt Shamira, who sat there with their mouths hanging open. She felt the feeling inside of Kashinka like someone had slapped her across the face, and she remembered all the times that Rhee had been hurt so badly by her sister and her mother and hadn't been able to do anything about it. And she knew, and was fiercely glad, that they would never be able to harm her friend again, ever.

When they got back to Grandmother Urnhild's house, Andy and Ytahu were still talking.

"I'll be a few minutes, Bee," said Andy. "Can you wait a little?"

"Sure," Bina said, "we can find things to do, right, Rhee?"

"Actually, I need to take this book back to the library; I promised Master Nikor. Do you want to come?"

"Okay," said Bina, feeling all light and bubbly inside from her friend's happiness, "let's go!"

They took each others' hands and ran across the marketplace, just for fun, giggling the whole while, and raced up the front steps of the library. Suddenly Bina found herself confronted with the heavy handle of the big carved door, and she gave a little gasp. The scary face! But then she looked at Rhee beside her, and she saw again in her memory the strong face of her friend as she stood up to her mother and Kashinka. So Bina took a deep breath, stared that carving right between the eyes, grasped the handle and pulled.

The chess set was sitting prominently on the big reading table in the middle of the library, and the pieces gleamed in the sunshine that fell through the skylight into the room. There was a game in progress, although neither of the players was in sight. Bina heard a noise from the stacks, and put her head around the corner.

"Hi, Mumma! Who's playing the chess game?"

"Oh, hello, dear! Randy started it, against Nikor. Nikor got distracted and wandered off, so I kept playing in between what I'm doing, but I've been busy. I think Randy went to see if Nikor wants to take over again."

Apparently he didn't—Randy came out of Nikor's room with a scowl on his face. "Come on! *Somebody's* got to finish the game! It's no fun by myself!"

Rhee came out from between the stacks, where she'd gone to find the next volume of the book she had brought back.

"I'll play," she said. "What colour are you?"

"White," said Randy.

Bina wandered over to where Mumma was putting away books, picked up a few, and found their places on the shelves.

"Mumma?" she said.

"Yes, sweetie?"

"Have you ever had a day like this? A day where you felt sad, and happy, and angry, and glad, all at once and over and over?"

Mumma put her arm around her shoulders and gave her a hug.

"Lots of times, sweetie. It comes with the territory."

"Of being an Unissima?"

"Of being human, Bina. And of having a heart that can love."

The chess pieces clicked, and Bina felt Rhee be proud, and she was proud of her too.

"Checkmate!"

NOTE

P ORCELAIN REALLY WAS CALLED 'white gold' when it was first imported into Europe. It was so valuable that smuggling the secret of its manufacturing out of China in the early eighteenth century became one of first cases of industrial espionage. But by then, European scientists had already discovered the technique for themselves. In the late eighteenth century, Josiah Spode found that if you replace a certain portion of the composition of the clay with bone ash, you get a lovely translucent ware, a porcelain that is still known as 'bone china'.

Grandmother Urnhild's dancers are similar to some figurines of sleeve dancers that date to the Chinese Tang Dynasty (ca. 800 AD). And if you want to get an idea what Andy and Ben's chess set is like, look up the Lewis Chessmen, a collection of medieval ivory chess figures that are in the British Museum—except that the Shapers of Ruph made their pawns more interesting, and the figures far more detailed, than those of the Lewis Chessmen.

GLOSSARY

PEOPLE

Cat (Catriona). Librarian, mum. Also called Book-woman or Septimuswife.

Guy (Dyniselm), Cat's husband. Potter, Septimissimus.

Bina (Ysbina, Bibby). Guy's daughter from his first marriage.

Cory (Coryell), Cat and Guy's first son.

Kell (Kelroda), their second son.

Dyllie (Aldyl), their third son

Yaya (Iawar), their fourth son.

Sepp (Rysil), Guy's brother. Woodworker.

Nicky (Monica), Sepp's wife. Designer, mum.

Tor (Torym), their son.

Ari (Ariana), their daughter.

Andy (A'verelm), Guy's apprentice. Clay sculptor.

Ben (Br'oldyn), Andy's twin, Sepp's apprentice and Nicky's adopted nephew. Woodcarver.

Uncle (Sardor), Guy's Uncle. Brewer.

Aunt (Ouska), Uncle's wife. Wisewoman.

Yldra, Guy's cousin, Ouska's daughter. Pastrybaker.

Randy (Randor), her son.
Chonyk, Yldra's brother. Farmer.
Yokan, Guy's brother. Fish farmer.
Nygelis (Liss), his daughter.
Kim (Kimira), her sister.
Dola, a Septimus cousin.
Lahni (Sulahna), her daughter.
Rhitha (Rhee), Bina's cousin.
Kashinka, her sister.
Shamira, their mother.
Urnhild, Shamira's mother.
Belock, Urnhild's late husband.
Ytahu, Shamira's son.
Ekinoru, potter master.
Bel'ris'oem (Osera), his journeyman
Nikor Archivist, town librarian.

PLACES
Ruph, the town
Isachang, the country
Ilim, a city
Rhanathon, a city on the coast; trading port for the Moon Sea
Chaelia, Andy and Ben's home world

ACKNOWLEDGEMENTS

A big shout-out to all of you who helped to made this book happen:

-Most of all Peter, who not only was my first reader, but designed the chess game in this story. Without his input, the game would have been a complete shambles, as I barely know how chess pieces are meant to move, let alone what makes for a good game. He made sure that all the moves are legal ones and actually make sense.

-And of course Anna, who was involved in plotting this story right from the beginning. I believe it was her idea to have a contest for the twins' chess set played out at a big local fair. And she helped me straighten out plot details and cut unnecessary extra characters, so the scenes are only half as confusing as they started out being.

-My intrepid beta readers and friends, Louise, Desi, Linda and Lee, thanks to whose excellent feedback the profusion of characters in this story was tamed a little and the plot rearranged more than once.

-And all my faithful readers who kept asking when the next book was coming out and let me know they enjoyed my stories and wanted to hear more about Cat and all the people of Ruph.

THANK YOU.

ABOUT THE AUTHOR

Angelika M. Offenwanger lives in rural Western Canada with her family, which includes two cats, numerous dust bunnies, and a small stuffed bear named Steve. She hardly ever plays chess, but loves losing herself among the stacks in a library.

Online she can be found on Facebook and Instagram, and on her website at www.amoffenwanger.com.

www.ingramcontent.com/pod-product-compliance
Lightning Source LLC
Chambersburg PA
CBHW020242180626
46810CB00006B/2319